"Bestselling and award-winning novelist [...] beloved empathy in *What a Wave Mus[...]* personal loss that becomes a beacon of [...] end. With her trademark insight into a contemporary woman's mind, Angela keeps us turning the pages into the wee hours to see how God can beam light into utter darkness."

JERRY B. JENKINS, *New York Times* bestselling author

"Honest, tender, heartfelt. Hunt examines the topic with such gentle insight we realize how anyone can be impacted . . . and find hope."

BILL MYERS, bestselling author, Rendezvous with God series.

"Angela Hunt delicately and expertly takes the confusion, depression, and traumatic effects surrounding suicide and transforms them with hope and a family's unconditional love in *What a Wave Must Be.*"

DIANN MILLS, author of *Facing the Enemy*

What a

Wave

Must Be

ANGELA HUNT

FOCUS
ON THE FAMILY.

A Focus on the Family resource
published by Tyndale House Publishers

A Focus on the Family book published by Tyndale House Publishers, Carol Stream, IL 60188

Focus on the Family and the accompanying logo and design are federally registered trademarks of Focus on the Family, 8605 Explorer Drive, Colorado Springs, CO 80920.

Tyndale and Tyndale's quill logo are registered trademarks of Tyndale House Ministries.

All Scripture quotations, unless otherwise noted, are from *The Holy Bible, English Standard Version*. Copyright © 2001 by Crossway Bibles, a publishing ministry of Good News Publishers. Used by permission. All rights reserved.

What a Wave Must Be is a work of fiction. Where real people, events, establishments, organizations, or locales appear, they are used fictitiously. All other elements of the novel are drawn from the author's imagination.

Cover photograph of water by Dave Hoefler on Unsplash.com.

Editors: Jerry B. Jenkins, Larry Weeden

Cover design: Libby Dykstra

For information about special discounts for bulk purchases, please contact Tyndale House Publishers at csresponse@tyndale.com or call 1-855-277-9400.

Library of Congress Cataloging-in-Publication data can be found at www.loc.gov.

ISBN 978-1-64607-149-4 Hardcover
ISBN 978-1-64607-045-9 Softcover

Printed in the United States of America
29   28   27   26   25   24   23
7   6   5   4   3   2   1

The Bustle in a House

The Bustle in a House
The Morning after Death
Is solemnest of industries
Enacted upon Earth—

The Sweeping up the Heart
And putting Love away
We shall not want to use again
Until Eternity—
—EMILY DICKINSON, 1866

Chapter One

Susan

I never imagined that Frank and I would live anything but a charmed life. But when I tripped over a dog toy and broke my right arm on an ordinary November day, I began to wonder if God was trying to tell me something. I listened and looked for writing on the wall, but if God was speaking, I couldn't hear him.

Three weeks later, Frank and I were upstairs cleaning our guest apartment. With one hand, I pulled the wrinkled sheet from the laundry basket and struggled to toss it to my patient husband. "I never thought having my arm in a sling would make me feel so helpless," I said.

Frank grabbed the sheet and fitted the corners to his side of the mattress. "You need help over there?"

"I've got it." I used my left hand to ease the seams over the corners of the king-size bed. "Thanks. I know you'd rather be teaching than helping me with this stuff."

"The school has other substitutes," he said, taking the top sheet from the laundry basket. "I'm certainly not irreplaceable."

"To me, you are." I caught the edge of the sheet Frank had flung toward me. "A man is never more attractive than when he's helping his wife with the housework."

He grinned as he tucked the edge of the sheet under the mattress. "My mother said I should beware of women who tried to sweet-talk me. Next thing I know, you'll have me doing the grocery shopping."

I laughed, realizing that he'd done more than help me make beds—he had also lifted my spirits, which had lately taken a downturn.

"Don't worry. I can fill a cart with one hand." I finished smoothing my side of the bed and walked around to do his. "And I know better than to send you to the grocery. You'd come back with nothing but snacks and cookies."

"Susan." Frank pointed at my hip. "Your shorts are buzzing."

"What? Oh—my phone." I glanced at the caller ID. "It's Rachel. Wonder what she wants?"

"The best way to find out"—Frank sat on the bed—"is to answer."

I pressed the speakerphone. "Rachel?"

"Susan." Our daughter-in-law's voice sounded tight, so something had to be wrong. She rarely called us, except when she wanted to suggest gifts for Maddie's birthday or Christmas.

"Is everything all right, hon?"

"I don't know."

I frowned. "Is everything okay with Maddie?"

"Sure, she's at school. But I was wondering . . . have you heard from Daniel? I was wondering if he hopped on a plane to visit you."

I shot Frank a look of alarm. Daniel and Rachel lived in Atlanta, only an hour's flight from our home in Florida, but Daniel had never *hopped on a plane* to visit us.

"Rachel"—I sank to the bed—"are you two having problems?"

"It's not like Daniel to ignore my calls. It's probably nothing, but last night he seemed preoccupied. He barely spoke at dinner, and he didn't even tease Maddie about the Falcons losing to the Buccaneers."

"Maybe he's dealing with a problem at work." Our son was a top sales rep for a pharmaceutical firm.

Rachel sighed. "Maybe you're right. Let me know if you hear from him, okay? Give Frank my love. I'll talk to you later."

As I put the phone down, Frank crossed his arms and nodded. "Male menopause. How old is he, forty?"

"Forty-two. And male menopause is a myth. You didn't go through it."

His mouth drooped. "I almost spent our savings on a boat."

"Yes, but you didn't."

"That was male menopause. I thought a boat might fill some void."

I winced. "Do you still feel that way?"

A smile crossed his face. "It was a phase, sweetheart. I haven't missed a thing—in fact, my cup runneth over."

"Good to know."

"Daniel's a grown man, a good husband, and we raised him right. If he wants a boat, he can afford one, but he's not about to leave his wife and daughter."

I wasn't so sure. The news overflowed with celebrities who walked away from their families on a whim. Daniel wasn't a celebrity, but any man could indulge a wandering eye or imagine he'd be happier living another life.

"If he's having an affair, I'll—"

"Not answering his phone doesn't mean he's having an affair." Frank walked over and squeezed my hand. "Maybe his battery died. Maybe he dropped his phone in the toilet. Or maybe he just wanted a little peace and quiet."

"Maybe." I forced a smile. "I hope you're right."

That night, as I struggled to brush my teeth with my left hand, I thought only of Daniel. I didn't want to turn a dead cell phone into a torrid affair, but I couldn't shake a feeling of foreboding.

I rinsed and went back into the bedroom. "My intuition keeps telling me something's wrong," I told Frank, who was sitting up in bed and absorbed in the History Channel. "I'm worried about Daniel."

"No news is good news," he said, idly petting our pug, Ike. "I'm sure he's fine."

"But what if he's not? What if he's been abducted? Some junkie could have seen the samples in his car and—"

"Daniel calls on hospitals and doctor's offices, not drug dens."

"Still, it's not like him to ignore Rachel's calls. They must have had an argument."

"So why don't you call him?"

"I tried. I got no answer."

"Did you leave a message?" Finally a look of concern crossed Frank's face. "Did you tell him Rachel wanted to talk to him?"

"I asked him to call me—the first time. The other times, I hung up. He'll see how many times I've called."

"And when he does call you back, he'll say you were silly to worry about him. Relax, honey. He's a grown man. He can take care of himself."

I blew out a frustrated breath and crawled into bed. Ike left Frank's lap and waddled over to me, snorting in my ear before settling his head on my shoulder.

I closed my eyes, hoping the drone of the documentary would lull me to sleep, but too many dire possibilities crowded my brain. Daniel could be unconscious in a ditch or in the clutches of a drug lord. Or considering Frank's cardiac condition, he could have had a heart attack.

"Honey," Frank said, "you need to stop worrying."

"Who says I'm worrying?"

"You're jiggling your foot. You haven't stopped since you got into bed."

"I can't help it."

"Pray for the boy and go to sleep."

"I've been praying since Rachel called."

"Is that what you call it?"

He had a point. Fretting and praying weren't the same thing at all.

I sighed and closed my eyes again. "Lord, let Daniel call us as soon as possible so we can all get some rest."

Chapter Two

Maddie

For hours Mom paced the house, calling Dad's friends and coworkers. He should have been home by six.

After midnight I crawled onto my bed, shoving books and electronics out of the way, and buried my face in my pillow. Mom usually conked out by eleven, because she insisted on seven hours of sleep before work.

I doubted either of us would get any rest tonight.

I rolled onto my back and closed my eyes to block an eruption of tears. Dad wasn't the type to disappear for no reason. He was the dependable parent, the one who never had work emergencies or forgot to pick me up. He was the one who slipped notes into my backpack and sent text messages to ask about my day. He was the one who took me to the mall when I needed something or had a craving for Chipotle.

Not even my boyfriend, Tris, loved me that much. I thought

he did until he went to Miami to visit family for Thanksgiving. I thought he was still there until Emily, my best friend, texted that she had seen Tris at a movie with some cheerleader.

No wonder he wasn't answering my texts.

I ignored him at school yesterday. Today he made a point of making out with the cheerleader right outside my first-period classroom. Dad would say Tris was a classless jerk.

I thought about calling Emily, but I knew she'd ask if my parents had been fighting and declare they were about to divorce. Because divorce had messed up her family, Emily figured it would eventually do the same to everyone else's.

Had my parents been fighting? They usually didn't disagree in front of anyone, especially me. If they were fighting, they'd argue in the privacy of their room on the far side of the house, after Mom put away her laptop. Because Mom never put her computer away until nine or ten, they didn't have much time to fight.

This whole thing was beyond weird. I couldn't believe Mom actually thought Dad might have taken off for Florida, but nothing about this made sense.

Who disappears without a word unless something really bad has happened?

Hours later, I heard the delicate chime from the alarm system. It was 5:45 a.m., which accounted for the weird, gray light seeping in beneath my curtains.

I jogged downstairs. "Dad! Where have you been?" I threw my arms around him, relieved he hadn't been kidnapped or abducted by aliens.

He gave me a sheepish grin. "It's a stupid story, and you won't believe it. Is your mom ready to kill me?"

"She was pretty upset last night. Everybody was."

His brow shot up. "Everybody?"

"Mom called Nana and Pop and pretty much everyone else she could think of."

He groaned. "I'd better go apologize. Meanwhile, get ready for school and I'll take you. It's the least I can do to make up for the kerfuffle."

Riding with Dad was infinitely better than taking the bus, plus I'd have an extra thirty minutes to get ready.

He dropped his briefcase onto the foyer table, then headed toward their bedroom. I knew I shouldn't, but after a minute I tiptoed to their door and was able to make out "problem at work," "needed time to think," and "fell asleep on the couch." I heard tears in Mom's voice, and Dad said something about his phone's battery.

That was all I needed to hear, so I turned and ran upstairs. The problem at work must have been hugely important, because Dad hardly ever let work get to him. Had he made a mistake and cost the company money? That didn't sound like him, because he was always getting promoted. But maybe he lost out on a promotion, or maybe he had to fire someone who worked under him. Who knew?

I went into the bathroom to brush my hair and put on my makeup. Whatever had happened was done, and Dad was home. Nothing else mattered.

Chapter Three

Susan

I had just put the coffee on the next morning when my cell phone rang. "It's Daniel!" I shouted, hoping Frank could hear me in the bedroom.

"Hey, Mom," Daniel said. "I'm sorry about yesterday."

"Where were you? You had all of us worried sick."

"My phone died," he said, "and I didn't realize it because we had a big meeting at work. The sales department has to cut some personnel, and all of us left feeling like we had an axe hanging over our heads. I didn't want to go home in that kind of mood, so I drove to a park to chill for a while. After about an hour, I went back to my office to get some papers, and I was so drained that I stretched out on the couch and fell asleep. Next thing I knew, the sun was coming up. I tried to call home, but—"

"The battery was dead," I finished, relieved. "Couldn't you have used a landline? You scared all of us to death."

"I'm so sorry. By that time, I thought I'd better get home. I didn't mean to worry you. I never dreamed Rachel would call you and Pop."

"She did, and she was right to, because she thought something horrible had happened. I didn't sleep a wink last night."

"Well . . . you could take a nap this afternoon."

I ignored the teasing note in his voice. "I can't. We have guests coming, and I want to bake some breakfast muffins. Not easy to do with one hand, you know. But you should think about getting rid of that couch in your office. Oh—here's your father."

I handed the phone to Frank, who had come out of the bedroom with a broad smile on his face. "Danny boy! You alive and well?"

"Yes. Sorry about the scare."

"Your poor mother jiggled the mattress all night. Kept me awake a couple of hours."

"Sorry. I promise to keep my phone charged from now on."

"Good man. Trouble at work, eh?"

I waved and mouthed a message: *Can I speak to Maddie?*

"Yeah," Daniel was saying, "the company wants to make some cuts. We're not sure what's going to happen."

Frank glanced at me. "Your mother wants to know if Maddie's able to come to the phone."

"Sorry, but she's getting ready for school. Maybe she can call later."

"Okay. Listen, take care and we'll see you after Christmas."

"Right. And don't even think about booking a hotel. Rachel has redone the spare room, and she wants you to be our first guests."

"Your mom will look forward to that. Bye now." Frank ended the call. "That boy will be the death of us some day."

"Did you hear his explanation?"

"Most of it. Have you ever known Daniel to sit in a park?"

"Maybe it's a meditation garden. Maybe he's established some new routines."

Frank shook his head. "Daniel is like you, always in motion. I can't imagine him sitting anywhere for very long. And considering how picky he is about his orthopedic pillow, I can't see him falling asleep on a couch."

"What does it matter? He's home and he's fine."

"Yes, he's home. But I'm not so sure he's fine."

Exasperated, I poured a cup of coffee and slid it across the counter. "And you say I'm the one who worries too much?"

Frank opened his hands. "I'm not worried; I just don't find his story convincing. In his entire life, Daniel has never disappeared like that. Something's not right."

I waved his comment away and turned to get another mug. But later, when I considered the events of that day, I realized I had ignored Frank's concerns not because Daniel's story made sense, but because I desperately wanted to believe it.

On the first day of December, the unofficial start of our holiday rental season, Ike and I stepped outside at the sound of slamming car doors. Joshua Wiggins, our next guest, and his six friends spilled out of a van. Joshua looked to be in his early twenties and said he was on leave from the army.

"We promise to take good care of your place, ma'am."

Ike barked, and the young man grinned. "Hello, little dude."

"Walk that way," I said, pointing to the stairs that led to the apartment over our garage, "and you can't miss the door. Do you remember the unlock code?"

"Yes, ma'am."

I nodded to each of Joshua's friends as they followed him, then went back into the house. "They seem like a nice group," I told Frank. "They're young, but the guy who booked the place is very polite."

Daniel had disapproved when we first told him we had signed up with a short-term rental platform, his flush visible even on the computer screen. "What if some crazy person books your place and refuses to check out? You two aren't exactly young anymore."

Frank lifted his chin. "Your mom and I still feed and dress ourselves."

"Very funny, Dad. But why would anyone even *want* to stay with you? You're not on the beach, the house is weird, and—"

"The house is quirky," I said. "And that's what sets us apart. Guests like this place because it's different."

I fell in love with our unconventional house the moment I saw the stained-glass windows, the Gothic architecture, and the native Florida landscaping, which Daniel described as "Florida rain forest." Plus, the place had a real caboose in the yard, which we painted a brilliant red.

I liked that the place looked nothing like the others around it. The main home, small compared to the mini mansions on the same street, offered only two bedrooms, which caused the house to sit empty for years before Frank and I discovered it. Meanwhile, the trees and shrubs grew wild, and the wood-frame house suffered termites and rot.

But the artist who originally built the home also built a detached studio that made a perfect guest apartment. Frank and I realized its potential immediately, so we added a small kitchen, a deluxe bathroom, and a loft with three twin beds.

"The rental deal is good for us," Frank assured Daniel. "We found damage our home inspector hadn't noticed, and the rental income helps pay for those repairs. This has become a FORD house."

"A what?"

"Fix Or Repair Daily. Anyway, we enjoy guests. Your mom makes them feel welcome, and I enjoy talking to people from all over. The other day I was talking to a guy from Europe while a family of otters played in the creek out back. You ought to bring Maddie and Rachel down for an extended visit. You'd love the place."

"And we're not doing it only for income," I had added. "This property is magical. I'd feel selfish if we didn't share it."

Clearly, Daniel didn't understand that we were maintaining the house for his sake. Someday he would inherit this place, and we didn't want to leave him with a derelict property.

Daniel *had* brought his family to visit—twice in five years. Rachel always walked the property as if she expected a snake to drop from the trees at any moment, but Maddie loved it. She was twelve when they first visited, and she climbed the oaks, took pictures of the wild rabbits, and even videoed a raccoon fishing in the creek.

As I relaxed on the front porch with Ike, I remembered how Maddie used to enjoy the tire swing Frank hung from a horizontal branch. Frank would turn it as many times as he could, then let go. As she spun, Maddie's squealing alarmed Ike, who barked so forcefully that his front feet left the ground. Afterward, the poor dog would collapse, panting at Maddie's feet while she begged Frank to spin her again.

I missed Maddie something fierce. I doubted she'd still climb trees at seventeen, but if Daniel needed to chill, why couldn't he do it here? The moss-draped tree canopies, the birds' cheerful songs, and the rippling creek never failed to relax me.

Frank stepped onto the porch, wearing dress pants and a long-sleeved shirt. "A teacher got sick," he said, adjusting his tie. "When I get home, I'll haul out the pressure washer and clean that north side of the caboose."

Ever mindful of his health, I blew him a kiss and reminded him to be careful. "Don't let those kids raise your blood pressure."

Two days later, Frank and I sat in the orthopedist's exam room, where the young doctor said I should start taking my arm out of the sling as much as possible. "We don't want your wrist or elbow to freeze in a bent position, so you'll need to start exercising those muscles. Just don't lift anything heavier than five pounds."

When Frank pulled into the driveway at home, we found Joshua near the front porch. "I hope you don't mind," he said, "but I invited a few friends over."

I forced a smile. "You have friends in town? Your profile said you were from Michigan."

"I grew up here. My friends should be coming by this afternoon, but now I'm heading to the beach."

An hour later, a small horde came down the driveway—twelve, fifteen, twenty people, including several families with young children. And Joshua was still at the beach.

His guests climbed the stairs to the apartment and punched in the unlock code.

"I don't like this," I told Frank as I watched from the window. "If one of them trips over a rock or something, we're liable—and Joshua isn't here to supervise. What should we do?"

"Nothing," Frank said. "We're going to stay put and not look out the window."

"But *twenty* people, plus the six already staying with Joshua— that's way too many for that apartment."

"If you don't want additional folks," Frank said, "you should spell that out in the rental agreement. But he told you he had friends coming, and you didn't object."

Frank had a point, but I couldn't help feeling concerned. Our rental agreement did have a "no party" rule, but who defined *party*, the host or the guest?

What if some of these people smoked in our no-smoking apartment? What if someone burned the house down? What if one of them refused to leave? What if one of the children fell into the creek? What if someone started horsing around on the widow's walk and fell off the roof?

Frank would say I was driving myself crazy over things that might never happen, that I should wait until Joshua and his group checked out and then assess the situation. My logical husband was nearly always right about such things, but I watched the strangers milling around on the deck and wondered which one would fall into the creek and break his neck.

Sunday dawned bright and clear, and our guest apartment hadn't burned down. Joshua's extra guests had disappeared, most leaving after dark, and we hadn't heard any noise that might have disturbed our neighbors.

"See there?" Frank said. "You worried for nothing."

"Just because you didn't worry," I countered, "doesn't mean something bad couldn't have happened."

I took a peek at my calendar. We had guests booked over Christmas, but I had blocked several days afterward so Frank and I could squeeze in a visit to Atlanta before New Year's. I looked forward to having a second Christmas with Daniel's family and personally giving Maddie her presents. Watching a grandchild open gifts was much better than hearing about it later.

I'd have to run the idea past Rachel, of course, but she was usually agreeable, probably because we saw little of our son's wife when we visited. Even on holidays, she worked between sixty and eighty hours a week. Daniel always reminded me that lawyers were paid by the hour.

Because Maddie adored him, Ike would travel with us. Rachel had never complained about hosting our little dog, and we were careful not to let him hop on her leather sofa or scratch her wooden floors.

Daniel and Rachel were easy to shop for, but Maddie . . . I sighed. The girl was growing up too fast. One morning she was a child; by afternoon she was a mini adult. One day she slept with stuffed animals; the next she was critically eying her body. And things had only gotten worse: Seventeen-year-old girls were chameleons, changing from one day to the next.

I could ask Daniel or Rachel for ideas . . . or ask Maddie herself.

I had three weeks to prepare for our trip and do my Christmas shopping before seeing the three of them . . . and assuring myself that all was well in their world.

Chapter Four

Maddie

Braced against a mountain of pillows with my earbuds in, I didn't realize Dad had come into my room until he squeezed my foot.

I nearly dropped my phone. "Dad! You scared me."

"Have you forgotten what time it is?"

I glanced at the clock. "Sorry—I was texting Emily."

"Last one to the family room has to make the popcorn."

I darted past him, but Dad laughed because he always made our snacks. I settled into a corner of the sofa in front of the TV.

Dad had been watching the 4 p.m. Saturday Creature Feature with me since I was in fifth grade. When I was new to horror movies, I loved sitting beside him and hiding my eyes when the movie got too intense. Even now, whenever the theme music began, I'd hug a pillow and pretend to shiver. I didn't have the heart to tell Dad that aliens and monsters no longer scared me.

"What's playing today?" he called from the kitchen.

"*The Thing from Outer Space*," I yelled back. "The version that's older than you."

"Don't mock it." He came around the corner and handed me a bowl of buttered popcorn. "It was the first alien-comes-to-earth story the American public ever saw."

"I'm not mocking," I said. "It's fun to see how things have changed since the Dark Ages. And I hear it's not bad."

"Listen to you." Dad settled into his chair. "Spoken like a real film critic."

I munched as we watched, but I could tell Dad wasn't really into the movie. He didn't flinch when the frozen alien began to defrost, and he didn't smirk at the hokey effects. He seemed a million miles away.

He had been acting weird lately. And that crazy story about falling asleep in his office . . . Not even a sick dog could sleep on the pleather-and-chrome monstrosity he called a couch. But where else could he have been? I'd imagined a thousand scenarios, and only one made sense: Dad was cheating on Mom.

I could understand why he might be interested in another woman. He and Mom got along fine as far as I could tell, but she spent so much time either working or thinking about work that I wouldn't have been surprised if he took up with someone who actually listened when he talked. But if he was having an affair, when was he having it? Most days he was home by six, and he spent his evenings either watching TV or helping me with my sketches. He was home nearly every weekend and filled his Saturdays with yardwork and Creature Features. He and Mom reserved Sundays for church and family dinner, usually at the country club.

Dad pinned the TV with a glassy-eyed stare, but his brows were wrinkled.

"Hey, Dad."

He blinked. "Yeah?"

"The guy who stars in this—didn't you tell me he was famous for another show?"

"Right. Played Marshall Dillon in *Gunsmoke*. Huge back in Nana and Pop's day."

"Was it black-and-white, too?"

"Yep."

"Was *anything* in color back then?"

"Color hadn't been invented yet," he said, his voice dry. "Even our clothes were black-and-white."

I threw a pillow at him. "So is Marshall Dillon going to kill the alien or what?"

"You'll have to watch till the bitter end." Dad leaned back in his recliner. "I'm not going to spoil the ending."

"Even if I want you to?"

"Even then."

Dad wasn't having an affair, I decided. Weirdness was just part of middle age.

After the movie, I left Dad snoozing in his chair. Mom was still working in the study, so I pulled a box of spaghetti from the pantry. I was breaking the noodles when Mom strolled into the kitchen. "You're cooking? Thanks, kiddo. Need any help?"

"Nothing to do but boil pasta and heat up the sauce."

Mom poured herself a glass of iced tea, then dropped onto a barstool at the island. "This case is going to make or break me."

I wasn't really into lawsuits, but her cases were usually interesting. "What's this one about?"

"An eight-year-old girl died because she wasn't fastened into a free-fall amusement park ride. The operators didn't check her safety belt, and because she was sitting on top of buckled seat belts, the electronic sensor didn't pick up the error."

I made a face. "Ugh."

"The park is going to shell out a ton of money for this one."

"They're going to settle?"

"They made an offer, but it wasn't enough to put the company out of business, so we're going to court. The family wants them shut down."

I closed my eyes, imagining falling away from family members on what should have been a fun ride. Would an eight-year-old understand she was about to die?

I slammed the door on that horrible thought.

"Hey, Mom, have you noticed anything strange about Dad lately?"

She raised a brow. "Other than his office nap and his phone battery? Not really. Why?"

"I don't know—he just seems a little off. This afternoon, he barely watched the movie. He stared at the TV, but I could tell he wasn't really focused on it."

Mom shrugged. "It is shopping season, you know. He's probably trying to figure out what to get us for Christmas. That would also explain his evasive replies."

I hadn't been aware of any evasive answers, but I'd seen him shop. He usually grabbed the first thing he liked and ran to the cash register. "So what's on his mind?"

Mom shrugged. "He's probably still thinking about that problem at work."

"Why doesn't he talk about it?"

"Because he doesn't want to bother us with the boring details of pharmaceutical sales." She sighed. "That's one of the things I appreciate most about him. When he's home, he's home."

Unlike you, I wanted to say, but didn't.

"What do you think—dinner in about twenty minutes?" Mom asked, standing.

"Yeah."

"Thanks for cooking." Mom inhaled the steam coming off the stove. "Smells good."

I stirred the bubbling sauce. She might be right about what was on Dad's mind, but for some reason I doubted it.

Chapter Five

Susan

On the thirteenth of December, with our rental guests checked out (after leaving the apartment in good shape), I decided to clean and decorate the unit. The place looked bland without holiday decorations, so I put a skinny Christmas tree in the corner and draped a garland over the bureau. I also put a manger scene in the yard, draped lights and greenery at the windows, and tied red velvet ribbons to the driveway lampposts. Next to the guest manual on the coffee table I left a Bible opened to the nativity story in the second chapter of Luke. As I pulled decorations from the storage closet, I found myself humming "Away in a Manger." Despite the seventy-nine-degree weather, December was beginning to feel like Christmas, and Christmas meant celebration and family.

Careful not to put too much pressure on my still-mending arm, I hung ornaments and prayed that Daniel would bring Rachel and Maddie to Florida. Surely Maddie deserved an old-fashioned holiday with a turkey on the table and pumpkin pie on the buffet, not the precooked holiday meals Rachel favored.

But I wouldn't be upset if they didn't come. Last year I realized that Daniel and Rachel were nearly at the point of saying goodbye to their own Christmas traditions. Maddie would soon be off to college, setting out on her own life adventure. Before Rachel knew it, she'd be hanging stockings and wishing that Maddie and her husband would come to Atlanta for the holiday.

That's when I decided to celebrate Christmas whenever and wherever we could. Frank and I would happily go to Atlanta or Alaska or wherever Daniel, Rachel, and Maddie were. We'd eat anything set before us, and we'd arrange our gifts on a coffee table at the Ramada Inn if we had to. Being together was what mattered.

And why was I feeling melancholy about missing Maddie when I had a phone in my pocket? I checked the time to be sure Maddie would be home from school, then dialed my granddaughter's cell. I heard the phone ring and braced myself for the inevitable transfer to voice mail. That was the disadvantage of caller ID—if someone didn't want to talk to you, they didn't answer.

But Maddie did. "Nana?"

"Maddie? I can't believe . . . How are you?"

"I'm fine."

"What are you up to?"

"Um, I'm reading a book for English."

"Is it good?"

"Sorta. Can't really tell 'cause I just started."

Conversing with a high schooler—I'd forgotten how challenging it could be.

"Hey, Pop and I were wondering what to get you for Christmas. Is there something you need? Something your parents aren't likely to get for you?"

"I don't know. Anything's fine."

"I'd hate to get you something you don't like or can't use."

"You don't have to get me anything."

"Of course I do. Christmas is for giving to those we love, and we love you to bits." My throat tightened. "We really do, more than you will ever know."

Silence rolled over the line; then Maddie cleared her throat. "Are you okay, Nana?"

"Just feeling sentimental." I blinked away tears and smiled. "If you can't think of anything, you'll have to be surprised. We're coming up a couple of days after Christmas, Lord willing, so we'll see you soon. I love you."

"Love you too."

The days before Christmas passed in a blur. Our apartment filled and emptied several times, and our Christmas guests, a Japanese family, posed on the deck of the decorated caboose while I recorded the moment with their camera phones.

I ended up doing my shopping online. For Daniel I found a beautiful chess set featuring resin Civil War soldiers painted in blue and gray. Abraham Lincoln and Jefferson Davis stood in for the kings, Mary Todd Lincoln and Varina Howell Davis represented the queens, and drummer boys served as pawns.

I got Rachel a honeysuckle spa basket—soaps, lotions, and bath bombs. If she didn't care for the fragrance of honeysuckle, I figured Maddie might.

"What'd you get the kiddo?" Frank asked as he helped me wrap presents.

"Since Maddie's not a kid anymore, I got her an electronic reader she might actually use. The kids seem to like anything high-tech."

"Smart woman."

I sighed and taped a bow on Daniel's gift. "You want to do anything special for Christmas Eve?"

"For us, you mean?"

"Sure. I could roast a turkey breast and maybe bake a pie."

"You don't have to do all that, hon. I'm sure we can find an open restaurant if you want to eat out."

"What about the rest of Christmas Eve?"

"We'll go to church. Maybe we can watch *It's a Wonderful Life* before we fall asleep."

I laughed. "Like last year?"

Frank wrapped his arms around me. "Truth is, I don't care what we do as long as we do it together."

Chapter Six

Maddie

On Christmas morning, I used to get up in the dark, sneak into my parents' room, and jump on the bed until they rolled out and let me sprint to the tree. All my presents would be waiting there, gifts from Santa, Mom and Dad, Nana and Pop, and Grandma.

But Santa stopped bringing gifts when I stopped believing. My maternal grandmother now sent gift cards in fancy envelopes. Nana and Pop stopped wrapping toys and tended to get me one big present, something expensive and educational.

This year I hoped they'd bring something that wasn't supposed to be good for me.

At nine, I grabbed my robe, went downstairs, and found Mom and Dad in the kitchen. Mom was checking something in the oven—a Christmas miracle!—and Dad was fiddling with the espresso machine.

"Something smells good," I said. "Cinnamon rolls?"

Mom smiled. "In the oven."

I peered into her mixing bowl. "So what's that?"

"Sausage casserole. We'll have the rolls for breakfast and cas-serole for lunch. And that will be the extent of my Christmas cooking, got it?"

"Yep."

I propped my elbows on the island while Dad grinned at me. "You want to eat first or open presents?"

I really didn't care, but the food wasn't ready, and the gifts were.

We made short work of the gift-giving. Dad gave Mom a cash-mere sweater; Mom gave Dad a new robe and slippers. Dad gave me a book about acrylic painting, and Mom gave me an easel. She also stuck a Nordstrom's gift card in my stocking.

"Buy clothes that will last for years," she said. "They'll always be in style if you buy classic designs."

Mom went into the kitchen to check on her casserole, so I turned to Dad, about to roll my eyes at her advice. But he had leaned back in his recliner and lowered his eyelids. A tear trickled from beneath his dark lashes.

"Dad? You okay?"

He looked up and dashed the wetness away. "I'm fine, Mads. Just a little nostalgic." He pointed to the top of the tree. "We bought that star when you were a baby. As soon as you were big enough to grip it, I'd lift you up and let you put it on the top. Somewhere along the way, you got too big for me to lift."

I stared at the star, which looked woefully battered and old-fashioned. "I would have put it up this year, but Mom hired a woman to do the decorating."

"Next year," Dad said. "Promise me you'll be the one to crown the tree. It's your job and no one else's."

"Now you're being silly." I walked over and kissed his cheek. "But if it means so much to you, I'll wait until you're here to watch me do it. Merry Christmas, Dad."

"Merry Christmas, Mads."

He caught my hand and held it until I jerked my thumb toward the kitchen. "I guess I should help Mom."

"Okay. Reserve a cinnamon roll for me, okay?"

I laughed. "You'd better save room for her casserole. It's all we're getting today, remember?"

He brought his index finger to his lips. "I've arranged for an entire dinner to be delivered later this afternoon. Turkey, dressing, cranberry sauce, even a pecan pie—a feast. And when we're done, I have a special surprise for your mom."

"Another present?"

He nodded. "An eternity ring with diamonds all the way around. After twenty years, she deserves one. Hope she likes it."

"Who wouldn't? But your anniversary's in May."

"And that's why it will be a surprise."

Chapter Seven

Susan

Daniel called on Christmas afternoon, and my heart warmed to hear his voice. "Merry Christmas, son."

"Same to you," he said. "Is Dad around?"

"He's right here." I put the call on speaker and gestured for Frank to come closer. "Was Santa good to you this year?"

He chuckled. "I can't complain. What about you? Did Dad book that trip to Hawaii you've always wanted?"

I smiled at Frank. "We're saving that for when we're older. Right now, we're too busy to go on a cruise."

"If you say so." Daniel cleared his throat. "Well, the girls are sure looking forward to seeing you. Rachel has the guest room all spiffed up."

"We can't wait to get there."

"Right." He sighed. "I'd better go. Rachel has Christmas dinner on the table."

"She cooked?"

"I had it delivered."

I laughed. "Such a thoughtful husband."

"Merry Christmas, Mom and Dad." He hesitated. "I love you."

"Love you too, Danny boy," Frank said. "We'll see you soon."

Chapter Eight

Maddie

We didn't have a white Christmas, and we had a gray day after.

I slept till eleven and woke to the unexpected sound of thunder. I pulled back the curtain as a car passed on the wet street, its headlights mingling with the holiday lights that had been coaxed to life by the storm-darkened sky.

I dropped the curtain and stretched out again, hugging my pillow.

No silence, I decided, was like the quiet of an empty house the day after Christmas.

I went downstairs to find the family room empty and the television off. A note on the fridge said Mom had gone to the office. I thought Dad might have gone to church on this Sunday, but through the dining room window I saw his car in the driveway. As rain rattled against the kitchen windows, I sat at the island and ate Pop-Tarts.

Emily and I had talked about going to the mall, but I wasn't wild about going out in freezing rain. Despite the rain, the place would be crazy with people returning gifts. The stores would have great sales, though, plus I had Mom's gift card, and my grandmother had sent me a Visa card loaded with two hundred dollars. Mom wanted me to buy classic, but I had plenty of time to buy old-lady clothes. I'd buy classic when I was thirty; now I wanted to look like my friends, only better.

I glanced out the window again. Maybe the rain would let up . . . or Dad would drive us so we wouldn't have to run through the storm.

I kept expecting him to pop into the kitchen. He never slept late, but yesterday had been a big day, and Mom had been stunned by his surprises. They might have had a late night. . . .

I went to my parents' bedroom door, my socks sliding over the polished wood. "Dad, you awake?" The door was partly open, so I gave it a push. The bed was made.

Back in the kitchen, I found two coffee cups in the sink. So Mom had gone to the office and Dad had gone . . . where?

Suspicion reared its ugly head. The beautiful ring Dad had given Mom hadn't been a cover, had it?

"You'd better be here, Dad."

I searched the study, the guest bath, the family room, the dining room, and the backyard. Mom's garage was empty.

I moved to the opposite side of the house, where Dad used his garage as a gym. My heart lifted when I saw a note on the interior door:

MADDIE, Do not open this door. Call 911 and wait. I love you. Dad.

Baffled, I pulled the note from the door. Had Dad been bitten by a snake in the garage? We never saw snakes this time of year. And anyway, wouldn't he have called 911 himself? Maybe he'd smelled gas. But he'd have called the gas company. People didn't tell others to call 911 unless they were strapped to a bomb or something.

This had to be a joke. I turned the knob, but the door wouldn't budge. "If this is a joke, Dad," I yelled, "it's not funny!"

I ran out the front door, keeping my head down, and hurried to the north side of the house, where rain bounced on Dad's car.

Shivering, I tapped in the garage code. As the opener hummed and the door rose, flooding the interior with light, I saw that a bookcase blocked the door that led into the house. I scanned the weight bench, the treadmill, the rower, the stationary bike, and the old desk in the corner. Dad was there, sitting in Mom's old chair, his head on the desk.

"Good one, Dad. What's up with the note?"

I walked forward, but Dad didn't move. How could he fall asleep out here?

An odd, faintly metallic odor filled my nostrils, accompanied by a sense of dread.

"Dad?" One arm lay bent on the desk, but his fingers were curled, as if he had fallen asleep. I couldn't see his face, only the back of his head, but no one could have missed the thick red puddle that reflected the overhead light and nearly covered the desktop. Another step brought me closer, and that's when I spotted the gun on the floor.

A ghost spider climbed my spine as I nudged his shoulder. "Dad?"

Gray threads I had never noticed in his hair gleamed wetly among the dark strands.

"Dad!" I shoved him hard enough to make the chair creak.

Horror overwhelmed all conscious thoughts. But like a recording on an endless loop, a voice in my head kept repeating, *Call 911 and wait.* Automatically, I obeyed.

I ran back through the rain and into the house. I couldn't

remember where I'd left my phone, so I used the landline in the study. My hands shook so violently, I don't know how I managed to punch 911.

"Help!" I whispered when a woman came on the line. "I think my dad's dead."

She asked for our address and wanted to know if anyone else was with me. "My mom's at work." I recited Mom's number, and the woman said she'd call and send a victim liaison officer to be with me. I didn't know what that was, but I said, "Okay."

After she hung up, I dropped into the desk chair, my arms and legs suddenly limp. I was staring at the desk calendar, trying to remember what day it was, when an unexpected impulse compelled me to lean over and vomit into Mom's trash can.

After that, I sank to the floor and curled into a ball, shivering with the memory of what I'd seen. I couldn't go back into the garage. I didn't want to see Dad like that again.

I don't know how long I lay there—probably not more than a few minutes—but I opened my eyes when I heard sirens, followed by the insistent chime of the doorbell. I pushed myself off the floor and went to the door, where I found a plump, middle-aged woman who introduced herself as Molly and asked if she could come inside.

I nodded as Molly gently pulled me away from the door. "Are you thirsty?" she asked. "Why don't we have a glass of water? Then let's get you into some dry clothes. You must be freezing."

"I'm not thirsty," I said, but I led her into the kitchen and took two bottles of water from the fridge, because it was the polite thing to do.

Then we went into the living room, where she draped a knitted throw around my shoulders and talked softly, but I don't remember anything she said.

All I remember is my teeth chattering because I was terribly, painfully cold.

Chapter Nine

Susan

The sun jabbed bright fingers through the clouds as I arranged our suitcases in the trunk. "I'll Be Home for Christmas" kept playing in my head, so I hummed along, thrilled that we would soon be on our way to Atlanta. Christmas had come and gone, but the best part of the season was only a few hours away.

My mind flooded with precious memories of Christmas: Daniel dumping handfuls of mini marshmallows into his hot cocoa, even as a grown man. Maddie at four, tenderly cradling her new baby doll. Rachel pulling a still-raw turkey from her oven. The poor woman looked on the verge of tears until Frank told her it was nice to know that even his brilliant daughter-in-law could forget to turn on the oven.

I stacked the gifts in the back seat and inhaled the sweet scent of Rachel's bath basket. I hoped she liked honeysuckle.

My phone rang. Who but a car warranty salesman would call the day after Christmas?

My heart twisted when I saw Rachel's name. Surely she wouldn't cancel our visit now.

I forced a bright note into my voice. "Hi, Rachel! We're about to be on our way!"

Silence.

I shook the phone, afraid I'd lost the connection. "Rachel? You still there?"

"I . . . have bad news," she said, and something in her voice sent gooseflesh rippling up my spine. I nearly hung up, not wanting bad news the day after Christmas. I didn't want to cancel this trip. I'd been looking forward to seeing them for days, working overtime to make sure everything went according to plan.

"Susan," Rachel said, drawing a breath. "I don't know how to tell you this."

Again I waited.

"Daniel shot himself this morning. He's dead, and Maddie found him."

No. Daniel couldn't be dead.

A lizard crawling over the roof of our car stopped and flashed his vibrant red throat.

Don't show off for me, you silly thing. I'm not your girlfriend.

"Susan?" Rachel asked.

Daniel's wrapped chess set sat atop a neat stack in the back seat. I had been looking forward to playing with him. He'd win, of course. He always did.

"Susie?" Seemingly from out of nowhere, Frank gripped my arm. "What is it?"

I shook my head, unable to dislodge the words in my ears. This wasn't real. Couldn't be. In a few hours we would pull into Daniel's driveway, and he would be waiting, as he always was.

Kill himself? Never. He was too full of life and promise. He had a wonderful wife and an amazing daughter. A man as successful and unselfish as our Daniel would not even *think* about such a thing. He had people who loved him, who would do anything to help him with whatever he might be facing.

Rachel was still talking, babbling about when we might come and how she had to wait for the autopsy before she could plan the funeral.

Autopsy? Funeral?

I could hear my thumping heart and ragged breaths, but I couldn't feel my arms or legs.

The lizard watched me. Wouldn't it be crazy if he slipped into the car? Daniel would laugh at a hitchhiking lizard.

"Maddie needs you," Rachel said, and Maddie's name hit me like a jolt of electricity. "*I* need you. Maybe you can help us make sense of all this."

"Come whenever you want," Rachel said, her voice lifeless. "The guest room is ready. And I know Maddie would appreciate your being here."

Rachel hung up, leaving me to stare at the phone. I squeezed it, marveling at how solid it felt against my palm.

"Susan," Frank said, stepping closer. "What?"

I couldn't repeat what Rachel had told me. She had to be mistaken, and in a minute I'd wake and life would be as it was a moment before.

"Who was that, Susan? What's happened?"

I met Frank's gaze, and the world fell away. A cloud blocked the sun, the scent of honeysuckle made my stomach churn, and a chilly breath of wind raised the hairs on my arms. I lifted my eyes to the sky, dropped my phone, and released a scream that drove me to my knees.

Frank knelt and wrapped his arms around me. "Who?" he said, his voice hoarse. "Not Daniel."

I nodded and stammered the awful news.

"Not my boy." Frank's face went gray. "How could it be Daniel?"

I shook my head.

Time stood still as we held each other. I couldn't look at Frank but stared into space, wanting to die myself. Death would be infinitely better than feeling this agony.

Finally, we helped each other stand and stagger into the house.

All I could think was that I should have listened to the sermon that morning instead of thinking about Daniel. I shouldn't have found so much joy in the thought of being with him, because God was a jealous God.

Frank guided me into the bedroom, and on the bed where we had conceived our beloved son, we clung desperately to each other while we fell apart.

Later, Frank and I sat at the kitchen bar and picked at leftovers we didn't want and couldn't eat. Frank lowered his fork and rested his head on his hand. "I don't understand any of this. I want answers. I need answers."

"So do I." I tilted my head toward the door. "The car's ready to go. And she did say we could come whenever we wanted."

"Should we—?"

"Everything's ready."

"We don't have any guests, right?"

"Not until Friday. The Lord must have known." The words came automatically, but once spoken, they stung. How could the Lord have known about Daniel's death? If he had, wouldn't he have stopped it?

I turned to Frank, whose eyes brimmed with pain. "Where was God this morning? How could he allow Danny to pick up a gun? He has never been a gun guy."

"I don't know." Frank placed his hand over mine. "And right now, I don't want to ask. I want all this to be a bad dream."

I stood and rubbed my broken arm, which had begun to ache. Six weeks had passed since I broke the bone, and this morning I'd felt fine. But now every movement brought pain, and with every breath I felt as though a boulder had taken up residence between my lungs.

"We need to get to Atlanta. Can you stay awake to drive?"

"I wouldn't be able to sleep if I wanted to."

I picked up our plates and carried them to the sink. As I scraped the untouched food into the disposal, a troubling thought struck me. "Frank, are we still parents? If we no longer have a child—?"

"Of course we are." Frank walked over and put his arms around me. "We still have a son. He didn't disappear."

"Didn't he?" The tears came again, so I wept them against my husband's shoulder.

How could this be happening? Only a few hours ago, I had considered myself blessed. Just this morning I had joined in the praise music, joyfully singing that God was wonderful, he was great, he was over all.

Where was God while Daniel struggled? If he was wonderful, why didn't he answer Daniel's cry for help? Why didn't he work a miracle to deliver Daniel from *his* lions' den? If God was over all, why didn't he preserve the life of my child, his child, *our* child? My mind bulged with questions, and I knew Frank had to be wrestling with the same thoughts.

"I don't know," Frank said, his voice trembling, "how we're going to survive this."

I met his gaze. "I don't know how we're going to survive, but I *do* know one thing—we have to help Maddie. She was a daddy's girl, and she's going to need us."

"Right." Frank nodded. "You finish up here. I have to look for my black suit."

My throat tightened. I no longer owned a black dress, but I couldn't think about that now. "So we're definitely leaving tonight?"

"We are. No sense staying here with a thousand questions and no answers."

Chapter Ten

Susan

At 5 a.m., Frank pulled off the interstate to a roadside restaurant. I nodded in grim approval. After nine hours in the car, we needed to wash our tear-streaked faces. I also needed to feed Ike and take him for a walk.

I looked like a train wreck in the restroom mirror. I splashed my face, applied lipstick, and ran a comb through my hair, not caring about anything beyond the loss that had gutted us.

And the haunting questions.

I felt guilty for even thinking about food, but since we had to keep going, we ordered breakfast. The waitress quizzed me about my preferences—how did I want my eggs, apple or orange juice, biscuits or toast?—and I could barely respond because so many other questions filled my head: Why was I allowed to live while Daniel died? Why were we having to bury our son? And why hadn't Daniel reached out when he ran into a problem he couldn't handle?

Rachel had always been more rational than emotional, and she would probably soldier through the funeral in her own disciplined way. But Maddie was a kid—mature for her age, but she'd never experienced this kind of grief. And when I thought about her discovering Daniel's body . . .

"Frank—" My voice broke. "When I think about what Maddie must be going through . . ."

He stopped mid-chew and lowered his head. "Don't."

"But she's at that age where—"

"Susie, please!" He shook his head. "I can't."

We didn't speak again until we made our way back to the car.

I couldn't imagine a world without Daniel. The very idea was ludicrous.

I usually enjoyed watching the forest as we drove north through Georgia, but the trees along the interstate seemed faded and the dawn a faded gray. How could life go on? The people in other cars zipped by, oblivious to the shift in the universe, and I wondered how they could sit so placidly when the world had lost all its color.

As badly as I needed to see Maddie and Rachel, dread overwhelmed me as we neared the sprawling development of showplace properties where Daniel lived. How could I be of any use to his family when I wanted to die myself? The constant sob in my throat finally erupted when we pulled onto the brick courtyard where Daniel's silver Lexus—the car he'd won as salesman of the year—sat in front of his garage as if nothing had happened.

I wanted to be strong, especially for Maddie, but the house repulsed me. Covered in gray stucco, the French country home featured a mansard roof and quoins at every corner—square blocks designed "to give it a look of strength and permanence," Rachel had said when they bought it.

Strength and permanence? What a cruel joke. Daniel should have lived long enough to pay off the mortgage and welcome grandchildren to this place.

I snapped the leash onto Ike's collar and walked him to a patch of grass. I shivered, trying to adjust to the chill and the skeletal trees.

Frank came over, took my face in his hands, and thumbed away my tears, clearly fighting his own. "Let's try to—"

"I know." I scooped up the dog and led the way to the door.

Maddie peered out and rushed into Frank's arms, burying her head in his chest as she burst into tears.

"My one and only," Frank said, the words coming out as a ragged whisper.

I rubbed her back. "We came as soon as we could," I whispered. "Do you think your mom will want us to stay here, or should we get a hotel?"

"I want you to stay here," Maddie said, lifting her head. "We're not expecting anyone else, so come on in." She scratched Ike's head. "Ikey! I've missed you."

"I'll get the luggage." Frank turned toward the car.

I put Ike down and followed Maddie into the huge foyer. "You'll have the guest room," Maddie said, managing a tearful smile as she led the way up the curving staircase. "Mom finished redecorating it a couple of weeks ago."

I didn't care about the guest room; I wanted to ask a thousand questions. But Maddie looked as if she'd been sleeping before we arrived, and she probably needed time to wake up.

"Are you sure it's okay if we stay here?" I asked, gently probing. "Is your other grandmother coming?"

Maddie shook her head. "She might drive down for the funeral," she said, pushing her dark, curly hair away from her face. "But she won't be staying."

As we climbed the stairs, I looked over the railing. From there I could see into the family room, where the Christmas tree stood dark and lonely, with a few unopened gifts still waiting on the red-and-gold skirt. A trash bag stood off to the side, colorful paper spilling from its mouth.

"What time did you leave home, Nana?"

"Um . . . we left last night, right after dinner."

"You didn't stop?"

"Only for breakfast."

"Wow." Maddie opened the door to the guest room. "You probably want to get some sleep."

I didn't, but Maddie looked like she wanted to go back to bed, so I stepped into the room and dropped my purse into an upholstered chair.

That's when I remembered—the last time I talked to him, Daniel mentioned that Rachel had redone the guest room and wanted us to be her first guests. Had he known we'd be coming for his *funeral*?

Somehow I found my voice. "Maddie? We love you. You know that, don't you?"

She blinked rapidly. "Sure. I love you too."

Frank brought in our suitcase, then looked at me as if awaiting instructions.

"Well," Maddie said, twiddling her fingers, "I'll let you two get settled while I get dressed. If you need anything, Mom should be up in a little while."

When she left, Frank dropped onto the bed, shoulders slumping, his face rippling with anguish. "What do we do now?"

I sat next to him, weary with grief, yet knowing I'd never be able to sleep. "I think I'll start breakfast."

"We just ate."

"For Maddie and Rachel."

"Right." He pulled himself off the bed, breathing hard.

"Did you take your pills?" I asked.

"They're in the suitcase."

"Honestly, Frank, we have enough to be stressed about."

"Don't worry. I'm fine."

"I'm not worried—I'm concerned."

"Whatever." He shot me a sidelong glance. "I've got a little more on my mind than pills, you know."

Before going to the kitchen, I followed Frank outside to help bring in the gifts. I was halfway to the car when a woman walking her dog stopped, shaded her eyes, and called a greeting. "You must be family."

For an instant I was confused; then I nodded.

"Such a shame about Dan," she said. "Simply a shame."

I started at her referring to Daniel as *Dan*. "We're Daniel's parents."

The woman nodded. "I'm Elaine, and my husband and I have lived next door for six years. Dan and Rachel were great neighbors, and Dan was close to my husband. We were so shocked."

I folded my arms. "We . . . we don't know much."

Elaine glanced down, then met my gaze. "It happened in the garage. Apparently Dan put a note on the inside door and blocked it, but Maddie found a way in. I'm sorry, but that's all I know."

I pressed my hand over my mouth. I was standing only a stone's throw from where Daniel died.

"He—" I cleared my throat. "He hadn't seemed upset or mentioned any sort of problem?"

Elaine shook her head. "He and my husband were friends, but they didn't confide in each other." She scoffed. "Does anyone do that anymore?"

"Some people"—my voice broke—"do."

Elaine squeezed my arm. "I'm very sorry for your loss. It's a horrible thing, just terrible."

I struggled to meet the woman's eyes. "Are the police sure it was . . ."

Elaine's brow arched. "No one has suggested otherwise."

"But Daniel was so positive, I can't imagine—"

"People get depressed."

"Not Daniel."

"Again, I'm so sorry."

The woman walked on.

Frank had set the gifts on the grass. "I don't think she knew Danny at all," he said. "What should we do with his present?"

"Let's give it to Maddie. Daniel would like that."

I was frying bacon in Rachel's gleaming gray kitchen when she appeared, her hair up in a messy ponytail and wearing the robe I bought Daniel for Christmas last year. She glanced from me to Frank to Ike, then gave us a thin smile. "Hey. When did you all arrive?"

"Early," Frank said, rising. He gave her a hug, and I left the stove to do the same.

"Maddie let us in," I explained, "and we moved into the guest room, which looks beautiful, by the way. I thought you might like to have breakfast when you got up."

Rachel walked to the island bar and slid onto a stool. "I'm not hungry. But if you have coffee . . ."

"I can make some," I said, moving toward the complicated coffee maker. "As soon as I figure out how to work this thing."

I hoped she would come over and show me how to operate the machine, but she propped her elbows on the counter and lowered her face into her hands.

"We couldn't stay away," Frank said, placing his hand on her back. "A family needs to come together at a time like this."

"Thank you," Rachel said, so faintly I could barely hear her. "I wasn't thinking much yesterday. After I heard the news, I was— I think I was acting on instinct. I don't even remember coming home from the office."

I lowered my voice. "Do you want to talk about it? There's so much we don't understand."

"You're not alone." She lifted her head. "I spent twenty years with the man and never dreamed he would do anything—like that."

"Had he been depressed?"

"Not that I could tell. About a month ago he mentioned problems at work, but when he didn't bring it up again, I assumed everything had been worked out. We had no secrets. At least, I didn't think we did."

"Did the police investigate?"

Rachel sighed. "They confirmed it was suicide. He wrote a note to Maddie, blocked the door, and only his fingerprints were on the gun. I didn't even know he'd bought one, but the police found the receipt in his car."

"Things were okay between the two of you?" Frank asked. "I mean he hadn't . . ."

"No. He was always home at night, he had no problem with me seeing his text messages, and he never lied to me—at least, not to my knowledge."

I bit my lip. "Could he have been depressed?"

Frank scoffed. "Daniel's always been as steady as a rock."

"But anybody can—"

"He wasn't depressed at Christmas," Rachel said. "He seemed happy, even sentimental. But the police pointed out that he had bought the gun, waited until after Christmas, waited until I went to work before he wrote the note and put it on the door. But he should have known Maddie would do anything to get to him."

She gulped, tears slipping over her cheeks, and I covered my mouth to restrain my own sobs. Nothing about this made sense, and maybe it never would.

Chapter Eleven

Maddie

Ike and I cuddled in my room while neighbors and friends of my parents came and went. From my window I watched people walk to the front door, usually with a dish or platter, and a few minutes later they drove away.

Nobody wanted to stay, and I didn't blame them. Mom was a mess. I was glad Nana and Pop had come, but they had to be messed up too. They looked at me with such pity and sadness that I nearly told them I was okay, though I wasn't. I kept seeing Dad in the garage, his head on the desk, and I knew those images would never, *ever* leave my brain. Even if I managed to shove those memories aside, how could I adjust to the idea of life without Dad?

I put off going downstairs, knowing everyone would stare once I entered the room. People were bound to be asking about me, and I was pretty sure the story about my finding Dad had already made its way around the neighborhood. Everybody had to be saying I'd be scarred for life, and they were probably right.

I had never known anyone who committed suicide. I'd heard about famous people who killed themselves, but they weren't ordinary, so it made a weird kind of sense that they'd choose an extraordinary way to die.

But Dad? I gave Ike a squeeze and fondled his velvety ears. "Dad wasn't dramatic," I whispered. "So what was he thinking?"

Ike stared at me, as clueless as I was.

Something else bothered me too. When our favorite influencer killed herself with an overdose, Emily said the girl was going to hell.

I stared at her, astounded. "Why would you say that?"

Emily shrugged. "Everybody knows it's true. Suicide is the unforgiveable sin. You kill yourself, you go straight to hell."

I'd never heard anything like that at our church, but I hadn't actually been to a service since middle school. Still, I was pretty sure my parents didn't agree with Emily. Dad wouldn't have shot himself if he did.

Or would he?

I pulled Ike into my arms and turned to the window.

Someone knocked at my door.

"Who's there?"

Mom's face appeared in the doorway. "Are you coming downstairs?"

"Do I have to?"

"Some of your friends might drop by. Or their parents."

"Okay."

When I finally went down, I found Nana and Pop answering the door, accepting food, and listening to the same words over and over: "I'm so sorry for your loss." I was surprised to find them on their feet—after all, they were *old*, and they'd driven all night to get here.

But they were far from 100 percent. I could see the quiver at Nana's chin and hear the quaver in Pop's voice. They were definitely struggling to hold it together.

Most of the visitors avoided speaking to me, which was fine. A few of them glanced over and then looked quickly away, as if I had a flashing *Danger!* sign on my forehead. I was The One Who Found Him, and no one wanted to ask me about *that*.

So I stood helplessly in the foyer, trying to think of something to do, but nothing would make the situation any better. I leaned against the wall and tried to distract myself from the horror of what Dad had done by imagining that he'd been killed in a wreck or died from cancer—*anything* that would have changed the looks on people's faces. Sadness and sympathy were one thing; shock and horror were entirely different. I knew what everyone was thinking— something must have been really, terribly wrong in our family.

I couldn't shake the feeling that Dad had disrespected not only himself, but me and Mom, too. *Especially me.* Even though I wasn't perfect, I knew Dad loved me. I think he tried to show that every day . . . until he didn't.

How could he leave me in such a horrible way—knowing, *knowing*, I would find him like that.

I closed my eyes, wishing I could unplug the movie in my mind.

Trying to distract myself, I walked over and studied the food spread over the dining room table—macaroni, potato salad, chicken salad, pot roast, mysterious casseroles. Ordinarily I'd have been drooling over so many choices, but I couldn't eat a bite.

I went into the kitchen, where desserts crowded the island— pumpkin pie, sweet potato pie, cherry pie, banana pie, chocolate chess pie. That last one got me. It was Dad's favorite.

Was I going to spend the rest of my life obsessing over things that reminded me of him?

Nana brought in a coconut cake and squeezed it between a Bundt and a German chocolate creation that oozed with icing. After placing the latest offering, she gave me a *Sweetheart, I'm ready to fall apart too* look and squeezed my hand.

I wanted to hug her more than anything in that moment, but she was desperately trying to stay busy. In a minute she would hurry back to the foyer, so I touched her arm. "Do people really think we'll eat all this?"

The firm line of Nana's mouth softened. "You'll have visitors after the funeral," she said, the lines around her eyes softening, "and they'll need to eat something."

"Nobody wants to stick around today though, huh?"

Nana shrugged. "They left," she said, her eyes gentle, "because most people don't know what to say at times like this. They bring food because they care. They leave because they don't know what to say."

Or because they were afraid something similar might happen to their family.

I opened the back door so Ike could go out, then took a plate from a cupboard. Except for the heaps of food, I could almost pretend this was like any other visit from Nana and Pop. Mom usually stayed in the study while Nana fussed in the kitchen, asking Dad what he wanted for lunch or dinner. Pop always sat on that same stool, folding his arms as he teased Nana and joked with Dad.

I swallowed to bring the lump down from my throat. If I tried really hard, I could pretend Dad had just left for the grocery, but why would he do that when we had all this food?

I set my plate on the counter and felt my appetite shrivel even further. Fresh tears stung my eyes when Pop came into the kitchen, and I saw the tenderness in his eyes.

"How are you doin', hon?" he asked.

"I'm—" My throat closed, and I couldn't say anything else.

Pop wrapped me in a bear hug, groaning as he rocked me. "I know," he said, his voice gruff. "I know, my one and only Maddie. I loved him too, more than my own life. One day"—he bent to look into my eyes—"we'll be with your dad again."

I wanted to scream that I wasn't in the mood to hear that stuff, but my throat felt too tight for more than a whisper.

So I looked up and gave him a wobbly smile. "Promise?"

Chapter Twelve

Susan

In all my years of imagining the worst, I had never imagined the funeral of my son. Nothing could have prepared me for its stark reality.

The scent of lilies and carnations permeated the chapel as we entered. The mortuary director had suggested that the four of us sit down front, but I said Frank and I would rather be inconspicuous and sit in a middle row. I could tell from Frank's look that I should have discussed this with him, but I was hoping to overhear whispers that might give us a clue why Daniel had ended his life.

When we were settled, Frank draped an arm around my shoulder and pulled me close. "This is a mistake," he whispered. "It looks like we've abandoned Rachel and Maddie."

I hadn't even thought of that. "Should we join them?"

He shook his head. "Too late."

I felt even worse—for Rachel and Maddie, and because I'd

upset Frank. I'd heard that the loss of a family member could strain a marriage, and that was the last thing I wanted.

At the viewing the night before, a floral spray had arrived from Florence Johnston, Rachel's mother. Rachel tucked the card in her pocket without comment. Apparently, her mother would not be attending the funeral after all.

The mortician had done a masterful job. Rachel told us Daniel held the gun at an angle, so the bullet exited near his left eye. Not only had the hole been filled in, but Daniel's face had an almost healthy glow, though Frank muttered that the makeup looked more orange than tan. The laugh lines around Daniel's mouth had been smoothed, the crinkles at the corners of his eyes filled, and the arms that used to hug me were rigid.

At quarter to eleven a song came over the speakers, the lyrics telling of a man whose life had changed when he met Jesus, and if people called him a loser, well, he was happy to have lost his guilt and sin.

The song had been a favorite of Daniel's. We had taken him to church ever since he was a baby, but he found Jesus—*really* found him—when he turned eighteen and was preparing to follow his friends into a season of collegiate carousing.

The summer before his freshman year, he came home one night, woke us, and apologized for all the times he'd lied to us. He said he would never do it again because a Christian should honor his parents.

Frank and I listened, dumbfounded. I was skeptical—after all, he'd been "saved and baptized" when he was seven. I'd spent years thinking of him as backslidden, while Frank called him confused.

In the end, we were both proved wrong, because Daniel's life changed after that night. He began to read his Bible, he prayed about his decisions, and he decided not to go to a party school but remain at home until he was sure what the Lord wanted him to do.

Frank and I nearly fell over when he began to ask our opinion about the girls he dated. After he'd dated Rachel more than a year, we were delighted to learn they had decided to commit their lives to loving God and each other.

When Daniel placed the wedding band on Rachel's finger, I felt I had run a marathon and won. My joy at their wedding was eclipsed only once—the day Rachel had given birth to our one and only Maddie.

The memory made my throat ache. A sob rose in my chest, so I drew a deep breath and tried to force it down. The chapel had nearly filled, and Maddie and Rachel had taken their places on the front row. The service would soon begin, a short ceremony to honor the life of a man who could never be summed up in fifteen or twenty minutes.

I gripped Frank's hand, knowing that in both our minds, thoughts of *how* and *why* were chasing each other on an endless track.

The question that haunted me was whether Daniel had really known and loved God. Had his faith been a mere facade? If he was a true Christian, his life belonged to God, so how could he wrest control from God's hands and act on his own? Why would he do such a thing?

Nothing about this made sense. Daniel was a good man, a moral man, and as far as I knew, he behaved as if he belonged to God. For years he had taught a Sunday school class of middle school boys, and nobody did that just for the fun of it.

I leaned toward Frank. "I won't be able to stand it if Rachel allows people to parade up there to sob and ramble, especially if anyone tries to guess at Daniel's reasons."

"Don't worry," Frank said. "Rachel said the service would be short and sweet."

But what would the pastor say? Would he blame Daniel for his decision? Would he say Daniel had disappointed God? Would he admit the truth about Daniel's death, or would he offer Daniel's friends a nebulous word salad?

I steeled myself as Maddie walked to the lectern and unfolded a sheet of paper with trembling hands. "Jesus said to them, 'I am the bread of life; whoever comes to me shall not hunger, and whoever believes in me shall never thirst. But I said to you that you have seen me and yet do not believe. All that the Father gives me will come to me, and whoever comes to me I will never cast out. For I have come down from heaven, not to do my own will but the will of him who sent me. And this is the will of him who sent me, that I should lose nothing of all that he has given me, but raise it up on the last day. For this is the will of my Father, that everyone who looks on the Son and believes in him should have eternal life, and I will raise him up on the last day.'"

I gripped Frank's hand as the minister stood.

Chapter Thirteen

Maddie

I hoped the preacher would say something about my reading, even a thank-you. I mean, he had to know how hard it was for me to stand up there and not cry. But he wasn't even looking at me or Mom. Maybe it'd be weird if he had. Maybe he didn't want to make us uncomfortable.

"We are here today to celebrate the life of Daniel Lawton," he said. "And to express our grief over his untimely and unexplained death. We don't know why Daniel took his life, but we do know he was a believer who had entrusted his life to Jesus. He was a charitable man, a loving father to Maddie, and an adoring husband to Rachel. He was successful and hardworking, a good neighbor, and generous with his time."

I didn't know the preacher well—church had been Mom and Dad's thing, not mine—but he sounded as if he actually knew Dad.

"We trusted Daniel when he was alive," he went on, "and because we saw that his actions were always carefully considered, we can conclude he was in one of life's greatest pains or challenges to have taken such action. We do not have to agree with what he did—I'm sure he had reasons that seemed powerful—and one day we can ask Daniel to explain why he chose to die by suicide. Though he has caused us heartache, after we are reunited, the grief that shredded our hearts on earth will no longer be relevant. We will be with our loved ones again, we will hug them and laugh with them, and we will behold the glory of Jesus, who makes all things new. Nothing from this world will ever be able to cause us grief again. Pain, separation, and death will be forever banished.

"We who loved Daniel are suffering now. The pain can be intense, and it doesn't vanish overnight. But a day is coming when we will no longer remember the agony because our joy at seeing him again will be so great, we'll have no room for memories of our grief.

"I know that hearing about the future may not help you feel better now. And God understands too. He grieves the deaths of his children. He understands our suffering because his son, Jesus, suffered agonies you and I will never experience.

"The psalmist says God keeps track of our sorrows and collects our tears in his bottle. He records everything we experience in his book, the one in which he has already recorded everything we will say, think, and do in this life. He understands us because he made us."

The preacher paused and cleared his throat. "So, though we weep now, in heaven we will sit with Daniel, smile at his dad jokes, and cry tears of joy over our reunion. So, cry when you need to, but don't despair as if you have no hope. If you have Jesus, you have all the hope you need. He is always close by, ready to comfort you, challenge you, and change your life forever. Just like he changed Daniel's. Just like he changed mine."

I respected the preacher for being honest and actually talking about Dad, which I liked more than hearing a bunch of theology.

After praying, the preacher lifted his head. "After a brief grave-side service, friends and family are invited to the Lawton house. Thank you so much for coming to help us remember Daniel, a truly fine man."

Everything was quiet for a minute. Then music began and Mom stood.

I followed her out. So was that it? All the things my father had been, said, and done wrapped up in a five-minute speech?

Maybe that's why Dad shot himself. Because he didn't think he'd accomplished anything that couldn't be summarized in five minutes . . . including being my dad.

The funeral-home limo took Nana, Pop, Mom, and me to the cemetery, the four of us wrapped in a cocoon of silence.

When we arrived, Dad's casket lay on a table by the grave. A green canopy sheltered us from the sun, and we lined up like sol-diers on a carpet of artificial turf.

The pastor read a single verse: "As it is written, 'What no eye has seen, nor ear heard, nor the heart of man imagined, what God has prepared for those who love him.'"

He lowered his Bible and looked like he was about to pray, but Pop's groan shattered the stillness.

My eyes flew open. Pop's face had gone gray, and sweat covered his upper lip as he clutched Nana's arm and crumpled to the fake grass.

"Frank!" Nana fell to her knees and tugged at his collar, while the preacher pulled out his phone and said he was calling 911. When I finally heard the sirens, I turned away and covered my ears. If God took Pop from us, I was done.

In minutes the EMTs had torn open his shirt and applied sensors to his chest. After another minute, Pop opened his eyes. "What's all the fuss?" he growled.

Nana stroked his face. "We thought—"

"I'm fine," he said, swatting away one of the medics.

The man nodded. "EKG normal," he said. "But get him checked out."

Pop sat up and ripped the wires from his chest. "I'm here to bury my son. Let me do that, please."

One of the EMTs helped Pop to his feet as the pastor said, "We can be done here. I'm sure you all want to get home."

Pop stared at the casket as if he could see Dad through the lid. "That is my son," he said, his voice low and desperate. "I loved him. I protected him. And I taught him that a man doesn't quit until the job is done." He lifted his chin. "I'm staying until Daniel is in the ground."

The pastor slipped his arm around Nana's shoulder and guided her toward the car. Mom and I followed, but Pop stood as straight as a soldier as the funeral people prepared to lower the casket.

I turned away. I didn't want to see that.

After the graveside service, we hurried home so we'd be ready for the guests. Mom's fretting over how the house looked made everything surreal. We had just buried my father, and Mom was wondering if she'd remembered to vacuum.

Funny how life could switch from one extreme to the other in a matter of minutes. The day Dad died, the police and EMTs came to the house with shrieking sirens. They left in absolute silence. Pop was a picture of strength at the funeral. At the graveside, I thought we were going to lose him.

Now he seemed okay. Nana insisted he go get checked out and shook her head when he refused, but I knew she'd keep an eye on him.

People began to arrive about twenty minutes later, most of them strangers to me, but I recognized some of them from the day everyone brought food to the house.

Mom sat in a wing chair, and people approached with bowed heads, as if visiting a queen.

I heard one couple whispering about our house. "So, what do you think?" the man said. "Seven figures?"

The woman said, "She may want to stay."

"Where her husband . . . Not likely."

Three hours before, I missed my father so badly my throat hurt. Now my longing for him vanished, swallowed up by rage.

Why had he done this—to himself, to Mom, to me? If he hadn't been dead already, I'd have killed him.

Chapter Fourteen

Susan

Daniel's coworkers and neighbors seemed nice enough, but I felt like a loaded mousetrap, ready to snap at any provocation. When people told me how sorry they were, I had to bite my lip to keep from saying, "Not as sorry as I am."

People who had nothing to say felt compelled to fill the silence.

"At least he's not suffering anymore."

None of us knew he was suffering. How did you know?

"I know it hurts now, but the pain will pass."

I doubt it. The hole in my heart feels permanent.

"I read a wonderful book that will really help—" and they rattled off a title.

I know they meant well, but my pain was unique, different even from Frank's. We had both lost a son, but I lost the baby I carried for nine months. I lost the child who nursed at my breast, who clung to me when he was frightened, and who drew me crayon pictures on Mother's Day. I unconsciously modeled what he later sought in a wife.

I was Daniel's *mother*, and our relationship was different from the relationships he had with Frank, Rachel, and Maddie.

Fortunately, the visitors didn't stay long. They ate, admired the flowers, and murmured all the standard stock phrases. They regarded us with what seemed a mix of pity, fear, and curiosity, then gave us perfunctory embraces and left.

When they were all gone, I collapsed into a chair. Rachel slumped on the sofa. Frank dropped to a footstool.

Maddie had disappeared long before.

"Well, that was torture," Rachel said, closing her eyes. "I felt sorry for some of them. The fixers were frustrated because they couldn't figure out how to make things right, and the handwringers seemed surprised that we had already pondered the unanswerable questions."

"If those were your friends," I said, "I'd hate to—well, you know."

"Most of them are only acquaintances," she said. "Honestly, Daniel and I were so busy, we could count close friends on one hand. And I saw only two of them at the funeral."

"They probably don't know what to say," I said, softening my voice. "I've experienced that myself. Words seem so inadequate."

"Sometimes they are," Frank said. "And an entire dictionary can't make this right. Daniel chose to leave us, so we have no choice but to accept what happened. We don't have to like what he did, but we have to figure out how to go on without him."

A tear ran down his cheek—the first I'd seen him shed since morning.

"I've always thought my faith could get me through anything," he went on, his voice hoarse. "But I'll be honest—after we heard the news, I didn't want to pray. I didn't want to throw myself at God's feet, because I didn't like what he had allowed." He lowered his head. "I guess this is one of those times God's power needs to show up in my weakness. Because I don't have the strength."

Rachel's chin quivered and her eyes filled. "I've been asking," she said, "if I did something to deserve this. Was I not a good-enough wife? Was Daniel punishing me, or was God?"

"Rachel, honey." I leaned toward her. "Daniel adored you. And God wouldn't punish you this way."

"Then why?" Her anguished voice broke on the last word, so I got up and wrapped her in my arms, realizing she'd had no one else to hold her while she sobbed. Rachel, introverted to the bone, would open her heart only to someone she trusted.

"Go ahead," I whispered. "I'm here, and I love you."

I don't know how long we sat there, but Frank and I wept with her until all of us were spent. "Thank you," Rachel said. "I needed that."

"I'm glad we could be here for you," I said. "And now, I think Frank and I will tackle that mess in the kitchen."

Rachel lifted her hand. "Before you start, I want to ask you two something."

Frank's usually lively eyes looked weary.

Rachel sighed. "I know we're all struggling, but I have so much on my plate—a big case, and Maddie—so I wondered if you'd be willing to help me out."

I folded my hands. "Rachel, anything. What do you need?"

Guilt flickered across her face. "Raising a teenager is not easy, and all this makes it worse. Is there any way you could take Maddie until the end of the school year? I think—I *know*—you would be good for her. And I know she'd enjoy being with you."

"I—we—" Frank's shoulders slumped. "Whaddya think, Susie?"

I pressed my hand over my mouth. We loved our grand-daughter, but . . .

"Of course we want to help," I said, "but doesn't she need her friends? What if we stayed here a few weeks?"

"Maddie's friends aren't good for her," Rachel said, her voice sharpening. "More than once, we could tell she'd been drinking. She was dating a guy we didn't approve of, though that might have ended by now. Daniel thought he smelled pot on her one night, so of course we worried about stronger stuff. You know peer pressure."

"Yes, but—"

"She loves you," Rachel went on, "nearly as much as she loved Daniel. Maddie was a daddy's girl. He was always there for her, and she's not going to know what to do without him. I'm afraid she'll resent me for not being Daniel. Frankly, I don't have the energy to deal with mourning, my job, and a troubled teenager. Please, say you'll take her. I don't think I can survive otherwise."

I caught Frank's eye. What could we do? Rachel had surprised us with this, but she was family.

"Why don't we sleep on it?" Frank asked. "There's a lot to consider—school and how we're going to arrange things . . ."

"Like what?"

I turned as Ike trotted down the stairs and came running to us. Maddie stood behind him in her bare feet. No wonder none of us had heard her.

"Hey, kiddo," Frank said, grinning like a man who'd just won the lottery. "How would you like to live with Nana and me until summer?"

Maddie turned to her mother, her expression unreadable. "Are you trying to get rid of me?"

Rachel lifted her hands. "I thought a change would be good for you. You like Florida."

"Dad's gone, and now you want to ship me off?"

"It's only for a few months, Maddie. You can come home in plenty of time to get a summer job. You can still enjoy your senior year here."

"Hey," Frank interjected, "I've got an idea."

We turned.

"The caboose." He winked at Maddie. "How would you like to have your own place?"

A flicker of confusion crossed Maddie's face, and she gasped. "You mean—I could really stay in the train?"

"You can have the place to yourself."

"I don't think—" Rachel began.

"We wouldn't leave you unsupervised," I said, warming to the idea. "You'll eat breakfast and dinner with us, have to check in with us if you go out at night, and we'll set a curfew. That is not up for debate."

Rachel rested her chin on her hand, her eyes narrowing, then she turned to her daughter. "I'm being honest with you, Maddie," she said. "You know I have an important trial coming up. A woman can do only so much, and I don't think I'm going to be able to give you the time and attention you deserve."

Maddie lowered her head. "You don't have to explain."

"If you were with Nana and Pop—"

"I get it."

Rachel held out her hand. "Maddie, you know I love you, right?"

"Sure, Mom. And so did Dad."

I glanced at Frank as Maddie turned and went into the kitchen.

"She loves you," Rachel said, hugging her bent knees. "I know you'll be good for her."

I watched Ike follow Maddie, probably hoping for a handout. I *hoped* we would be good for her, though in that moment, I wasn't sure we had much to offer.

Chapter Fifteen

Maddie

I sat on my bed, surprised and bewildered. I was moving to Florida, and Mom was actually okay with it. Though I'd often dreamed of living minutes from the beach, I couldn't believe it. I wanted to be thrilled, but while part of me wanted to dance, another part of me knew I wouldn't be going anywhere if Dad hadn't died.

And Mom wanted to send me away. That news came as a complete surprise. I had assumed she would become super-protective after losing Dad, but apparently she trusted Nana and Pop to take care of me.

So she could focus on her work.

So how was I supposed to feel about all that? Sad . . . sure. Excited? Maybe. Only one thing was certain: When Dad picked up that gun, he changed everything for me and Mom. Nana and Pop, too. Like a tornado, his death had lifted us from the smooth paths we'd been walking and dropped us into uncharted territory.

And I didn't have a map.

I drew a deep breath. I was moving to Florida, so who would care? Emily, for sure. Maybe some of my other friends. I'd miss them, but I could always FaceTime them or get them together online.

I picked up my phone and stared at the photo I'd chosen as my wallpaper. Dad's face grinned at me. Last year, he'd won a week-long trip to any city in the U.S., and he let me pick the location for our mini vacay. Of course I chose Honolulu.

"I guess I ought to thank you," I whispered, staring into his brown eyes. "If you hadn't died, Mom would never have agreed to let me stay with Nana and Pop. I know Mom's trying to get me out of her hair for a while, but living in St. Pete will be easier than being Atlanta's poster child for kids whose fathers committed suicide for no apparent reason."

I texted Emily.

> Guess what? Moving to
> Florida. See you next summer.

For real? What about Tris?

> You know I'm over him.

Not what you said last week.

> Lot's happened since
> then. Not thinking bout him.
> Focusing on FL.

Happy bout it?

> Hard to be happy bout
> anything, but yeah.

Lucky you!

> Fill you in later. Got to pack.

Tell me all about it. Wow.
Beach. Hot guys. Tan all over.

> I know, right? I get my own
> place. A train car.

Get out! Too good to be true.

No kidding. Pretty sweet.

Send pics.

Maybe you can come down.
Leaving tomorrow.

Wildly jealous.

No need. Nana and Pop are
wardens.

LOL

See you. ♥

Chapter Sixteen

Susan

Frank was already in bed, propped up on Rachel's oversize pillows and staring at the TV.

I sat on the edge of the mattress and tried to remember what day it was. Wednesday? Yes, the day of the funeral. The two days we'd spent here felt like a week.

And we had just promised to take Maddie for the next six months.

The sheets rustled behind me. "Ready to turn out the light?" Frank asked.

I shook my head.

"What's wrong?"

I pressed my hands over my burning eyes. "I don't know how we're supposed to do this."

"What do you mean?"

"This is going to sound horrible, because I love Maddie more than anything. But how are we supposed to take care of her when I don't know how to take care of *us*?"

Frank stroked my back. "We're going to be fine, Susie."

Frank was grieving too, so why didn't he admit it? "How can we be fine?" I said. "I know we have to do our best to give Maddie a normal life, but how can we when—when—" I paused, my chin quivering. "When you faint during the graveside service and I can't talk without crying?"

Frank drew me into his arms, but I didn't want to be comforted. I wanted to make him see how difficult, even impossible, our task was.

I pulled away. "You asked Rachel if we could sleep on it, so I know you had doubts."

He frowned. "Not really, but I knew we needed to talk about it."

"But as soon as Maddie showed up, you invited her. You made the decision without me."

"Sorry. I thought you'd be all for it."

"I am, but . . . well, it's not like we have any choice. It's not going to be easy. How are we supposed to carry on as if nothing happened? We've lost our only child, and I haven't had even a second to process it."

"Neither have I. Maddie hasn't either." His voice cracked. "We will process it when we need to, but we don't have the luxury of managing the schedule. And think a minute, Susie. You're wondering how you can grieve and take care of a teenager, and that's the same situation Rachel faces. Except she also has a demanding job."

I opened my mouth, about to say I had a job too, but renting out a guest apartment was not nearly as demanding as a law career.

Frank read the expression on my face and softened his tone. "Rachel needs help, and so does Maddie. And because they're family, we're going to do whatever we can to see them through this."

"And who's going to see *us* through this?"

"We're going to take care of us." Frank gripped my arm. "I'm going to take care of you, and you're going to take care of me. And the Lord will take care of us both."

Again with the spiritual clichés. I knew he was speaking out of his beliefs—*our* beliefs—but I was still reeling. Frank might have forgotten how difficult raising a high schooler could be, but I hadn't. I remembered every minute I spent pacing our living room, one eye on the clock, the other on the driveway, waiting for Daniel to come home. I remembered finding vomit in the yard, evidence he'd been drinking, and plants trampled beneath his window, proof that he'd sneaked out. Maddie was a good kid, but even good kids pushed at the boundaries.

All I wanted was to go home and tend my shattered heart. I didn't want to have to set curfews and fret when Maddie didn't come home on time, let alone worry about a new set of teenage friends.

But Frank was right. If we didn't help Rachel, who would?

I loved Maddie. She was my only grandchild, and I was so grateful when the Lord sent her our way. I cried the first time I saw her. That same morning, Frank held our swaddled grandbaby to his chest and prayed over her.

When Maddie was a toddler, she and I put on floppy hats and held tea parties in the backyard, drinking imaginary tea and nibbling invisible cookies. That was the age of tutus and parasols, and I loved buying full-skirted dresses and watching Maddie twirl.

Though we were separated by miles, our bond remained strong as the years passed. On one of our visits to Atlanta, I took her shopping for her first bra—something she was too embarrassed to ask her mother about. Eleven-year-old Maddie beamed because she would no longer be one of the few in gym class without that garment. "Now I feel like a woman," she told me, and it had taken all my self-control not to laugh.

If someone kidnapped Maddie tomorrow, I would willingly give my life for hers. So why was I so anxious about bringing her with us?

Frank would say I was worrying again, but I chalked my reluctance up to *concern*. I was terrified we would not be at our best.

I bit my lip and told myself not to cry. I could dump buckets of concern over this situation, but Maddie was going home with us. For better or worse, we were going to grieve together.

How many sermons had I heard about depending on the Lord during the tough times? How many songs had I glibly sung about trusting God in all things? We were about to venture into the darkness with our granddaughter, and our faith—along with our strength—would be tested as never before.

The next morning, Frank and I hugged Rachel and watched as she gave her daughter a bittersweet smile. "Don't worry," I said. "We're as close as a phone call."

Rachel nodded, but her chin quivered as Maddie and Frank slid suitcases into the back of the car.

"Take care of yourself, hon," I said, taking her hand. "Frank and I love you, and we'll be praying for you."

Maddie hugged her mother once more, then got in and snapped her seat belt as Frank started the car. After more waving and brave smiles all around, we headed for the highway.

Ike settled next to Maddie. "Good," I said, checking to be sure he was comfortable. "He'll be snoring before you know it."

"How far is your place from the beach?" Maddie asked.

"About twenty minutes, depending on traffic," I said.

Maddie leaned forward. "I have my driver's license, you know."

I glanced at Frank.

"We'll see about that," he said, glancing at her in the rearview mirror. "But the school is only five blocks from our house. You could walk, or we have a bike."

I was afraid Maddie would scowl, but she tilted her head and looked thoughtful. "Sweet."

I tried to stay awake in case Maddie wanted to talk, but by the time we passed through Macon, she had fallen asleep.

Relaxed by the hum of the tires, I drifted into memories mingled with fragments of dreams. I saw myself at the funeral, but this time Daniel sat beside me, watching with an amused expression. "Don't worry, Mom," he said. "You're 'Can-Do Susan,' remember? The woman who can do anything she sets her mind to."

I smiled. That had been my nickname since high school. During my campaign for senior class president, we staged a press conference, complete with pretend security guards, flashing cameras, persistent reporters, and fans who yelled my campaign slogan: *We can do it!* We won by a landslide, and we *did* have the best prom in history.

But how could I be 'Can-Do Susan' when I couldn't keep my own son from killing himself? As a mother, I must have failed to teach him that life was priceless and not to be thrown away. Now we would all pay for my failure.

As I drowsed on the edge of sleep, reality mingled with the gossamer cobwebs of dreams. A professional woman behind a desk questioned me. "Was Daniel's suicide your fault? You were his mother."

Reclining on her office couch, I couldn't answer. My mouth wouldn't work, and my thoughts roiled with troubling questions.

I had watched dozens of movies in which the root of the main character's problem was his mother. She had either been too aloof, too domineering, too sexual, or too strict.

Yet I had always tried to do my best with Daniel. I loved him, set firm guidelines, encouraged him to go to church and love the Lord. Frank and I tried to model a good marriage, postponing any heated discussions until after Daniel's bedtime. Had he heard our occasional arguments? What if he came to believe that a healthy marriage was impossible? Maybe he and Rachel had had a fight, and Daniel gave up on life.

"Suicidal people want to escape," the woman behind the desk said, her voice flat. "What was Daniel running from? His marriage? His job?"

Tears rolled down my cheeks.

"You were his mother!"

"Susie?"

My eyes flew open. Frank was pulling into a truck stop. "I'm going to get coffee. Need anything?"

I shook my head and glanced in the back seat.

"She's exhausted," Frank said. "Let her be."

"Where are we?" I asked.

"Just north of Valdosta. Not far from the border."

I checked the back seat again. Ike had his head in Maddie's lap, and Maddie had propped her head against the door. I didn't see how she could sleep with her neck bent in that position, but she was young. And worn out.

We all were.

The sun had set by the time we reached the house. "You can stay in the spare room tonight," I told Maddie. "Tomorrow we'll empty the caboose and move your stuff in."

"We can do it together," Frank said.

"Only if you get plenty of sleep," I said. "After nine hours of driving, you need to rest."

"I can do it," Maddie said. "I didn't bring that much."

"I'm fine. Your grandmother worries too much."

I pressed my lips together, determined not to utter another word, but I couldn't help worrying about Frank. I couldn't imagine surviving the loss of Daniel. Losing Frank would be the end of me.

Chapter Seventeen

Maddie

For the first time since The Incident, I didn't wake up in a cloud of gloom. I still thought—and dreamed—about Dad, of course. I mean, it had been only a few days. But it was nice to have something else to think about too.

After breakfast I crossed the brick driveway, with Ike trailing me, to find Nana already busy in the caboose.

I have loved Nana and Pop's compound—and the caboose—ever since my first visit. An artist built it ages ago, and I could totally tell the design sprang from a creative brain. Nana once showed me the artist's original sketches. Apparently, he wanted his home to be a series of oddly shaped buildings, but his unconventional ideas freaked out the county building officials. So he settled for a main house and a second building for the garage, office, and art studio. Then he bought the antique caboose and parked it next to a workshop he designed to look like an old-fashioned train station.

But the best thing about the place was the jungle. A creek ran along the back edge of the lot, and towering oak trees covered the property—more than fifty, I'd guess. The artist removed only the trees he absolutely *had* to, so huge live oaks shaded the structures and the driveway. Between the giant trees, sawtooth palmettos, vines, and ferns grew wild, along with dozens of other plants I didn't recognize. The place looked like a rain forest, and all those plants hid the buildings from the street. When we drove up the driveway, I always felt I was entering a hidden paradise, complete with giant tree frogs, exotic orchids, and screech owls.

The caboose had been sitting on its rails over thirty years. Trees had grown around it, shading it in the summer and providing homes for dozens of squirrels. I climbed the iron steps to the front platform and found the door standing open. I stepped inside and inhaled the scent of cedar, which lined the walls. The caboose had a front room, with a window on each side and another in the door; a middle section with a shower, toilet, and sink; and a back room that held a table and about a dozen painted canvases.

Nana was standing by the sink, eyeing a box filled with paint tubes.

"Your art is pretty good," I said.

She looked up and grinned. "You don't have to be nice to your grandma," she said, winking. "I paint for fun. And it's relaxing. You like art, too, right?"

I shrugged. "I like to sketch. Dad would draw with me sometimes."

Nana lowered her gaze, and I almost wished I hadn't mentioned Dad. Thinking about him hurt me, too, but I wasn't going to stop talking about him.

"Maybe he got that artistic gene from me," Nana said, her voice artificially bright. "Seems like most kids today don't have time for hobbies like painting. Too busy texting and buzzing around the Internet."

I lifted my chin, feeling a need to defend my generation. "Some of my friends play sports. And my friend Emily plays the guitar."

"Good. Now, let's get this place cleaned out. We can keep this stuff in the workshop while you're here."

Nana and I got busy, filling cardboard boxes and carrying them to the workshop. Considering her sore arm, Nana did pretty well, but more than once I caught her wincing as she reached for a painting. "Let me do that," I told her. "Pop wouldn't want you to hurt yourself."

"I'm fine," she said.

I kept an eye on her for the next couple of hours, making sure she didn't lift anything too heavy.

When we'd removed all the paintings and paint supplies, she pointed at the TV on the wall. "I know you'll use that, and the computer has wi-fi."

"Sweet."

Videos would look fantastic on that big screen.

She showed me the microwave and mini fridge, then pointed to the AC unit in the bathroom. "The air conditioner works, but you probably won't need it until March or April. There's a space heater in the closet if we have a cold snap."

She took a deep breath and suggested we go in for lunch. "We can bring your stuff in afterward."

I turned for the door, but Nana wrapped me in an unexpected hug. "You are our precious girl," she said, squeezing me so tightly I could barely breathe.

A minute ago, she'd seemed happy and matter-of-fact—though I knew neither of us really were. But now her voice wavered.

"Um, Nana? Do you really want me out here? I hate to take your painting place."

"Oh, sweetheart. I can paint anywhere. I want you to have a place you'll love."

"I love the caboose."

"Then it's settled."

After lunch, I told Nana to rest, and Pop helped me wrestle the bed into the caboose. I thanked him and said I could handle everything else.

I went to the house and dragged out my suitcases, each of which Ike sniffed, then sat and grinned as if he approved.

"Maybe you can spend the night with me sometime, Ike. Want me to ask Nana?"

His tail beat double time. I scratched his head, then wheeled the suitcases over the brick driveway. Ike barked and tried to bite the wheels. His darting in and out, trying to attack my suitcases, made me laugh for the first time in a week.

Chapter Eighteen

Susan

I had nearly forgotten I had a family coming for the weekend. When I heard them pull in, I got up from my nap and met them in the driveway, where the couple were looking around with wide eyes as their two children clambered out of their safety seats.

As I welcomed them to our tropical paradise, hoping my smile wasn't too frayed, I directed them up to their door and apologized for the Christmas decorations' still being in the apartment. "Life has been a bit—"

I froze, aware the dam was about to break. If I said another word, or even implied what had happened . . .

"Sorry," I whispered, my voice strangled. And then, before I washed my guests away in a tsunami of tears, I turned and hurried back into the house.

Chapter Nineteen

Maddie

I had just pulled a few shirts from my suitcase when my phone rang. Mom. I gulped, remembering that I'd promised to text her as soon as we arrived.

But she sounded as bubbly as a cheerleader. "Have you moved into the caboose?"

"Doing it now. It's a sweet setup. Pop calls it their hurricane bunker."

"Nana and Pop are okay?"

"Yeah."

We fell silent, and I got the impression Mom was too tired to make conversation.

"How about you, Mom? I suppose it's quiet there without me."

"The place feels like a mausoleum and smells like lilies. I hate lilies."

"I thought you liked them."

"Not anymore."

Guilt spurted through my veins, and too late I realized I wasn't the only one who'd left. Dad had gone too, and he wasn't coming back.

"Turn on the TV," I suggested. "I do that when I'm home alone. Hearing another voice makes me feel better."

"Great idea," she said. "Thanks for the tip."

I wondered if she missed me, or if she was still numb. "How's your case coming?"

"Fine," she said, "considering everyone is still in holiday mode, so no one wants to talk business. I've been doing some research. The Internet doesn't go on vacation."

"Unless there's a power outage," I said. Dad would have howled at that, but I wasn't sure she even realized I was trying to be funny.

"Well, I wanted to make sure you were okay," she said. "Do you need anything?"

"Just school clothes. They have a dress code. Collared shirts, jeans or long shorts, the typical stuff."

"Ask Nana to take you shopping and I'll put extra money in your account. And you have your debit card."

"Sure."

"Okay, then. Happy New Year."

Did she think that was actually possible? At least she was trying. "Is that tonight?"

"Yes. I'll be thinking of you when the ball drops."

"Me too, Mom. Thanks."

I opened one suitcase and found a framed picture of me, Mom, and Dad. Mom must have slipped it in before we left. Pop had put a little table beside the bed, so I set the picture on it. It would be the first thing I saw in the morning and the last thing at night.

I studied Dad's face. He was grinning, almost laughing, and his personality shot right through the glass and hit me in the heart. How could a man so full of life decide to end it? How could a man who loved me leave without so much as a goodbye? One day he had been my dad, grinning while he opened presents he would never use, and the next day he simply stepped out of the world.

I flipped the picture facedown. I didn't have time to cry, not now. I had a caboose to organize, a place where I could be alone with my thoughts.

School wouldn't start until January 10, so I had time to get my act together, get the tears out of my system, and sort through my jumbled thoughts. I would go to school as a new person: Maddie Lawton, the fatherless girl who lived in a little red caboose.

My life was beginning to sound like a TV pilot.

Chapter Twenty

Susan

From the living room window, I watched the lights come on in the caboose and hoped I was doing the right things for Maddie. Teens could be tricky, and it had been years since I'd dealt with one. Plus, Frank and I had raised a son, completely different from a daughter.

My right arm ached from wrist to shoulder, but no one, especially not Maddie, needed to know.

I sighed and rested my feet on the coffee table. A moment later, Ike jumped up and put his front paws on my leg. "What do you think?" I asked, looking into his eager brown eyes. "What do you think about our girl coming to stay with us?"

The dog wagged his tail.

"Good boy." I patted his head. "What would we do without—?" My voice broke, and my eyes filled. I didn't want Maddie to see me crying, but she was in the caboose. Frank would understand.

The tears were more from an overflow of grief than physical

pain. For Maddie's sake, I had forced an artificial smile ever since leaving Atlanta.

But behind the facade, a dark spring churned with grief, exhaustion, and devastating confusion. If Daniel had been killed in a car crash, if he had been sick, or even if he'd been the victim of random violence, there would have been a *reason* for his death, an awful understanding. But *suicide*?

If Daniel had been clinically depressed, having problems at work or with Rachel, his decision might make some kind of sense. But Rachel said their marriage was strong, and Daniel was up for a promotion. Daniel had no money problems, he didn't drink, and he wasn't addicted to drugs or gambling.

Rachel had mentioned only one unusual event. "The day I called you, when we couldn't find him? He said he'd fallen asleep in his office. That didn't make sense, but after that, he was back to his usual self. Maybe even better than usual. He kept saying he was looking forward to Christmas. Why? Because of what he had planned for the day after?"

I heard the front door and gave Frank a teary wave. He told me our guests seemed settled in the apartment. "Nice couple. Drove all the way from Texas to celebrate New Year's on the beach."

I glanced at the clock. "I should wish you a happy new year, but I don't feel like celebrating."

"Oh, love." He sat and squeezed my knee. "I know."

"I just can't understand *why*." I forced the words out between sobs. "Danny seemed to have everything. And he loved the Lord. So how does that kind of man do what he did?"

"The same way a person who *doesn't* belong to Jesus does," Frank said, his voice heavy. "We don't know what he was thinking. He might have been deceived. Or maybe his problem, whatever it was, outweighed his faith."

"I can't believe that. Daniel's faith meant everything to him."

Frank seemed at a loss for words. "Maybe something weighed so heavily on him that quitting seemed the only way out. Maybe he did something so out of character that he couldn't live with the guilt."

"Daniel would never do anything like that."

"No one is perfect, Susie. Truth is, we may never know what brought this on. Like the preacher said, we don't have to like it, but we have to know he must have been in tremendous anguish and believed the powerful reasoning in his own mind."

"But if something was bothering him that badly, why didn't he come to us? Why didn't he trust God with the problem?"

A light rain began to patter against the window. "Seems like the whole world is crying tonight," Frank said.

"And what about Maddie?" I blew my nose. "She hasn't cried since she's been here, but I know she's as devastated as we are."

"Sure she is."

"So how do we help her?"

"Did you notice she seemed okay today when she was busy? The work took her mind off everything else. Maybe we just need to keep giving her things to do."

"But we don't want her to *not* deal with what she's going through, do we? The only way to survive this is to face it, isn't it?"

"Sure," Frank said, "but sometimes mindless activity can free a person's mind to sort through other problems."

I nodded slowly. "But what can we ask her to do? I don't want her to think we invited her because we needed cheap labor."

Frank smiled. "We could ask her to paint the inside of the caboose. Right now the walls are spattered with thirty different colors."

"My fault," I said. "You think she'd want to?"

"Why not? It's her space. Let her choose the colors and make the place her own."

I leaned against Frank's shoulder, imagining Maddie smeared with paint in that tiny space, running rollers and brushes over the old shiplap. "That's a *great* idea, honey. It might help us—" My voice choked.

"What?"

"What I want more than anything," I whispered, "is to send Maddie back to Atlanta happy and on the road to healing. If we can do that for her, all this will be worthwhile."

Chapter Twenty-One

Maddie

Living in St. Pete was definitely different. In some ways I felt free and independent, as if I'd left home for college, but hanging over what should have been a thrilling adventure was a dark cloud that kept bringing me back to the truth. I hadn't gone off to college; I'd been sent away because Mom couldn't handle me and Dad's suicide in the same lifetime. And though Nana and Pop welcomed me, they wouldn't have invited me to stay if they didn't pity me. They had to be whispering about how horrible it must have been for me to find Dad in the garage, and they probably worried that I'd been scarred for life. Maybe I had been.

One thing was certain: The sight of Dad and that bloody desk had been seared onto the back of my eyeballs.

During those first few days, I found myself thinking a lot about Dad and wondering what he was doing. I didn't know if I believed in pearly gates and streets of gold, but Dad certainly did. So it figured that he was floating around in heaven, which had to be in another dimension. Could he see me? Did he know what I was doing? Or was he caught up in some kind of mystical experience, thinking only of God the Father and Jesus?

Did he even remember me?

I wish he'd thought more about me before he went into the garage with a gun. Yeah, he wrote me a note, but had he really thought about what his actions would do to me? Did he think I'd be able to shrug off *that* experience?

Maybe Dad wasn't thinking straight that morning, or maybe he overestimated my abilities. Maybe he didn't love me as much as he said he did . . . because no one should do that to their kid. Or wife. Or anyone they loved.

Dad might not have been thinking about me that morning, but Nana and Pop were sure thinking about me now. They weren't about to let me sit and mope in the caboose. They were up and busy every morning, and they expected the same of me. Even on weekends.

On Sunday, the second day of the new year, I heard the caboose door open and felt Nana's hand on my shoulder. "Hey, kiddo," she said, "it's time to get up. Can you help me clean the guest apartment?"

I covered my eyes to block the sunlight radiating through the square window. "What time is it?"

"Noon."

As I groaned into my pillow, Mom's voice filled my head: *Be sure to help Nana and Pop. Act grateful.*

"Sure. Meet you up there in a few minutes."

I stumbled out of bed and stared into the mirror. My hair was a mess, my face pale, and I hadn't put on makeup since the funeral. But I had promised to help Nana clean, so I might as well get it over with.

Nana had brought me a cinnamon bun—a bribe, no doubt, but a good one. I grabbed it and left the caboose, eating as I walked to the apartment. The guests, whoever they were, had done a decent job of cleaning. Other than the unmade beds, I couldn't tell anyone had been there.

I spotted Nana at the kitchen sink. "What do you need me to do?" I walked closer and realized she was washing dishes. "Those people didn't wash their dishes?"

"They washed *some* of them," she said. "But sometimes people hide dirty dishes under clean ones." She dropped the sponge into the water and stretched out her arm. "My arm is still a little weak, so it hurts to scrub. Can you wash these dishes for me?"

I started scrubbing, and Nana moved to the bed and piled the linens in a laundry basket, then went upstairs to strip the beds in the loft. Sheets sailed over the railing and landed on the floor.

When I finished the dishes, she asked me to dust the furniture and windowsills while she started the laundry. "After you dust, there's disinfectant under the sink for any high-contact surfaces— doorknobs, keypads, countertops."

By the time Nana came back, I'd finished. She gave me a high five. "Thank you, sweetheart. You've been a big help."

Ike scampered up and stood between us, his tail wagging and eyes bright. He looked so overjoyed to see me that I was tempted to scoop him up and take him to the caboose. But he was Nana's dog, and I could almost hear Dad telling me not to be selfish.

"He wants to be with you, Maddie. Let him follow you."

"Are you sure he won't miss you?"

Nana scoffed. "He'll miss his food bowl, but it's not good for him to graze all day. So you bring him over at breakfast and let him spend the day with me while you're at school. After you get home, you can take him to the caboose."

I liked that idea and had always loved Ike. Mom had pictures of me holding him as a big-bellied puppy and then as a longer-legged adolescent. For the past several years he had been chunky, but I could still see the happy puppy in his eyes. "Whaddya say, Ike?" I patted my knees. "Want to sleep with me in the caboose?"

He barked and wagged his tail double time.

Nana laughed. "See? If he's any trouble, bring him back to the house."

I didn't think Ike would like the caboose as much as he enjoyed being with his people, but I was thrilled he wanted to be with me. Dad used to be that way, but now I couldn't say the same about either of my parents. Or even Emily, my supposed best friend. She hadn't called or texted since the funeral.

"Okay, puppy, let's go."

As I walked Ike across the driveway, I looked up and smiled . . . in case Dad was watching.

I had always loved the first day of school, but I'd never been the new kid on a back-from-vacation day. I spent hours obsessing over January 10—sometimes dreading it, sometimes feeling grateful for a chance to start fresh in a new place. No one at St. Pete High knew me, and no one knew what had happened to me over Christmas. That alone was worth enduring a few stares and wisecracks.

I toyed with adopting a completely different persona, like faking a British accent and telling people I'd just moved from London, but finally decided against it. I'd heard so many different British accents on TV that I was sure to mix the upstairs and downstairs, and anybody who'd watched *Downton Abbey* would see through me in no time.

On the big day, I woke early, dressed in jeans and long-sleeved collared shirt, and walked over to the house. Nana opened the door in her nightgown.

"Sorry," I said. "Guess I was overeager."

"Nervous?"

"A little."

"You'll do fine. You look beautiful, and light blue is a good color on you. Your dad"—her chin trembled—"would be proud."

She glanced at my backpack. "Do you have everything you need—paper, pens, whatever?"

"Yep, and I have my phone."

"After I throw on a robe, I can pack your lunch. Last night I made egg salad for sandwiches."

I resisted the urge to make a face. "I'll buy something in the cafeteria, Nana. I have my debit card."

"Okay." She drew a deep breath and took a step toward the bedroom. "How about some breakfast? You want eggs and sausage? There's plenty of time for me to whip something up, as soon as I get my robe—"

"I'll help myself to a doughnut and a diet soda, if that's okay."

Nana frowned, but Pop's arrival distracted her. He came out of the bedroom and stopped to adjust his tie in a mirror. I'd almost forgotten that he worked as a substitute teacher at a nearby middle school.

"Well, look at the early bird," he said. "I'll drive you because it's your first day. Gotta get you registered."

"You sure? I don't want to make you late."

"The middle school starts later." He kissed Nana on the cheek.

"I'm ready." I grabbed a diet soda from the fridge, popped the top, and took a swig. I started toward the door, then grabbed Nana's arm. "Oh—I left Ike in the caboose. Can you get him? He was still asleep when I left."

She smiled. "No problem. Ike is *not* an early riser."

I waved to her and followed Pop.

I kept my head down as I walked to the school office with Pop, and within a couple of minutes he was filling out forms. No one asked about why I was living with my grandparents, and no one questioned why Pop signed as my official guardian.

A woman asked about the classes I'd been taking in Atlanta, and she did her best to put me in the St. Pete High equivalents.

Pop guided me toward the door. "Want me to help you find your homeroom?"

"I can do it. You don't have to stay. Thanks, Pop."

He walked away, and a minute later a bell rang, the doors opened, and students surged into the building.

I studied my schedule and started searching for room numbers.

I always felt sorry for new kids at my Atlanta school. They usually entered the classroom late and adopted one of two looks—Let-Me-Be-Invisible or Aren't-You-Lucky-to-Have-Me?

I just acted like I belonged and walked purposefully through the mob, sliding into an empty desk two minutes before the bell rang.

Fortunately, my homeroom teacher, Mrs. Barcher, didn't make a big deal about me being new. She worked my name into the roll as if I'd always been part of the class.

"Lahon?"

"Present."

"Lawton?"

"Here."

"Matthews?"

"Yep."

Mrs. Barcher's classroom screamed "history teacher." An old American flag—one with only a few stars—was thumbtacked to a bulletin board, and a life-size cutout of George Washington stood behind her desk. On the whiteboard she had written, *Those who do not remember the past are condemned to repeat it.*

When she finished calling the roll, Mrs. Barcher worked at her desk while kids talked, stared into space, or put their heads down for a nap. The loudspeaker squawked and a kid said, "And now, for a moment of silence."

Those who had been talking lowered their voices, but no one seemed to pray or meditate. And when the kid said, "Those who wish may stand for the pledge of allegiance," no one did.

Nana and Pop would have been upset by that. Dad, too, probably. The kid on the loudspeaker ran through a series of announcements, and then a louder, deeper voice came on. "This is Principal Sweet. Let me remind you that no student, unless involved in an extracurricular activity, will be allowed to remain on campus after school. Any such student found on the property will be subject to disciplinary action or arrest for trespassing."

Did all principals sound alike? A dark-haired girl across from me caught my eye. "As if I'd want to stick around this place," she whispered, and I smiled.

At the end of homeroom, everyone headed out.

"Madison Lawson?" Mrs. Barcher said, waving. "May I see you a moment?"

I walked to her desk.

"I hope you enjoy it here," she said. "Do you know where your next class is, or do you have any questions about your schedule?"

"My next class is English," I said. "With Mr. Wright."

"I can show her," the dark-haired girl said. "I'm in the same class." She wore all black, including fishnet stockings.

Once we were in the hallway, she said, "I'm Hester. And you're Madison?"

"Maddie," I told her.

"Where'd you come from?"

"Atlanta."

"Why'd you come?"

I bit my lip, debating how much to tell her. "My mom's preparing a big court case, so she thought I should stay with my grandparents awhile."

"She's a lawyer?"

"Yeah."

"Cool. Your dad's out of the picture?"

My stomach dropped, but I nodded. "Yep."

"No worries. I haven't seen mine in months." We stopped outside a classroom. "Welcome to American Lit."

I sighed. "Looks like my classroom in Atlanta. Same posters on the wall."

"Was your teacher boring?"

"She was okay. We spent three weeks reading Puritan poetry, though, and I thought we'd never finish *The Scarlet Letter*. Hey, you're not named after *that* Hester, are you?"

"Know anyone else with the name?"

I laughed. Though this Hester had short, dark hair, it wasn't hard to imagine her in Puritan dress with an A embroidered on the bodice. Along with her startling blue eyes, she certainly had Hester Prynne's spunk.

Everyone stopped chattering when the bell rang. Up front, a middle-aged man in a cardigan surveyed the room. When he saw me, he glanced at his roster. "Would you be Madison Lawton?"

I nodded, my face burning. Someone whistled, and Mr. Wright frowned.

"Open your books, please," Mr. Wright said, "to page 149. Mr. Westfield, since you are feeling your oats this morning, would you please read the Emily Dickinson poem on that page?"

Someone near the windows—presumably the dark-haired guy who'd whistled—turned to the assigned page. Then, in a voice as dark and deep as a well, he read: "This is my letter to the world/ That never wrote to me . . ."

I parked my chin in my hand and listened, losing myself in the sound of his voice.

Chapter Twenty-Two

Susan

I nearly wept with relief when Maddie and Frank left for school. For the last two weeks, grief had been like a corpse tied to my back. I staggered beneath it, exhausted myself doing the simplest tasks, and found it impossible to sleep beneath its moldering heaviness. I did my best to comfort, help, and wear a pleasant expression for Maddie, but I needed to acknowledge my own grief. I needed private, uninterrupted time to mourn my son.

I went into the spare bedroom, locked the door, and sank to the floor in front of my old hope chest. I lifted the lid, inhaled the aromatic cedar, and pulled out the half-dozen or so scrapbooks I had filled over the years with everything from grade school pictures to accounts of Daniel's sports activities.

On the first page of Daniel's baby book, I had written *Daniel Joseph Lawton, born December 6, 1980. Six pounds, five ounces. Twenty inches long. Miracle of God.*

He'd been delivered by the doctor who held my hand through three miscarriages and rejoiced with us when God blessed us with a son.

I found Daniel's first smile, first word (*Dada*), first step.

A collection of cards and notes from shower gifts spilled from the middle of the book. At the very back, tossed in like confetti, lay photos that ignited dozens of memories: Daniel's first Christmas, where he lay swaddled beneath our spindly Christmas tree. Daniel smiling, his face smeared with chocolate icing from his first birthday cake. Daniel standing in his first swimming pool, an ankle-high inflatable from Walmart. Me sprawled in a chair while a naked Daniel ran by, testing the allegedly surefire method for potty-training boys.

I ran my fingertips over each faded photo, reliving every moment. Tears dropped onto the yellowed pages, but I didn't wipe them away. They would be part of his history too.

In the first-grade photo, the cowlick at the front of his head made a hank of Daniel's brown hair stick out. He stood a head taller than anyone else in his fourth-grade class picture, on his way to becoming a man who would tower over me.

I smiled at Daniel's ninth-grade picture. That year I gave away all his jeans and skimped on groceries so I could buy new ones. That year Frank installed a basketball hoop over our garage, and he and Daniel shot baskets at least twice before the hoop rusted and fell.

Daniel liked sports, but he loved books. He devoured the writings of C. S. Lewis and classics like *Robinson Crusoe* and *Treasure Island*. He read *Black Beauty* and *Bambi*. Frank thought Daniel might be interested in hunting, but no man who loved Bambi would ever carry a gun into the woods.

I opened a box at the bottom of the chest to find a toilet paper corsage stemmed with florist's tape. The handmade card rested beneath the flower: *Dear Mom, Happy Mother's Day. If you get tired of this, you can blow your nose with it!*

"Never," I whispered. "Nobody touches this flower."

I shuffled through certificates and prizes—from Daniel's science fair projects, a trophy for second place in a high school debate team, another for placing second in the high jump.

A small manila envelope contained a five-by-seven photo of Frank recovering from his cardiologist-implanted stent. Though Frank spent only one night in the hospital, Daniel left work and drove without stopping so he could reach St. Pete General by morning. I snapped the picture when Daniel hugged his father. Frank was awake enough to realize Daniel was sobbing on his shoulder. Neither of them spoke—neither needed to.

I had printed the photo, not willing to risk losing it on my phone. I planned to give it to Daniel after Frank's funeral, never dreaming that life would upend my plans.

A sob welled in my chest and erupted, leaving me breathless. I felt a flicker of fear—what was this?—and then a stabbing pain beneath my breastbone.

I eased myself down to the tile floor on my back and focused on breathing. With each breath came a stabbing pain unlike any I had felt before.

Nausea swept over me, heating my skin. I pulled off my blouse and lay back down, grateful for the cool kiss of the tiles.

What would Frank think if he saw me like this?

Poor man would probably have a heart attack.

I pressed my sweaty palms to the floor and tried to push myself up. Again the wave of nausea, so I lay back.

Good thing Frank was not home. Or Maddie. This would pass, and I would wait until it did.

As I lay staring at the ceiling, I couldn't help thinking of Daniel. When he was alone and needing help, who embraced him? Who comforted him? No one, because not even Rachel knew he'd been overwhelmed. His handsome face had been a perfect mask, hiding a storm of . . . what, exactly?

Why, God? What was he going through? Why didn't you stop him from doing something so final?

The weight of grief kept me on the floor even after the pain eased. I curled up on a rug and wept tears I had repressed far too long.

When I finally opened my eyes, it was after two.

I pulled myself together and went into the kitchen, ate a sandwich, and wandered into the bedroom, surprised to find Frank napping. He must have come home early.

I lay beside him until he stirred. "Sorry," he said, taking my hand. "It's not like me to sleep during the day."

"It's okay," I told him. "I fell asleep in the spare room. I think our bodies are trying to recover . . . from everything."

"I'll need more than a catnap to do that." He slid closer to me. "I don't think I'll ever be the same."

I turned as his fingertips grazed my cheek. "I still can't believe it."

Frank drew me closer and we lay together, locked in inertia. Finally, Frank pressed a kiss to my forehead. "We've got to get ourselves together before Maddie comes home."

"Right." I reached for a tissue and wiped my eyes. "You came home early."

"The teacher I subbed for was only out half a day."

I caught his hand. "I know you don't feel much like working, but maybe you could ask to substitute at the high school. That way you could keep an eye on Maddie."

Frank hesitated. "You don't think she'd resent my being around?"

"It's not like you'd be there every day."

He grunted. "I'll ask. Going back to work is good for me. Keeps my mind off things."

Maddie had school and Frank had work. What did I have to keep me busy? Cleaning the guest apartment filled only a few hours a week.

I would need far more than that to fill the gaping hole in my heart.

Chapter Twenty-Three

Maddie

My first day at St. Pete High wasn't terrible. Hester was in most of my classes, and I was surprised when she asked if I wanted to hang out at her house after school. "My mom works until five," she said, snapping her gum, "and she'll drive you home, if you want."

I shrugged. "Okay. Just let me call my grandma." I told her about Hester and said, "We're going to hang out at her house, and her mom will drive me home after five, okay?"

I could almost hear the wheels turning in Nana's head. "Are you sure it'll be all right with her mother? Are you sure she can bring you home? We don't want you walking after dark, so if you need me to come get you—"

"I'm sure, Nana. See you later."

I clicked off before she could find more things to worry about.

Hester lived less than a mile from St. Pete High in a neighborhood of tree-lined streets and cinderblock houses, most covered by climbing vines. I figured most of the residents were older, because I didn't see any kids playing outside.

At a pink house with white shutters, Hester said, "*Mi casa es su casa.*"

"Pink! My dad used to sing a song about little pink houses."

Hester groaned. "John Mellencamp. That stupid song is the reason Mom painted our house pink. Anyway, ours is the only pink house on this street, so it's easy to find."

We walked into hot air, but Hester immediately lowered the temperature.

"Mom's a penny-pincher," Hester said. "Drives me crazy about the thermostat."

"You could open the windows."

Hester shook her head. "Not the best neighborhood."

Her bedroom was painted white, but it was hard to tell because she had plastered the walls with posters. One featured Emily Dickinson, and another Sylvia Plath. On the opposite wall, she'd hung a poster of a white-haired, bearded man with a cigarette dangling from his mouth.

"Reminds me of the guy who lives across the street from us in Georgia," I said.

Hester laughed. "That's Ernest Hemingway. Haven't you read him?"

I shook my head. "Did you study him last year?"

"Not in school." She tugged the short strands of her hair. "He hated adjectives and adverbs. Someday I'm going to write like him, but right now the teachers want *creative* writing. The more adjectives, the more Mr. Wright seems to like it."

"You want to be a writer?"

"Why not?" She stretched out on her stomach and rested her head on one hand. "I have the personality for it. Mom says I'm moody, and Dad, when he's around, says I have a gift. So maybe." She tilted her head. "You get along with your parents?"

I shrugged. "Mom's okay. She wants to become a partner in her law practice, so she puts in all kinds of hours to impress the other partners. She's working on a huge case right now."

Hester's eyes widened. "Murder?"

I laughed. "She's not that kind of lawyer. She handles civil cases, and most of her work involves amusement parks. If you owned a Ferris wheel and someone got hurt on it, you'd hire her."

"Wow. I would imagine people get hurt on those rides almost every day."

"Well, not that often, but it happens." I traced the pattern on her bedspread with my finger. "You asked about my dad, and I let you assume something that isn't true."

"Your parents aren't divorced?"

"My dad shot himself the day after Christmas."

There, I'd said it. And it felt like a boulder rolled off my shoulders and landed smack in the middle of the room. I was almost afraid to look at Hester.

"Whoa." Her mouth dropped open. "That's insane."

I tightened my jaw to stop my chin from quivering. Now Hester would ask questions I didn't think I could answer.

"You mean"—Hester shook her head—"like two weeks ago?"

"Sixteen days. And yeah, we're all still messed up by it."

Hester let her head drop to her arm. "Do you know why?"

"No, and that's the worst part. My dad was the calmest, nicest man you'd ever want to meet."

"Could he have been murdered?"

"The police investigated, and no. He definitely pulled the trigger."

Hester's eyes filled with horror and pity. "That's sick. I can't even imagine. I mean—" She drew a deep breath. "I'm so sorry. Here I am, blabbing about Hemingway while your dad . . ."

"What does Dad have to do with Hemingway?"

She blinked. "He shot himself too. Some people think his family was under some kind of curse."

"What?"

"No kidding. Hemingway's father and grandfather, brother and sister, even his granddaughter committed suicide. A lot of great writers are obsessed with death. Hemingway wrote seven novels, and the main character died in five of them."

"Depressing."

"And Sylvia Plath taped off her kids' bedrooms so they'd be safe, then put her head in the oven and turned on the gas. Not a bad way to go, I guess, considering the alternatives."

I closed my eyes, imagining a woman applying duct tape to the doors of her kids' rooms. In my imagination, she was crying. Did Dad cry when he wrote that note for me?

"Plath was a great writer," Hester said. "A prodigy, even. Wrote her first poem when she was eight, and later wrote *a lot* about death and dying. Tried to kill herself three times—once with pills, and another time she drove her car into a river."

"But why'd she do it?"

Hester shrugged. "Some say because her husband left her for another woman. Some say she was clinically depressed. No one knows."

"That's the problem," I said, staring at her bedspread. "That's what bothers me. If my dad had been depressed, or sick, or if he and Mom were breaking up, maybe I could at least halfway understand. But I had no clue, not one, so none of it makes any sense. Sometimes I'll wake up in a good mood, then remember Dad's gone. It's been sixteen days, and I still can't believe it."

"I'm really sorry," Hester whispered, leaning toward me, "but maybe you shouldn't dwell on stuff you can't do anything about. Hey, I've got Cokes in the kitchen and can find some chips."

"Thanks, but Nana will be cooking dinner soon. I should call Pop and have him come get me."

"But it's only four."

"They eat early. But I will have something to drink while we're waiting for him."

"Come on." Hester led the way to the kitchen.

I called Pop and drank a Coke, grateful I'd found a friend who didn't melt down when I told her about my family. But honestly, all that talk about people who committed suicide was enough for one day.

After my first week at St. Pete High, I joined Hester and her friends at the Pizza Palace. "It's a Friday night tradition," she explained. "We go to the Pizza Palace, hang out, and eat. Whoever has money pays, or we all chip in. We've been doing it since we were freshmen."

I'd met most of the others during lunch, but Matthew and Avery, who came in holding hands, weren't in any of my classes. Matthew had short hair and broad shoulders and looked like a football player. His girlfriend, Avery, had long, blonde hair that fell in perfect messy curls. She could have been a runway model.

Hester crossed her arms and smiled at me. "Have you met everybody?"

I looked around, trying to match names and faces. "I think I know everyone. Logan, Jackson, and Mia are in our English class, and Sofia has gym with me." I recognized Logan right away as the guy with the deep voice who had read the Dickinson poem in class my first day.

Hester looked at the waitress, who had arrived with menus. "I think we know what we want, right?" She glanced around the table. "You guys okay with pepperoni and pineapple?"

"No." Logan, who sat across from me, smiled when our gazes met. His dark hair was long, but only in the front, where it often fell into his blue eyes. He had a runner's body, tall and wiry, and stunning cheekbones. Emily would swoon over him.

"Pineapple," Logan said, "goes with ham, not pepperoni."

"It's all *pork*," Hester said, the corner of her mouth twisting. "What's the difference?"

"How about one with pineapple and ham, and another with pepperoni and mushrooms?" The suggestion came from Mia, who was probably as smart as she was cute. She pushed at her glasses and smiled at the waitress. "And water all around, okay? We've all agreed to go a week without carbonated drinks."

"I'll probably die." Sofia's brows drew together in an agonized expression. "I drink Diet Coke for breakfast, lunch, and dinner."

"You're not gonna die," Mia said. "You'll probably never go back to that stuff once you detox."

I folded my arms and tried to look pleasant. When Hester invited me, I had no idea we'd be sitting in the center of the restaurant. But Hester's friends were a lot like her—outgoing, welcoming, and smart. Mom would take one look at them and declare them artistes. Dad would have said they seemed a little crazy.

While we waited, Logan waved to catch my attention. "So, how was your first week?"

My cheeks heated as the others turned to look at me. "Okay. Not so different from my other school."

"Hester says you went to a prep school," Sofia said. "Fancy?"

I shrugged. "A lot like St. Pete."

"I knew it." Logan thumped the table. "If you were fancy, you wouldn't be hanging out with Hester."

Hester made a face. "I'm not sure how to take that."

"So . . ." Avery turned away from Matthew. "Has anyone else seen *Before I Go*? Matt and I saw it last night."

Jackson lifted his head. "Theater or streaming? Because if you say streaming, I've got a feeling you didn't watch much of the movie."

Everyone laughed, but Avery only flicked her hair over her shoulder. "We watched every minute, and it was *wonderful*. This girl was dying of leukemia, and her new boyfriend wanted to—" She stopped. "Well, you can figure out the plot from that. Anyway, I liked it. I cried at the end."

"A love story." Jackson snorted. "If you want to watch a love story about death, you have to see *Harold and Maude*."

A couple of the kids laughed, and Logan slapped *ba-da-boom* on the table. I turned to Hester. "What's *Harold and Maude*?"

She leaned forward. "A movie about this kid obsessed with death. He meets Maude at a funeral, and they fall in love—"

"That's not what it's about," Jackson said. "Harold is obsessed with death, right. But Maude is obsessed with life and getting the most out of it because she's eighty. They *do* fall in love, and then—"

I covered my eyes. "A young guy and an old woman?"

"Yes," Jackson said, laughing as he pulled my hands from my face. "They do it. And when she turns eighty, Maude decides to go out on her own terms."

"Let's talk about something else." Sofia stiffened. "It's not right to talk about suicide. I don't even want to think the word."

"Impossible," Logan said. "If someone says, 'Don't think about bananas,' you can't help thinking about bananas."

"Talk about something else," Mia said. "How about our English term papers? We have to give our topics to Mr. Wright on Monday."

"I'm choosing survival," Jackson said. "I'm going to get the CliffsNotes for *Call of the Wild* and write about survival of the fittest."

Hester slapped his hand. "CliffsNotes are for cheaters."

Jackson grinned. "What are you doing your paper on?"

"Death." Hester lifted her chin. "As portrayed through the poetry of Emily Dickinson. The woman wrote about it almost constantly." She turned to me. "What about you, Mads?"

I startled. No one but Dad ever called me Mads. "Um . . . sorry to bring it up again, but I was thinking I might write about suicide." I expected the table to go suddenly silent, but Hester must not have told them about Dad.

"And how are you tying that into literature?" Sofia asked, mimicking Mr. Wright.

"Um . . . maybe I can find a copy of the *Harold and Maude* screenplay. If not, a lot of movies mention suicide."

"*Dead Poets Society*," Mia said. "And *The Sea of Trees*."

"*A Long Way Down*," Sofia added. "And it's based on a book. I read it last year."

"Even *It's a Wonderful Life*." Jackson lifted his chin when Hester snickered. "I know it's an old movie, but my parents made me watch it over Christmas. George Bailey is about to jump into a river before an angel stops him from killing himself."

"I'll find something," I said, my mouth suddenly dry.

Hester caught my eye. "What's up with them?" she mouthed, nodding toward Matthew and Avery. They had dropped out of the conversation and were whispering, their heads inches apart.

I shrugged. I tried to smile. The restaurant suddenly seemed a lot noisier and busier. A woman across the room was on the phone, but I could hear the person talking to her. Had I suddenly developed super hearing?

"Hey, Matthew," Hester called. "Trouble in Paradise? What's up with you two?"

Avery turned. "Nothing."

"Really?" Hester's voice dripped with sarcasm. "I thought we were talking about movies. What are you two whispering about?"

Matthew crossed his arms. "Nothing that concerns you."

Hester lifted one shoulder. "The lovers have secrets," she said, loud enough for everyone to hear. "That's why I hate it when people start hooking up."

My heart began to pound. Though everything in me wanted to take deep gulps of air, I did my best to breathe normally. Darkness crowded my peripheral vision, making everything fuzzy. What was *wrong* with me?

The subject shifted to Mr. Wright and whether he was really married. Everyone had a different idea about the sort of woman who might marry the bookish teacher, but my ears were ringing.

My stomach had tightened so much I wouldn't be able to eat, and I might actually throw up.

I tapped Hester's arm. "I'm going to the restroom."

She squinted. "You okay? You look a little pale."

"Might be something I ate at lunch. I'll be back."

I slipped away and turned into the narrow hallway that led to the restrooms, carefully following the wall, not trusting my eyes or my sense of balance. Once inside the ladies' room, I went into a stall and sat, letting my head drop between my knees.

I couldn't be sick; this had to be only momentary. But until I felt myself again, I was staying put, no matter how long it took.

Chapter Twenty-Four

Maddie

I was supposed to spend the night at Hester's, but as we drove away from the Pizza Palace, I told her what had happened. "It was like my body freaked out for no reason."

She stared at me and nodded. "I'll bet you had a panic attack. I mean, we were talking about suicide, plus it was noisy and hot in there. It's a wonder you didn't pass out."

"You should probably take me home. If I'm sick, I don't want to give you whatever this is."

"Probably too late for that," she said, grinning. "But I'll take you home. I'm just glad you got to meet everybody. We've all been best friends a really long time." She flashed a sly smile. "When you left, Logan asked if you were okay. I said I thought you were. Sweet of him, though, wasn't it?"

I didn't answer. Was Logan the kind who asked about everybody, or was he interested in me? It didn't matter.

"So . . ." I was ready to talk about *anything* but panic attacks and death. "What did you all talk about while I was gone?"

Hester sighed. "The usual. Sofia is worried about getting a date for prom, and Mia doesn't want to go to college."

"I'll bet her parents aren't happy about that."

"They're not, especially since she's a superbrain. She could probably get a scholarship to Florida State, but she won't even apply."

"Why not?"

Hester sighed. "Because Jax isn't going. He wants to become an electrician or a plumber—he says that's where the real money is. So he's going to stay home, go to a technical school, and start working."

"I didn't know he and Mia were dating."

"They're not—at least, not yet, but Mia's been in love with Jax since forever. We all know it—everybody but Jax, that is."

I snorted. "Guys can be blind."

"I know, right? Logan keeps telling Jax it wouldn't hurt him to go to college for a year or two, and Sofia keeps telling Mia she could go to community college first and save her parents a ton of money. Mia would be glad to do that, I think, but her parents want her to aim higher. She's got potential, blah, blah, blah."

I tried to imagine what my parents would want in a similar situation but drew a blank.

"My mom probably feels the same way," I said finally. "We haven't talked much about college, but I know she wants me to go."

"My mom never mentions it," Hester said, "because she can't afford to send me. I'll do community college. It never hurts to learn all you can."

"Turn here—this is the place."

Hester dropped her jaw as we pulled onto the brick driveway of my grandparents' house. "Good grief," she said, "which building?"

"I live in the caboose," I said.

"Get out!" She smacked my arm. "You live in a *train*? Girl, why didn't you tell me? That's the coolest thing ever."

"I'll have you over next weekend, if you want." I forced a smile. "Thanks for bringing me home."

"Anytime."

I waited until she drove away, then walked toward the main house.

Nana and Pop were in their bedroom, propped up by a mountain of pillows as they watched TV. Pop lowered the volume, and Nana searched my face. "Are you okay, honey? I thought you were spending the night with your friend."

I sat on the corner of the mattress, resisting the urge to curl up between them. "I wasn't feeling well."

I told them what had happened. "Hester thinks I might have had a panic attack. She could be right, considering we were talking about suicide." I looked away. "I'm fine now. I even managed to eat some pizza."

Nana's eyes narrowed. "I've had moments like that too. Grief can do that." She swallowed. "Today I was talking to a friend who lost her husband last year. She joined a grief support group and said it helped a lot. This group meets Saturday afternoons at a nearby church. Everyone who comes has lost someone." She reached for my hand. "I was thinking that kind of group might be good for the two of us."

She looked at Pop, who nodded agreement, then turned back to me. I wasn't wild about the idea, but I didn't want to disappoint her . . . and I sure didn't want to have another panic attack in front of my friends.

So I nodded too.

The next afternoon, Nana and I sat in a circle of folding chairs at a Methodist church. Colorful banners hung from the walls, and someone had loaded a table with cookies, plastic cups, and pitchers of iced tea and water.

I was definitely the youngest person in the room. Most of the others had gray hair, but a few were my parents' age. I didn't see anyone who appeared to be in their twenties or younger, and I felt oddly relieved to know that not as many young adults needed grief support.

I imagined a cartoon in which a kid was telling his therapist, "My parents dragged me to a support group when my gerbil died, and I haven't been the same since."

Dad would have chuckled at that.

At two o'clock, an older man in a cardigan sweater—the grief-group version of Mr. Rogers—took a seat and shot a smile around the circle. "Welcome to Hearts Together," he said, focusing on each face before moving to the next. "I'm Bob Halsey. If you're struggling with grief, you've come to the right place. Whether you've lost a parent, spouse, partner, child, or a dear friend, we'd like to hear your story whenever you're ready to share it. We learn from one another.

"A few guidelines: First, avoid graphic descriptions, as some people are particularly sensitive. Second, we do not allow weapons of any kind. Third, we ask that you come to this meeting sober. Fourth and finally, please be respectful of other people's stories and opinions—do not interrupt, and do not share anyone else's story outside this room.

"And now, let me offer my weekly bit of wisdom: Grief is invisible trauma. Grief is a very real wound, and it throws even the strongest of us out of balance. Grief can hinder our ability to think clearly. It can make us physically ill, and it can cause us to make serious mistakes. That's why you should never make a permanent decision based on a temporary emotion."

Bob leaned back and crossed his long legs. "Who'd like to share first?"

He waited a full minute, but no one answered his invitation. I couldn't blame them—who would want to share the traumatic event they didn't want to even think about? But someone had to go first, and after a moment a middle-aged man in a dark T-shirt cleared his throat.

"Hi," he said, pulling a small notebook from his pocket. "I'm John, and I'm living with grief."

I flinched when the group responded in unison: "Welcome, John."

"I lost my wife two years ago, and I'm still struggling. They tell widowers it usually takes a year to get over the loss of a wife, but that's not been true for me. I wrote this poem to help me work through my feelings. I hope it'll help you, too."

He cleared his throat and read:

They said it was cancer, and you had a chance.
So you fought and we cried, and we prayed like mad.
But God was asleep, or off doing his thing,
And six months later, your soul took wing.
I miss you, Debbie, I miss you, my love.
So much I would follow on wings like a dove.

Most everyone responded with soft murmurs. The woman next to John patted his back, but I looked away. John might have been a nice man, and I felt for him, but his poetry was lousy. Of course, that wasn't the point. But the poem was saying he wanted to die to be with his wife, and that seemed like a cop-out. I thought this group was about learning to survive, not give up.

I glanced at Nana, wondering what she thought of the guy's poem, but her face was as blank as a mask.

"Oh," Bob said, smiling, "I forgot to welcome our new members." The hair on my arms lifted when he smiled at me and Nana. "Welcome, ladies. Would you care to share your names?"

Nana stiffened. "I'm Susan," she said, giving him a polite, no-teeth smile. "And this is my granddaughter, Madison."

"And the source of your grief?"

Nana's voice trembled. "My son took his life the day after Christmas."

A heartfelt groan ran around the circle, and everyone adopted a pained expression. Why did *they* look hurt? They didn't know my dad, and they didn't know us.

Bob welcomed us and reminded us we could share whenever we felt ready, today or anytime later.

A woman lifted her hand. "Hi," she said, her smile utterly life-less. "I'm Caroline, and I live with grief."

"Welcome, Caroline."

"I had a miscarriage six months ago. This week a friend in the grocery store asked how I was doing and said, 'Cheer up! You'll be pregnant again in no time.'"

Caroline swallowed hard. "She acted—and others have done the same thing—as if the baby I lost didn't mean anything. That I should just forget about her and wait for the next one to come along. That was really hard to hear. It was all I could do not to scream in the middle of the cereal aisle."

She burst into tears, and a woman three seats over fished a pack of tissues from her purse and passed them down. Again the group murmured in sympathy, and Bob's flexible face shifted into a compassionate expression.

"People often say thoughtless and cruel things," he said. "But we have to remind ourselves that others don't understand because they've never walked in our shoes. A woman who'd had a mis-carriage would never have been so flippant, would she?"

"No," the group responded.

Bob nodded. "We all have a collection of memories, good and bad, but everyone has a different catalog of experiences. I may not understand yours, and you may not understand mine. But the gift we can give anyone is to *listen*, to restrain ourselves from taking over the conversation, and to validate the grieving person's feelings. That woman shouldn't have said, 'You'll feel better in no time,' because she doesn't know how long it will take you to reach acceptance. She should have said, 'I am so sorry you had a miscarriage.'"

"But how do we respond when people say stupid things?" a red-haired woman asked. "I never know what to do or say, so I just stand there and stutter."

Bob smiled. "I'd encourage you to be the more compassionate person. Instead of responding in anger—though it may be deserved—remind yourself that this other person simply doesn't understand. So thank her for her attention and move on. Walk away if you must. Or respond to the person in the way you wish she had responded to you, with compassion and understanding. What did the apostle Paul say? Faith, hope, and love—but the greatest of these is love."

When it was finally over, Nana and I were the first ones out the door. When we were in the car, I asked her, "Did you hate it too?"

She hesitated. "I didn't hate it, but I'm not sure those people can help us. I could be wrong, though."

"Will you go back?"

"You don't want to?"

"I was the only teenager in the room."

She sighed. "I think I need to give it a fair shot."

"I'm not going." I crossed my arms. "Nobody there could possibly know what it's like to lose your dad."

"You might be surprised," Nana said, putting the car in gear.

Chapter Twenty-Five

Susan

I opened the email and had to read it twice:

> *Dear Susan:*
> *We've received a report of a dangerous animal at your listing.*
> *Your account has been suspended until we resolve this. Please*
> *call me at your earliest convenience.*
>
> *Rick with GuestRoom's safety team*

"Frank! We've been suspended!"

He looked up from papers he was grading. "From what?"

"Our rental unit. Someone reported us having a dangerous animal."

"Would that be me or you?"

"Be serious. They had to mean Ike, unless they saw a palmetto bug, or maybe a snake." None of my guests had said anything about Ike or bugs. "Maybe they saw a roach."

"There'd have to be an infestation to qualify as dangerous," Frank said.

"And the exterminator comes every month. I have to call this support guy. We have a vacancy this weekend, and now we're not listed."

"Maybe the Lord knew we needed a weekend off."

We *were* working hard, and a weekend with no guests would be a welcome treat. But this was our busy season, and a weekend booking could pay off our Christmas bills.

I finally reached Rick, who told me that on the fifth of January, "a guest reported that your dog was aggressive. Apparently, he stole a bag of potato chips."

I blinked. "Our dog weighs twenty pounds, and he's never been aggressive."

"Well, the report says the dog growled, and your guest was afraid to retrieve his chips."

I shook my head. Ike *was* overly fond of food, but I'd never given him potato chips. He probably didn't even know what they were.

"My dog has short little legs, a big belly, and can reach things only less than eighteen inches from the ground. The guest must have been dangling the bag in front of his nose."

"I don't have any details about the incident."

"Ike has never acted aggressively before. Did he nip at the guest? Was he or she injured?"

"I'm not allowed to tell you that, ma'am."

"Why not? If this was a big deal, why didn't the guest say something to me? My door is only a few feet away."

"I'm sorry, ma'am. I can repeat only what's written in the report."

"This makes no sense."

"I'm sure you understand, ma'am, my job is to guarantee the safety of our guests."

"I care about our guests too. Our listing mentions our little dog. Perhaps I should add that guests should guard the perimeter around their snacks."

Rick might have chuckled, but I couldn't be sure. "I just want to make sure you're aware of the problem and will take steps to remedy it." Computer keys clicked in the background. "Will you agree to do that?"

"Yes. And in return, can you reinstate our account?"

"Your listing will be reactivated in forty-eight hours."

"Why so long? If I can be suspended with a keystroke, why can't I be reinstated with another one?"

Silence.

"Anything else, ma'am?"

I sighed. "I suppose not."

"Thank you for being a GuestRoom host, and have a wonderful day."

I went outside, the one place I could rant without bothering Frank. The squirrels wouldn't mind.

I strode down the driveway, my thoughts racing. Dark clouds sagged, heavy with rain, and the scent of ozone filled the air. My nerves were still knotted from hearing the report about Ike. How could anyone be so wrong? Ike was about as dangerous as a marshmallow.

I left the driveway and waded into the foliage. At the end of summer, I had cut back the palmetto fronds and vines that obscured the trail through our tropical jungle. But since Maddie's arrival, I hadn't spent much time in the garden. I plowed through the overgrowth, dodging spider webs and weeds, until I arrived at the vine-covered gazebo that sheltered my favorite bench.

I sat, braced my elbows on my knees, and lowered my face into my hands. "Father," I cried, anguish shredding my voice, "how am I supposed to cope with all this? It's too much."

I had no sooner uttered the words than I sensed a gentle reminder: My situation, while bleak, was not nearly as dire as others'. Frank and I had a home, food in the fridge, and could usually pay our bills. This house, though in constant need of repair, was exactly what we needed for Maddie.

The Lord had known what we would need and when we would need it.

And though we invited Maddie to stay because we wanted to help her, she had also helped us. She gave me a reason to get out of bed every morning.

"There's something else, Lord," I whispered. "For the first time in my life, I'm not enjoying church."

I loved the people in our church, but they had begun to treat me and Frank like celebrities with a contagious disease. Those who dared approach regarded us with an odd mixture of pity, judgment, and fear as they asked, "How *are* you?"

How were we? Devastated.

Last Sunday Frank and I held hands as we walked out of the sanctuary, feeling dozens of eyes on our backs. I had never felt more lonely.

Daniel may have sought release from pain, but he only transferred it to me, Frank, Rachel, and Maddie.

We would suffer with it for the rest of our lives.

"I'm hurting, Father." I lifted my gaze to the swaying oaks beyond the gazebo. "And I don't know how to stop the pain. Maddie has to be hurting too, and I don't know what to do for her, especially when she doesn't want to talk about Daniel."

After that first visit to the support group, Maddie had clammed up. I kept going, hoping to pick up some ideas about how to help Maddie and Frank.

So who was Maddie confiding in? Not me. Not Frank, either, even though he was now substitute teaching at the high school.

When I asked how she was, he shrugged and said she seemed fine. "She's found friends," he said, but when I pressed for more information, he shrugged again. "It's hard to learn much about the kids as a sub, but I don't think she's hanging out with troublemakers, if that's what you mean."

I hoped Maddie would take up with young people who would encourage her to go to church, but since *like* attracted *like*, I doubted that would happen. At least she'd found friends and was talking to them, though I had no idea what they were talking about.

"Guide us, Lord," I prayed. "I don't know what to do. Nudge me when I should speak, and put your hand over my mouth when I should keep quiet. I love that girl more than I can say. I know you love her even more, so please touch her heart."

When I opened my eyes again, the clouds still shaded my garden, but my heart felt lighter. Grief still rode on my shoulder, but its grip had slackened, at least for now.

Frank and I were settling down to watch TV when my phone rang. Rachel was calling.

My heart leapt to my throat, because she never called on weeknights. "Is everything okay?" I asked.

"It's Maddie's SAT," she said, panic in her voice. "I nearly forgot, so I registered her online. The test is March 12, a Saturday, and you'll have to take her. Colleges require it. Juniors need to take it this year to apply to colleges next year."

"Where is the test center?" I asked. "Let me write it down."

"You don't need to," Rachel said. "I'll text the information the day before. Just be sure she gets to the place before they close the doors at eight. She'll need a photo ID, two number two pencils, a calculator, and her admission ticket. They allow the kids to eat and drink during breaks, so if you can give her a bottle of water and some crackers, that'd be great."

"You can relax. We'll make sure she gets there on time. Now how are *you* doing?"

She hesitated. "I'm okay. I get up, I get dressed, I go to work. I put in my ten hours, then come home and try to sleep. Being in this empty house . . . most of the time it seems pointless."

I softened my voice. "We're pretty much doing the same—trying to get through our routines."

"Dinnertime is the worst," she said. "That's when Daniel and I used to catch up with each other. Sometimes I'd cook, but now I think, *Why bother?* So I'm eating way too many frozen dinners. My blood pressure is probably through the roof from so much sodium."

"Rachel, have you thought about finding a grief support group? Maddie and I went once, but I've been three times. It's been helpful."

"Maybe once this case is done. Then I'll have time to take care of myself."

"Don't wait too long," I said. "Even if it's half an hour a day, I need time alone to vent and pray."

"I'm okay," Rachel said. "And thanks again for helping Maddie. Her future may depend on that SAT score."

Chapter Twenty-Six

Maddie

Every Saturday, Nana asked if I wanted to go to her grief support group. I always said no, but when she kept asking, I started to make sure I was gone on Saturday afternoons. I couldn't imagine anything more depressing than sitting with a bunch of people telling sob stories.

I enjoyed having my weekends to myself. I spent every Friday night at the Pizza Palace with my friends, and Saturday mornings I slept in. Hester and I spent the afternoon on the beach or doing homework.

I had been thinking about asking Mom if I could spend the summer in St. Pete. My Florida friends were way more creative than my friends in Georgia. The kids at my old school were all about preparing for college, but my Florida friends talked about movies, art, and poetry. They lived for *today*, not tomorrow. *Carpe diem.*

One Wednesday after school, I was sprawled out on Hester's shag carpet, my history book open as I filled in our study guide. Hester was doing the same on her bed, or so I thought.

"You ever been in love?" she said.

I tripped back to six months before, when I'd been crazy about Tris. Now I could barely remember what he looked like. "I thought I was, once."

"What happened?"

I shrugged. "He liked someone else better."

"Ouch. Do you miss him?"

I snorted. I missed my dad, but *Tris*? "No."

"Well . . . do you like any of the guys in our group?"

I sat up to see her better. "Have *you* ever been in love?"

She waved. "Dozens of times."

"Seriously?"

She laughed. "I used to make out with any guy who smiled at me until Logan said guys were talking about me in the locker room. So I stopped, 'cause a girl's gotta maintain her dignity."

I fell silent, wondering if Tris had ever talked about me.

"What's up with Avery and Matt?" I asked. "I saw them outside school. Avery was yelling at him."

Hester shrugged. "No telling with those two." She leaned toward me. "My turn to ask a question. Why don't you ever talk about your mom?"

"You never ask about her."

"You talk about your dad."

"I was closer to him."

"You and your mom don't get along?"

"We do. We're just different."

"So tell me about her. I keep wondering why she's such a mystery."

I blew out a breath. "Whaddya want to know?"

"What does she look like?"

"Like me, but older. Her hair is shorter and kinda gray around her face."

"Does that freak her out?"

"She says the gray makes her look dignified, and that's a plus for a lawyer."

Hester chewed on the end of her pen. "Tell me something else about her."

I thought a moment. "I have never heard her tell a joke. Ever."

"She doesn't have a sense of humor?"

"She laughs at other people's jokes. She just doesn't tell them."

"You said your dad told jokes all the time."

"Bad jokes." I pointed to the history book. "Which Confederate general surrendered to Grant in 1865?"

"Robert E. Lee," Hester said, drawling. "At Appomattox Court House."

"How do you remember all this stuff?" I wrote the answer in my study guide. "I bet you could get a scholarship."

"Does she take you shopping?"

"Who?"

"Your mom. Or is she a workaholic?"

"She takes me shopping when I need stuff. And yeah, she works a lot, but when the pressure's off, she's off. She and Dad used to take me to the lake, where we'd swim and lay around—though Mom usually read a book."

"Not a joke book, I presume."

"No." I grinned. "Not a joke book."

"But your dad told jokes all the time."

"Horrible jokes. Hardly worth telling."

"So your mom and dad were opposites."

"Pretty much." I lifted a brow. "What about *your* dad? I've met your mom, but I keep wondering why you don't talk about your other parental unit."

Hester snorted. "He's hardly a mystery. He lives in Tampa, he has another wife and two little kids, and I see him maybe three or four times a year."

"Do you miss him?"

Hester jiggled her pen between her fingers. "I used to; then I grew out of it. When I do see him, we pick up where we left off, but sometimes he forgets I'm not a little girl anymore. For my thirteenth birthday, he got me a Barbie." She laughed. "He is totally clueless."

She leaned forward. "My turn. Do you like Logan?"

"Sure. He's nice."

"That's not what I mean." She leaned toward me. "Would you go out with him?"

I bit my lip, thinking about how he read Dickinson's poem on my first day at school. "Yeah. I think I would."

Hester giggled. "Good to know."

"That's just between us, okay? And now it's your turn to answer something for me. Why did you speak to me on my first day? You already had friends."

I expected a sassy remark, but her eyes softened. "I don't know." She shrugged. "Maybe I sensed you were a kindred spirit."

I looked away as a lump rose in my throat. I had been super anxious that day—calm on the outside but churning like mad on the inside. Now I understood that Hester was anxious every day, but few people realized it because she always seemed cool and confident. But beneath her black outfits and fishnet stockings, she was as screwed up as I was.

We had never talked about it, but I knew Hester was a cutter. She wore long sleeves even to the beach, but when we went swimming, I saw the scars. She had to know I saw them. A couple of the scars were red and angry, so they were fresh.

I knew about cutting. Dad explained it to me one afternoon. He said he used to watch *Ben Casey*, an old medical show, and one episode featured a woman who suffered from headaches the doctors couldn't diagnose. They hurt so much she walked around like a zombie, numbed by the constant throbbing in her head. Dr. Casey needed to measure her discomfort, so he hooked her up to an electrical machine that caused sharp pain. He kept increasing the voltage until the pain caused by the machine was worse than the pounding in her head. I thought it was a brutal way to treat a patient, but Dad said she didn't feel the electrical pain until it overpowered her headache.

"I don't know if there really is such a machine," he told me as we sat by the pool, "but I think kids who cut are basically doing the same thing. The pain of the cut distracts them from the numbing pain of whatever they're going through. Sometimes it's mental pain, sometimes it's physical or social. But if you ever feel that kind of pain, Mads, I want you to come to me before you pick up a blade. Together we'll figure out a way to make things better."

Good advice, but ironic in light of what he had chosen. Still, I thought about telling Hester that story, though she didn't have a dad who'd help her figure things out. She had me and her other friends, and I didn't know how to make anything better.

I found myself wondering if cutting would ease the pain of missing Dad. If I tried it, could I become as nonchalant as Hester?

Chapter Twenty-Seven

Susan

When he got home from teaching, Frank usually sat at the kitchen bar and told me about his day, especially if he'd seen Maddie. I thought I'd seen him pull in, but when several minutes passed with no sign of him, I hurried outside. What if he was having a heart attack?

I looked everywhere I could think of and was half a breath from panic when I remembered that Frank liked to sit by the creek. I hurried to the back of the house, and there, on the deck overlooking the waterfall, I saw Frank in the swing. His shoulders were shaking.

I sat beside him and took his hand. Fear snaked around my heart when I saw tears in his eyes. If Frank crumbled, how was I supposed to make it through? And how could we help Maddie?

We might not be up to the task.

I laced my fingers through his. "Tough day?"

He nodded. "One of the toughest."

"What happened?"

He swiped tears from his face, then pulled a handkerchief from his pocket and blew his nose. "It's not easy, Susie."

I was pretty sure I knew what he meant, but I wanted to let him explain. "What's not easy?"

"For a father to mourn his son." His voice cracked, and I waited as he struggled to regain his composure.

"At first," he said, fighting to get the words out, "the thing I most wanted to know was why Daniel did what he did. Now I don't care why. Now all that matters is that Daniel deliberately chose to leave this world without saying goodbye."

I patted his hand.

"The choir had a concert today," he went on. "I wasn't going to go, but I had a free period, so I slipped into the auditorium. Everything was fine until this kid—probably a freshman, because his voice hadn't changed yet—stepped out and sang a song that tore me apart."

"Did—did he look like Daniel at that age?"

Frank shook his head. "He sang 'Danny Boy.'"

He didn't have to explain. Frank, who has a fine voice, used to sing that song to Daniel when he was little, but in those days he sang it with the light irreverence of a young man who had never experienced loss.

We sang it to each other when Daniel went away to college, feeling the sting of separation even as we looked forward to our empty nest.

We had not sung it at all this year, but as the words rippled through my soul, the yearning and passion of the father washed over me: "'Tis you, 'tis you must go and I must bide . . ."

I rested my head on my husband's shoulder as Frank sang through his tears: "Oh Danny boy, oh Danny boy, I love you so."

The gray February sky opened up just as I arrived at the church. I waited in the car, hoping the storm would let up, but rain continued to pound the roof. I grabbed the broken umbrella I kept by the front passenger seat and prayed the ribs would hold until I reached the portico. I was dripping by the time I reached shelter.

I left the umbrella in a trash bin.

Our circle held more empty chairs than usual, probably because of the weather forecast now coming true. Bob was arranging cookies on a platter as I walked in. "Hi," I said, using a napkin to wipe rain from my sleeves. "It's cats and dogs out there."

"Thanks for coming." He smiled. "I'm glad you're sticking with us, Susan. How's your granddaughter doing?"

I shrugged. "She seems to be okay. She's made some new friends at school."

"That's always good," Bob said. "New friends can lead to fresh thoughts and encouragement. And I'm sure she loves being with you."

I wasn't so sure about that, but I smiled.

At two o'clock, Bob took his seat, smiled, and introduced himself. After running through the guidelines, he spread his hands. "I'm sure you've all been waiting for my regular words of wisdom, and this week I learned a lesson from my wife. The other day she pointed out that I can't seem to fill the dog's water bowl without spilling all over the floor. I fill the bowl at the sink, carry it carefully to the mat where we keep his bowl, and always manage to spill at least a third of it.

"Then my wife shared her secret. 'To not spill a drop,' she said, 'you can't look at the water as you walk. But if you lift your head and look at something else, you'll be fine.' Well, what do you know, she was right.

"That lesson works for us, too. When you've suffered a major loss, it's easy to focus on the loss, but sometimes we need to lift our heads and look at something else for a while. That can make life a whole lot easier."

He settled back in his seat. "So who'd like to share first?"

The first to share was a new woman who appeared to be about

my age. Her hair was a shade of dark brown, ill-suited to her pale complexion. "I'm Helen," she said, a hard light in her eyes, "and two weeks ago I lost my forty-eight-year-old son, Harry, to leukemia. I was with him during his fight, of course, so I thought I'd be done with grief after he died, but I'm not. I'm angry—with the world and especially with God. Why didn't he help us? My son worked so hard to get better. He did everything the doctors told him to do and suffered through all the treatments, and for what? Nothing slowed his disease, and two weeks ago I buried him alone because his wife had left as soon as she heard the diagnosis. So why did Harry and I pray and give and work? None of it did a bit of good."

Helen was red-faced by the time she finished, and the rest of us held our breath.

Bob cleared his throat. "Anyone want to respond?"

I felt as though I'd been horsewhipped. Every time Helen had mentioned her son's working hard, I couldn't help feeling that if she knew my story, she'd say Daniel hadn't worked at all. When he met whatever his insurmountable obstacle was, he took the easy way out.

My stomach shriveled when Bob's gaze landed on me. "Susan," he said, "you've been coming a few weeks now. Do you have any wisdom to share with Helen?"

Lord, give me grace. . . .

I swallowed hard. "I lost my adult son too," I said, barely glancing at Helen, "and I know a little about what you're going through. I can't address your feelings about Harry's illness, but I can tell you that grief can make you angry and desperately sad. It can rise up out of the blue and knock you flat. When Harry was sick, you were probably fueled by hope, desperation, and adrenaline. But now you feel tired. There are mornings when getting out of bed requires more energy than you have. Some mornings, you look at your laundry hamper and figure it'd be easier to wear dirty clothes than to do a wash.

"But as weary as you are, you have to keep hope alive for the sake of the others in your life. If there's no one else in your circle now, there are plenty of folks outside your circle who could use a little help. When you start thinking about others, that's when you find motivation to start living again. That's what helps me and my husband. We're moving forward for our granddaughter's sake."

Helen sat stiff and unmoving when I began, but when I finished, her chin trembled, and fresh tears shone in her eyes. The sight of those tears assured me that her heart had not completely hardened.

"I'll pray for you," I said. "God may seem far away, but he's not. If you and your son are believers, you know your son is not dead. He is alive in heaven, and he's completely healed. You will see Harry again—and I will see my Daniel. My husband and I are counting on that."

Bob smiled. "Susan has given me an idea," he said, reaching for a notepad. "We're not Alcoholics Anonymous, but they have a system where every member has a sponsor, someone they can call if they're about to take a drink. We could do something similar."

I frowned, not sure I wanted to be responsible for another member. Frank and I had enough on our plate.

"I know we all have our struggles," Bob went on, "but I also know there is power in united prayer. So why don't we establish a phone chain? If you want to participate, write your name, email, and phone number on this tablet. And if you find yourself having one of those days where you can't rise above your grief, call the name beneath yours on the phone list, and ask that person to pray for you. They will pray, and they'll call the next name with your request. And in no time, we'll *all* be praying."

Bob passed the notepad to Ruby, an older woman whose husband had committed suicide. We watched as she wrote her name and number.

"What if the name below yours doesn't answer?" Ivano asked. He had recently lost his best friend to Covid.

"Then you call the next name," Bob said. "I'll compile the list and email it to everyone who wants to be a part of this chain. You don't have to participate, but if you sign up, please be faithful to pray."

Lucio signed the notepad and passed it to John, the man who had lost his wife to cancer.

"Bob," Caroline asked, "I have a friend who suffers from depression and has mentioned suicide a couple of times. I want to ask how she's doing, but I'm afraid if I bring the subject of suicide up, it'll only reinforce the idea in her head."

Bob groaned. "If she's talked about suicide, the idea is already in her mind. And some say that having someone ask if they're still feeling suicidal helps relieve their anxiety. It brings a taboo topic out into the open."

"Suicide isn't about dying," Isabell said, staring at the floor. She had told us about her brother, who killed himself with a drug overdose. "It's about stopping unbearable pain. That's what my brother told me the week before he died."

Bob clasped his hands. "I recently read a report about suicide notes. When a person is serious about ending his life, the notes tend to be matter-of-fact—Johnny gets the car, don't forget to feed my cat, that sort of thing. Rarely are they philosophical or even explanatory. It's as if the person simply wants to tie up loose ends and say goodbye."

When the notepad reached me, I hesitated, not sure I could commit. Then I realized I had *already* committed to these people. I had become part of their lives, and they were part of mine.

I jotted down my name and number and passed the notepad on.

Since Frank and I lacked the energy for a full grocery run, we decided to stop by the store on our way home from church. We walked through the door together, then Frank headed for the snack aisle while I moved toward the produce department. I gathered the ingredients for a salad, then added a few other basics to my cart. We met at the cashier.

I watched Frank place his selections on the checkout stand. "Chips, cookies, and salsa?" I lifted a brow.

"Salsa's healthy," he said. "It's vegetables."

I snorted.

We paid for the groceries, then Frank put the bagged items into the cart and wheeled it out the door.

We'd been lucky to get a parking spot near the front, so Frank loaded the trunk while I walked to the passenger door. I saw him close the door and give the cart a push—a move that left me speechless, especially when the cart rolled down an incline and crashed into a parked vehicle.

"Frank! Your buggy hit that car!"

He looked at me, his face hard. "So? God lets bad things happen."

I had no words.

At home, I walked into the house without speaking. Frank dropped the grocery bags on the table and left.

From the front window, I watched his car move down the driveway and turn right.

I wept.

My support group had taught me that grief has many faces and moods. "Even kind people," Bob Halsey once said, "struggle with anger during grief."

When I heard Maddie walking across the front porch, I dried my tears and started putting groceries away.

"Hi, Nana." She hopped onto a stool at the kitchen island. "What's for lunch?"

"Salad." I kept my back to her so she wouldn't see my blotchy face. "I want to boil some eggs, so it'll be a while before lunch is ready. You might want to come back in half an hour."

When she didn't answer, I glanced over my shoulder and saw her watching me, her eyes pensive. She'd noticed.

"I'm okay," I said, my throat tightening. "But why don't you come back in a bit?"

She slid off the stool and left the house.

I was boiling the eggs when Frank came through the back door, his head low. He shrugged out of his jacket and sat at the counter. "I'm sorry," he said.

I faced him. "Where'd you go?"

"Back to the store. I left my name and number with the manager—and yes, the owner of the other car had already complained. I'll take care of it."

I stifled a sob of relief.

I draped my arms around his shoulders. "You're a good man, Frank Lawton. Just in case you were wondering."

He patted my arm. "I needed to hear that."

Chapter Twenty-Eight

Susan

February and March are high season for Florida rentals, and we were booked nearly every day. I found myself doing countless loads of laundry and making several trips to the warehouse store, stocking up on paper towels, toilet paper rolls, and snacks.

Maddie often helped me clean the apartment, especially when I had a one-day turnover. I probably could have done the job faster if I cleaned alone, but I wanted her to feel that she was contributing. I *did* appreciate her help—though my broken arm had healed, the muscles around the bone were still bruised and sore. It was nice to have an extra pair of hands for hauling heavy laundry baskets up and down the stairs.

I also appreciated our time together. While we cleaned, I was able to talk to Maddie—not about anything serious, but at least the conversational doors were open. I hoped the mindless work of dusting and vacuuming kept her mind off more-troubling matters.

I asked her about school; she said everything was fine. I asked about Rachel; Maddie said her mom was doing okay and working on her big case.

Once, when we were cleaning the kitchen, I asked about her new friends. Maddie stopped scrubbing the counter long enough to widen her eyes and place her hand over her heart. "I promise, Nana," she said, exaggerating her words. "None of them takes drugs or has ever been arrested."

"All right, Miss Sassy," I answered. "Still, that's nice to know."

I met Hester Ackerman, Maddie's new best friend, when she spent the night after one of their gatherings at the Pizza Palace. Hester shook my hand and grinned at Frank. "I already know this man," she said, her smile broadening. "He had to babysit our class once."

Frank grinned. "You were one of the few I didn't have to reprimand."

Maddie grabbed Hester's arm and dragged her out to the caboose, so we didn't see them again until noon the next day. Hester seemed to be good for Maddie, so I was grateful she had found a friend.

Track-and-field began in early spring, and Maddie and Hester often stayed after school to watch. One of their friends, Logan somebody-or-other, had apparently caught Maddie's eye. I learned that Logan ran the 200 and the 400 meters. Frank told me those were basically long sprints.

"Logan's a nice kid. I can see why Maddie likes him."

"Have you ever seen him with Maddie?"

Frank nodded. "With others from that group."

"They're not dating, are they?"

"I don't think they've actually gone out."

I figured everything was going fine—maybe even better than fine. But one night I discovered I was wrong.

Our dinnertime discussion started out smoothly enough.

Maddie was eating leftover lasagna with us—a rare thing, since she was usually with Hester. "Did you ever run track, Pop?" she asked.

Frank nodded. "Yep. I was a distance runner—I ran the mile and the 4-by-400 relay."

"Set any records?"

Frank chuckled. "I once ran a mile in under five minutes. That wasn't a school record, but it was my best time."

"Did Dad run track?"

Frank swallowed a bite and nodded. "He went out for track in—what was it, Susie, tenth grade?"

"Ninth," I said. "I remember because he didn't like it. He only lasted two weeks."

Frank nodded. "That's right. He preferred team sports. He found track too solitary."

Maddie immediately turned stony, staring at her plate.

"Honey," I said, lowering my voice, "if you don't want to talk about your dad, that's okay. But since you asked . . ."

"You let him *quit*?" Maddie looked up, her eyes blazing. "You let him quit track?"

I blinked, stunned by her vehemence. "He was miserable. It wasn't what he thought it would be."

"So he learned it was okay to quit if he didn't like something."

Frank reached for Maddie's hand. "Just because a kid quits track doesn't mean—"

"Mom didn't let me quit gymnastics when I was eight," she said, spitting the words. "She made me stick it out until the end of the year."

"But—"

"Dad wouldn't let me quit tee-ball, either. He said once you commit to something, you shouldn't quit and disappoint your teammates."

"See?" I forced a smile. "Daniel wouldn't have said that if he thought it was okay to—"

"But you *let* him quit. And when life wasn't what he thought it would be, he quit because you said he could."

I knew she was upset, but surely she couldn't believe what she was saying.

"Maddie," Frank said, his voice firm. "You know better. Your dad had learned that important lesson, so that's why he told you not to quit tee-ball."

"It's your fault." Tears filled Maddie's eyes. She slid from her stool so abruptly it toppled over. "It's your fault, and I'll never forget it."

I had to talk to someone, but Frank was as confused as I was. I thought about calling Caroline, whose name was beneath mine on Bob Halsey's phone chain, but I wasn't sure a younger woman would understand the frustration of dealing with a teenager.

So I was the first to arrive at Saturday's grief support meeting.

Feeling about to burst, I sat and watched the clock until Bob took his seat. When he finally asked if anyone wanted to speak, my hand rose like a rocket, my cheeks burning. "I'm Susan, and some of you may remember that I brought my granddaughter with me about a month ago."

Bob nodded. "Your son committed suicide, right?"

Bless Bob for his memory. He had saved me the stress of having to tell the story again.

"Maddie's been staying with us since her dad's death, and I thought we were all doing pretty well, considering. But the other night, I mentioned that we'd let Maddie's dad quit the track team in the ninth grade. Well, she blew up and said we'd taught him to be a quitter, basically blaming us for his quitting on life. I was flabbergasted."

The others murmured in consolation, and Isabell, who had lost her brother to suicide, said, "Did you snap back at her?"

"I was too shocked. I tried to tell her Daniel wasn't a quitter, but Maddie ran out of the house."

"How has she been acting since then?" John asked. "Is she still angry?"

"Probably. That was Thursday night, and I haven't seen her smile since. She's been cool toward us."

"Ah." Ruby crossed her arms. "She's punishing you."

"What for?"

"Doesn't matter. She's angry and wants to blame someone. You and your husband are the most convenient targets."

"And you're safe," Bob added. "She knows she can blow up at you and you'll still love her. She wouldn't try that with her friends."

Ruby nodded. "The stages of grief, remember? Denial first. Then anger."

"She's probably angry with her father, too," Bob said. "You might not get to see that. But if you look, you can probably spot a few signs."

I stared at him, my heart pounding. Maddie had adored her dad. I couldn't imagine her being angry with him even for a New York minute. Then again, last week I couldn't have imagined her being mad at me and Frank.

"Let her vent and keep loving her," Bob said. "She's a teenager, and she's grieving. Her anger is passionate, so your love has to be even more passionate." He smiled. "I know you and your husband can handle this."

Lucio leaned forward. "I have a friend whose daughter was murdered. He was so angry, he destroyed almost everything in the house. When his wife called him crazy, he went out in the back yard and started digging. Every day, he'd come home from work and add more to his mountain of dirt. Last I heard, he was still doing it."

"That's why we need to move *through* the stages of grief," Bob said. "You can't let yourself get stuck. You have to keep moving forward."

"And how do we do that?" Caroline asked.

"You're already doing it," Bob said. "By talking and listening, by sharing your feelings, you are making progress. You're learning how to move forward, and we're praying for each other. That's the answer."

Just because Maddie's anger was normal didn't mean it was easy to handle.

I got out of the car and glanced toward the caboose. I couldn't see through the tinted windows, but I could hear the rhythmic thumping of music, so Maddie was home. Maybe she'd had time to cool off. Maybe she'd apologize for her attitude the other night.

I tacked on a smile and strode toward the train car. I knocked on the door and waited, praying her mood would be better.

My heart sank when she opened the door and stared, her face like a thundercloud.

I brightened my voice. "Do you want to help me make cookies?"

"I'm busy," she said, about to close the door.

I held it open. "Honey, I want to know how you're doing. I want you to talk to me."

"I don't have anything to say. Now I need to get back to my homework."

She closed the door.

"When you want to talk," I yelled, "you know where to find me."

Annoyed, I strode across the driveway. I couldn't believe she had closed the door in my face. My irritation flared into indignation. Then my blood began to boil.

I slammed my purse to the kitchen counter and stood in front of the sink, my chest heaving.

Bob Halsey said I should meet Maddie's anger with love, and I was struggling to dredge up a thimbleful of affection. I was stewing in a soup of resentment, exactly the opposite of what Maddie needed.

A wave of guilt slammed into me. I stumbled toward our bathroom, kicked off my shoes, and stepped into the shower fully clothed.

As water poured over me, I hung my head and sobbed, letting the rushing stream muffle my cries.

I didn't hear Frank come in, but suddenly there he was, turning off the water and pulling me into his arms.

"It's okay," he whispered, his breath warm against my ear. "We're going to make it through this, Susie. I promise."

When I was all cried out, I looked at him and struggled to smile. "We're pitiful," I said. "Fully clothed and dripping."

"People would say we're crazy."

I handed him a towel. "People don't have to know."

Chapter Twenty-Nine

Maddie

When Logan, Matthew, and Jackson didn't show up at the Pizza Palace, our tradition turned into a girls' night out. Hester, Mia, Sofia, and I hung out—no Avery, either—but the night was definitely missing something without the guys.

The next night we went back to the Palace. Julie, the waitress who usually took care of us, had just brought our drinks when Logan and Jackson strolled in.

"Where were you guys last night?" Hester said, pouting. "We thought you might have found better friends."

Logan slid in next to me. "My parents didn't want me going out, since I had to take the ACT today. They're convinced my future is riding on that test."

I made a face. "Your entire future?"

"Oh, yeah." Logan raked a hand through his hair. "They want me to go to Johns Hopkins or Cornell, and both have high standards for the ACT. If I can't get in, I can't go to medical school, and if I can't go to medical school, life is over as we know it." He grinned. "Or as I know it, at least."

Hester nudged me. "Logan's parents are doctors. His dad is a brain surgeon."

"Wow." I looked at Logan with new appreciation. "I had no idea."

He snorted. "Like that changes anything."

"So, how'd you do?" Sofia asked. "Was it hard?"

Logan shrugged. "The English and reading parts were cake. Math and science were more of a challenge." He jerked his chin at Jackson. "What'd you think?"

Jackson scoffed. "I was going to Christmas tree the answer sheet, but my mom would kill me if my score wasn't decent. So I answered the ones I knew and skipped the rest."

"How many questions did you answer?" Hester teased. "Your name and social security number?"

"Ha ha." Jackson gave her a humorless smile. "For your information, I answered at least half of them. I did okay, I think."

"Oh, wow." Jackson stared at his phone, then quickly flicked the image away.

"What's up?" Hester asked.

"Nothing."

"Come on, man." Logan grinned. "You can tell us."

"I can't," Jackson said. "It's bad."

Hester grew serious. "Someone we know?"

"One of us?" Mia demanded. "Who?"

Jackson's eyes darted. "No one at this table."

Hester narrowed her gaze. "So, Avery and Matthew?"

Jackson closed his eyes, and I felt sorry for him. He hadn't asked to receive that text, and whatever he saw had genuinely upset him. And if it involved one of us . . .

"I'm gonna take that as a yes," Hester said. "You might as well tell us so we can help. They're our friends."

Jackson leaned forward and lowered his voice. "There's a video . . . of something that ought to be private. I only saw a screenshot, but someone's gonna be in big trouble."

I gasped. Avery and Matt had been going together a long time, and if they had been recorded in a private moment . . .

Hester turned hot eyes on Jackson. "Who sent you that screenshot?"

Jackson slumped. "Some sophomore. I think he sent it to his entire contact list, along with a link to the video."

Hester grabbed her purse. "Let me out of this booth. Avery needs me."

Mia's eyes went wide. "What if she doesn't know?"

"She's going to know soon enough," Hester snapped. "And someone's going to need to talk her off the ledge—or keep her from killing Matt. Either way, I'm gonna be there for her."

Logan and I stood, letting Hester scoot out of the booth.

"Wow." Jackson shook his head. "If Matt made a video, how could some dweeb find out about it?"

"It's not impossible," Logan said. "All he had to do was share it once. It could be all over the Internet by now."

Mia and Sofia looked as shocked as I felt. I didn't know exactly what had happened, but I had a pretty good idea.

If I were Avery, I'd want to disappear forever.

Chapter Thirty

Susan

Maddie texted me Sunday after church: **At Hester's. Home later.**

We'd been hoping Maddie would be home so we could clear the air, but apparently that conversation would have to wait.

After lunch, I put a burger on a paper plate, piled it with the condiments Maddie liked, and carried it over to the caboose. I knew she snacked at Hester's house, but I wanted to be sure she ingested a decent amount of protein before the day ended.

I unlocked the narrow door and stepped inside. The front room was a mess, but I wasn't surprised. With little room for storage, Maddie had schoolbooks stacked on the futon, papers scattered over the foldout table, and a mountain of dirty clothes in the corner. I kicked a few pieces of clothing out of the way and put the burger in the mini fridge. Later she could warm it up in the microwave.

With that done, I put my hands in my pockets and resisted the urge to pick up the clutter. This was her space, and I didn't want to intrude. But I did want to leave a note so she'd know I'd left food for her. Given her current mood, I didn't think she'd stop by the house when she got home.

I saw a sketchbook on the floor and picked it up, intending to rip out a page and tape it to the door. But what I saw when I lifted the cover made my blood run cold.

She'd drawn a picture of Daniel as she must have seen him a thousand times—smiling, holding a soda while he relaxed in his recliner. She had real talent—she had even detailed his wavy hair and the cleft in his chin.

But at some point, Maddie had scratched out Daniel's eyes with marks so sharp she'd torn the paper. I couldn't tell when she had drawn the sketch, but I had a feeling she had defaced it in the last couple of days.

I flipped through other sketches—the house in Atlanta, Daniel practicing his golf swing on the front lawn, Daniel and Rachel at the dinner table. Maddie had crossed out the faces of both parents. Page after page, in sketches of Daniel or Rachel, she had obliterated the facial features.

I sank to the futon as if I'd stumbled upon a serial killer's journal. Was this normal anger or psychotic rage? I'd been angry too—with Maddie, Frank, and especially Daniel. But I hadn't done anything like this.

My mind drifted back to a morning when Daniel was about ten. We had gone to the grocery, and he asked if he could go get a bag of Doritos. I told him yes, then moved down the aisle, focused on my shopping list. I looked for Daniel when I reached the snack section, but he was nowhere in sight. I whirled my cart around and walked across the back of the store, peering down each aisle. I made it all the way to the dairy section, then turned and checked the aisles again, sure I'd missed him.

When I made it to the far side without spotting Daniel, I sped to the manager's office. "I can't find my son," I said, struggling to keep my voice from breaking. "Would you please ask Daniel Lawton to come to the front of the store?"

The manager must have seen the terror in my eyes. He went straight to the PA system and made the announcement. I stood, foot tapping, vowing to never let Daniel out of my sight again. I waited five minutes and asked the manager to repeat the announcement. "Maybe he was in the restroom," I said, trying to remain calm. "If you would please call him one more time."

I stood by the cash registers for what felt like an eternity, my head filling with reports of kidnapped children. I was about to ask the manager to call the police when a woman yelled, "Hey lady, look outside. Is that your kid?"

I spun and saw Daniel sauntering past the store windows, a shopping bag in his hand. I went weak-kneed with relief, but when I caught up to him, I grabbed his shoulders and squeezed so hard I probably left bruises.

Several times in the past month, I'd suddenly felt an urge to smack my son. Had he walked through the door, I would have done just that, despite being overjoyed to see him. How could he have been so thoughtless and cruel? Did he not think of us before he used that gun? Didn't he realize we would never think of him without remembering how deeply he had wounded us?

Desperate love compelled Maddie to draw these sketches, and anger drove her to deface them.

I found an index card and scribbled my note about the burger. Before leaving, I stood by the door and begged God to watch over my granddaughter. "Please don't let her friends feed this anger. I don't know much about them, Lord, but please let them be a blessing to her, not a curse.

"And calm my heart, Lord. Help me put aside my anger and love her as you would love her. Always."

Chapter Thirty-One

Maddie

I shoved my history book aside. "So, are you finally going to tell me what's up with Matt and Avery, or are you not allowed to say?"

Hester blew a stubborn curl off her forehead. "Honestly, I don't know who's more stupid, her or him. Let's just say there's a video."

"Jackson told us that much."

"Matthew shot the video."

"A *private* video, Jackson said."

"Right. I don't know why Avery agreed to it, but she never meant for anyone else to see it. Matt got stupid and showed it to one of his cousins."

"He was that careless?"

Hester nodded. "Apparently this cousin is older, and before you know it, he's on Matt's computer uploading the video to some website. Matt might never have known, except the cousin put a caption on it—something about hot St. Pete girls. He might as

161

well have pinned a target on Matt and Avery, because within two days, guys at school were asking Matt about it. He told Avery, she's furious, and Matt's in trouble with her, his parents, and her parents. They're talking about pressing charges since she's under eighteen and the video was posted without her permission."

I shuddered. "That's awful. And probably not what Matt wanted to deal with on Valentine's Day."

"No kidding. Even if they get the video taken down, there's no telling how many people have already downloaded it. Avery wants to kill Matt, but he keeps saying it wasn't his fault, it was his stupid cousin's." Hester shook her head. "If Matt drums up enough courage to give Avery a Valentine's present, I'm pretty sure she'd throw it back in his face."

Hester poured more tortilla chips into the bowl, then scooped up a hunk of melted cheese. "If I were Avery, I don't know what I'd do. She says she loves Matt, but she can't believe he was so stupid."

As Hester rattled on about the irresponsibility of guys in general, I dipped a chip into the cheese and stared at the resulting blob. I'd never been in a situation like Avery's—and never wanted to be—but I had dreaded the thought of going back to my old school with everyone knowing my father had blown his brains out.

In high school, some things were almost unsurvivable.

Chapter Thirty-Two

Susan

One of our next short-term renters looked so much like my daughter-in-law that I was reminded I hadn't talked to Rachel in several days. I needed to call her—especially today.

I dialed and waited for her to pick up. After three rings, she finally did. "Susan? Is Maddie okay?"

"She's fine. I was calling to check on you . . . because it's Valentine's Day."

"Is it? I didn't realize." She was whispering, so this was probably not a good time to talk.

"How are you doing, hon?"

"Good."

"Do you have a minute?"

"Not really. Can we talk tomorrow or next week? I'm at work, and things are really busy here."

"Sure. I'll let you go."

I lowered my phone, embarrassed.

Rachel was probably in a roomful of lawyers, and I'd interrupted an important meeting just because it was Valentine's Day.

At least she knew I cared enough to reach out.

Next time, I would text her.

Chapter Thirty-Three

Maddie

Hester and I were walking home from school when she said Mr. Wright had given her an A- on her Dickinson essay. "It wasn't my best work," she said, "but I think he felt sorry for me because I mentioned not having a dad at home."

I snorted, irritated because I got a B on that essay and my dad had permanently checked out. "Since when has Mr. Wright gotten sympathetic? When Sofia came in late the other day and said she'd been sick in the restroom, he sent her to the office."

Hester arched a brow. "Think she could be pregnant?"

"Does she even have a boyfriend?"

"Since when is that a requirement?"

"If she'd been with a guy, she wouldn't have kept it a secret from you or Mia."

"You'd be surprised. Some people have secrets they never share even with their best friends. Bet even you have a couple."

"Me?" I laughed, but the truth was I'd never told Hester about finding my dad or what I'd done to my sketches of him. Or that I had regular nightmares about finding him at that desk, but in my dreams he lifts his damaged head and asks why I let him down.

As if he hadn't ruined my life.

"You're pretty intuitive," I said, hoping to distract her. "So you're thinking Sofia isn't pregnant."

She shrugged. "She probably got her period, that's all."

We reached Hester's house, went inside, and dropped our stuff onto the couch. We were still studying the Civil War, and Hester thought it'd be easier to watch a couple of Civil War movies than read the assigned chapters.

We were three episodes into a series about a hot Union officer and a wasp-waisted Southern belle when Hester's mom turned into the driveway. She came in, gave us a quick smile, and switched on the lamp. "Why are you girls sitting in the dark?"

"Because we're at the movies." Hester grabbed another handful of popcorn from the bowl between us. "And we didn't realize how late it was. Can we order a pizza?"

"Go ahead." Mrs. Ackerman left the room while Hester called the Pizza Palace. She placed the order, hung up, and snorted when her phone rang again.

"It's Sofia," she said, reading the caller ID. "I hope she's not *really* sick. Hello?"

I watched as Hester's eyes widened. "That's not funny!" She listened again, then nodded, her eyes filling with tears. "Okay, we'll meet you there." Her hand trembled as she lowered the phone. "It's Matt and Avery."

"Did they break up?"

Hester blinked, her face a perfect mask. But when her mouth twitched in an odd grimace, I knew something bad had happened. "What?"

"They jumped from the water tower. Matthew's in the hospital, and Avery . . ."

"*What?*"

"She's dead." Hester's voice cracked. "Sofia said they made a suicide pact."

By the time Hester and I got to the water tower, the cops had cordoned off a large area around the base. Police vehicles ringed the site, their red-and-blue lights pushing at the dense darkness. At least a couple dozen people huddled in groups, drawn by the lights, the noise, and the horror.

A bald man told anyone who would listen, "I saw them from my front porch, so I called 911. But I couldn't stop them."

Hester spotted Mia, Logan, Jackson, and Sofia shivering beneath a pine tree, their faces pale in the headlights of a police car. Hester and I hurried over.

"How'd you hear?" Hester asked Sofia.

"Logan and Jax were playing basketball a couple of blocks away," she said.

"We heard the sirens," Jackson said, "and we ran over here. Logan recognized Matt's jacket."

Hester turned back to Sofia. "Where'd you hear they had a suicide pact?"

Sofia lifted her hands in a *don't shoot* pose. "I overheard a cop say it. I don't know if it's true, but that's what I heard."

"I didn't know anything until my mom drove by and saw the flashing lights," Mia said. "A cop told her two kids had jumped. The EMTs were in a hurry to get Matt to the hospital."

"How could he have survived?" Jackson asked. "They had to fall over 150 feet."

Sofia pressed her hands over her mouth, then vomited in the grass.

"Why'd they do it?" I whispered, trying not to think about my dad.

Hester kicked at the ground. "Avery's been humiliated, Matt's in trouble with the law. They probably couldn't see any way out."

She peered at Logan and Jackson. "Did Matt say anything? Drop any hints?"

Jackson frowned and shook his head.

"Not to me either," Logan said.

Mia whispered, "Avery was really quiet today, but . . ."

"She wasn't her usual self," Sofia added. "I thought it was because of the video."

I closed my eyes. My dad seemed fine too on Christmas Day. But that didn't stop him the day after.

Hester raked her hands through her hair. "Maybe they were up there goofing around. That catwalk could be slippery."

"I hope," Sophia said, rubbing her arms. "I couldn't stand to think Avery was desperate and I didn't know it."

"The other night," I said, thinking aloud, "Matt and Avery kept whispering to each other, and Avery seemed upset. Maybe that was when she learned about that video."

Hester shrugged. "They were in love. They were *always* whispering."

"But Avery seemed upset. What if that was right after she learned about Matt's cousin uploading that video?"

I stared at the ground, silently sifting through the rumors and observations that might have brought Matt and Avery to this horrible place.

Suddenly wanting to be *anywhere* else, I stepped out of the circle. "I need to get home. Can anyone give me a lift?"

"I can," Logan said, his voice gruff.

I nodded at Hester, then shoved my hands in my pockets and followed Logan through the overgrown grass. When we reached his car, he started the engine without saying a word.

We rode in silence until we reached Nana and Pop's mailbox. Logan shoved the car in park and let his hands fall into his lap. "Matt is one of my best friends." He stared at his steering wheel. "I can't believe he wanted to off himself."

"Maybe he didn't want to," I said. "Maybe you'll get to talk to him soon."

"I hope so. Because not knowing . . ." A muscle clenched along his jaw. "Sorry, I forgot about your dad."

"It's okay. I wish I could forget."

He killed the engine, making me hesitate before grabbing the door handle.

"You wanna talk?" I asked.

He shook his head. "Not really. I just don't want to be alone." He squinted at a solar-powered light that struggled to light the front of the caboose. "You're really staying there?"

"Yeah."

"Sweet."

"It is, sort of. It was built in 1921, so it's officially an antique. Pretty amazing that it's still standing."

The ghost of a smile flitted over Logan's face. "I like trains. My granddad used to take me to the train museum when I was little. Once he took me on a weeklong trip—Amtrak, so it was nothing like yours, but it was still a cool experience."

As darkness pressed against the car windows, we talked—not about death or dying or even Matt and Avery, but about trains and summer vacations and old friends. We laughed about some of our stupid dreams, and I even told him that I kept dreaming about losing Dad in odd places—at the beach, in a department store, and in downtown Atlanta.

When we were talked out, we stared at each other awkwardly for a few seconds. Logan said he'd better get going, and I said me too. By the time he drove off, the darkness seemed a little less dense.

Chapter Thirty-Four

Susan

Maddie's nightly check-in was part of our arrangement, but since she'd been dropped off at the caboose early, I let it go.

An hour later, Frank and I were in bed. I was working on a crossword puzzle while Frank clicked through TV channels. He was watching a local station when a teaser for the nightly news came on. "Local teens jump from water tower in suicide pact. Details at eleven."

I dropped my crossword puzzle book. "Frank—"

"I heard."

My blood chilled when the story came on. "Two seventeen-year-old, eleventh-grade students at St. Petersburg High School jumped from the Crescent Lake water tower shortly after sunset. The young woman died, and the young man is in critical condition at St. Pete General. Their names are being withheld at the request of their families."

The cameras panned the crowd around the water tower, and I thought I recognized a couple of Maddie's friends.

"Police confirmed that a bystander found a handwritten note at the base of the tower stating that the teens intended to die together."

I turned to Frank, who was watching with an agonized expression. "What were they thinking?"

Frank shook his head. "Could have been anything."

"I'm pretty sure I saw some friends of Maddie's."

"I recognized a few of them too."

"Maddie doesn't need this. If she knew those kids who jumped . . ."

"I know, Susie." He rubbed his temple. "Their parents must be wild with grief."

I brought my hand to my mouth, choking on the conviction that Frank and I had made a huge mistake. Why had we put Maddie at a school where kids were jumping off water towers?

Frank blew out a breath. "Father, be with the parents of these kids, and please preserve the life of the young man. And, Lord, give us wisdom to guide Maddie."

"We have to talk to her, Frank."

He leaned back on his pillows. "This might be a good time for her to see a counselor."

"She won't go. She didn't even like my support group. What about you? Aren't you taking her to school tomorrow?"

"I have to go in early," Frank said. "They're doing standardized testing for the ninth grade, and I said I'd come in and help set up. So Maddie will have to walk tomorrow morning." He gestured to his lips, his way of asking for a good-night kiss. "I'm not putting all this on you," he whispered. "But if the Lord sends an opportunity, take it. I'll do the same."

Everything would be easier if I could leave matters in Frank's hands, but he was right. I'd probably have more opportunities to speak to Maddie.

But I had no idea what to say.

Maddie didn't approach the house until it was almost time for her to leave for school. When I heard footsteps on the front porch, I stepped behind the kitchen counter, ready to whip up whatever she wanted for breakfast. I could talk while I cooked, and maybe she wouldn't realize I'd been waiting for her.

"Good morning, hon." I gave her a restrained smile. "What would you like to eat?"

"I don't have time," she said, picking up the newspaper.

"Maddie, you should eat something."

"Not really hungry."

"How 'bout I fix you a sandwich for lunch."

"I'll get something at school."

I sighed and waited for her to finish reading. When she finally lowered the paper, I said, "You know those kids, don't you?"

She nodded, her eyes glistening.

"I'm so sorry, hon. I imagine their parents are heartbroken."

Maddie sniffed and pulled a diet soda from the fridge.

"It's been on the TV news," I said, desperate to fill the heavy silence. "The young man is still in critical condition."

"I gotta go, Nana."

"Honey, if you need to talk," I continued, trying to connect with the soul behind those wet eyes, "I know how upset you must be. I'd do anything to help."

Finally, her gaze met mine. "I know."

"Do you? Would you like to talk to a counselor? Not a support group, but a trained counselor, someone who could help you make sense of all this."

"How is this ever gonna make sense?" She shook her head. "Maybe Matt and Avery didn't *want* to make sense. Maybe Dad didn't want us to know what was in his mind. Or maybe all of them wanted to hurt the people who loved them. What they did could be a form of revenge, you know."

Revenge? "Maddie, you know your dad loved you more than anything. He would never intentionally—"

"But he did." Her dark, wounded eyes rose to meet mine. "He loved you and Pop. And me and Mom. He loved us and he destroyed us. So how can that make sense?"

I gripped the counter, speechless. That's why we needed a professional. At seventeen, Maddie was smart enough to talk me into a corner.

"I'm begging you, Maddie. Please let me find a counselor. Pop and I would arrange and even go ourselves if that would help. We need help too."

"Right," she said, "but I'm gonna be late—"

"Maddie—"

She lifted a hand. "Would you mind if I did a little decorating in the caboose? Maybe paint the inside walls?"

I blinked. This girl could change subjects on a dime. "I was going to ask if you wanted to paint the place. Pop and I thought you'd get tired of looking at those paint-spattered boards."

"So it's okay?"

"Absolutely!"

"I was thinking about asking a couple of my friends to help."

I had imagined the three of us painting together, but this was a better idea. At least she would be thinking about something other than death.

Not all my rental guests earned five-star reviews. After checkout time, I went upstairs and found trash on the floor, unwashed dishes, and a broken lamp. I was running hot water in the sink when my cell phone rang. I didn't recognize the number and braced for a sales call.

"Susan? This is Ivano, and I need you to pray for me." He spoke in an aching, husky whisper I barely recognized.

I shut off the water. Ivano's name was above mine on the phone chain. He did not often share in our support group, but I could hear pain in his voice.

"I'd be happy to pray. Do you want to tell me what's happening?"

He drew a ragged breath. "It is not one specific thing, you know? My wife, she does not understand. I try to tell her Viktor was like a brother, and she says when her brother died, she did not carry on for weeks. But she was not as close to her brother as I was close to Viktor."

I closed my eyes and prayed for wisdom.

I knew Ivano and Viktor had emigrated together from Russia, married within weeks of each other, and they and their wives each had three children. Ivano and Viktor had been planning the trip of a lifetime. As huge baseball fans, they wanted to attend a game in all the Major League stadiums. But in the spring of 2021, Viktor caught Covid and died thirty days later.

"My wife says for me to cry for Viktor is unmanly. She tells me to watch baseball, but how can I without thinking of Viktor? Why can she not understand? Sometimes I think it is because she is American, but I think you would understand."

I took a deep breath and prayed for wisdom. "You and Viktor were closer than brothers, because you spent more time together. Maybe she scolds you because she wants to hold first place in your heart. When you grieve your friend, she may feel jealous."

"Oi!" he said, sounding surprised.

"Try this," I said. "The next time your wife says something negative about Viktor, take her in your arms and tell her you love her more than anything. See what happens."

He said, "*Ya ponyal,*" then apologized. "Sometimes I forget my English, but I'm saying I get it. If you say to do it, I will do it. If only I could sometimes stop my tears."

"Did I tell you about my broken arm?"

"*Nyet.*"

"Last winter I tripped over a silly dog toy, and when my husband took me to the emergency room, the nurse said my blood pressure was high because I was in pain."

"Your arm," Ivano asked, "it is better?"

"Completely," I told him. "I never cried over my broken arm.

Physical pain hurts until it doesn't. But emotional pain is deeper and more complicated. I think it will make us cry until we meet our loved ones in heaven."

"Thank you, Susan. I will do as you say."

"Do you want me to call the next person on the chain and ask her to pray for you?"

"Yes. Yes, please."

"Then I will."

Chapter Thirty-Five

Maddie

Mia, Hester, and Sofia stared at the gallon of paint I'd just opened. "Whoa," Mia said. "Your grandma's going to let you paint this place *black*?"

"She didn't say anything about color."

Sophia shook her head. "We're all upset about Avery. But *black*?"

"I think it's cool," Hester said, dipping a finger in the bucket and wiping it on the white wall. "It'll be atmospheric."

"It could be a base," Mia said. "And you could draw designs on it with neon colors and hang an ultraviolet light."

"I'll think about it."

We didn't have a lot of room—the caboose was only eight feet wide—but after losing Avery, it felt right to be together.

"So," Hester asked as she painted the trim above my head, "are we going to Avery's funeral tomorrow?"

"I think we should," Sofia said. "Avery would want us there."

"What about her parents? Did they approve of her hanging out with us?"

"Of course," Hester said. "Why wouldn't they?"

"Well . . . they might blame us for not stopping her and Matt."

Hester snorted. "How were we supposed to know? She didn't tell us anything."

"But we noticed they were acting weird—"

"And when we asked what was going on," Sofia interrupted, "Matt and Avery clammed up. So we couldn't have stopped them."

Hester and Sofia were right, of course. I couldn't have stopped Dad, either. The only strange thing I noticed about him was that he seemed super sentimental at Christmas. But if I'd asked him about it, he would have come up with some silly excuse. He certainly wouldn't have told me what he had planned.

We painted until our arms ached and the caboose's ceiling and walls were covered. When we finished, we put our brushes into the sink and dropped onto the futon to admire our work.

"This place is like a cave," Hester said, crossing her arms. "Or a tomb."

Sofia nodded. "I think it's comforting, like reentering the womb—or lying in one of those sensory deprivation chambers."

"It's a little spooky," I said, "like an abandoned subway tunnel."

"I've never seen a tunnel with a futon," Hester said. "Once we get all your stuff back where it belongs, this place will look chic. Like something from New York."

I sighed, too tired to care. "I hope so."

"Hey." Sofia picked up an unopened gallon of paint. "We have extra. You guys want to start on the outside?"

"No," Hester, Mia, and I said in unison.

"I can't paint another stroke," I said. "My arms feel like wet noodles."

"Okay." Sofia shrugged. "Now for step two. I could run home

and get my neon markers. We could put a few Emily Dickinson poems on the walls. Under a UV light, the words would glow."

"Sweet," Hester said. "Maddie, you could draw some pictures. Use your gift, girl."

I studied the black wall, trying to imagine it with an illustration of Pop, Dad, or Logan. Uh-uh. I should stick to neutral images like dogs, cats, and birds. Drawings of people might reveal too much of my aching heart.

I rode to Avery's funeral with Nana and Pop, then peeled off in search of my friends. Everybody came—Logan, Hester, Jackson, Mia, Sofia, and me. Matthew was still in the hospital, but Avery was with us—laid out in a pink casket on the school auditorium stage.

The music took me right back to my dad's funeral, and my feelings must have shown, because Logan put his arm around me as we climbed to the balcony. Most of the adults sat on the first floor with somber expressions.

Hester peered over the railing and whispered, "Everyone in town must be here."

"There's the mayor," Sofia said, pointing. "Reporters will be waiting outside for him."

"Why?" Jackson asked. "Did he know Avery?"

"The issue of teen suicide, goofball. As if he could do anything about it."

A gaggle of younger girls entered, wailing as if Avery had been their best friend. A blonde cried out, "I miss her so much!"

Mia snorted. "Who is that?"

"I was with her last week in Spanish class," the blonde continued. "When we left, she told me *adios*. If only I'd known what she meant!"

Hester shook her head. "Brace yourselves. Avery is on her way to becoming the patron saint of St. Pete High."

I hadn't known Avery all that well, but I couldn't help remembering that no one wailed at my dad's funeral. Most of the people in that chapel seemed embarrassed to be there.

"The newspaper said someone found a note at the water tower," I whispered. "Anyone know what it said?"

"I heard about it," Mia said. "My mom's friend works for the police department. The note was pretty simple. It was in Avery's handwriting and said if they couldn't be together on earth, they'd be together in death. That was it."

"Who said they couldn't be together on earth?" I asked.

Mia leaned closer. "After all that trouble with the video, Avery's parents said she couldn't see Matt anymore. She'd been thinking about breaking up with him, since he'd been dumb enough to show the video to his cousin. But when her parents told her she *couldn't* see him, she decided she and Matt were destined to be together forever."

Hester sighed. "That's crazy. So what if they had to break up for a while? They could have gotten back together later. People would forget that video after a few months."

"Not everybody thinks like you," Sofia said, glaring at Hester. "Some people are more romantic. Avery couldn't see herself living without Matt."

Logan, who'd been quietly looking over the balcony, turned toward us. "Hester, your mom still work at the hospital? Any news on Matt?"

"He's still in the ICU with internal injuries and a broken back," Hester said. "If he pulls through, he'll probably spend the rest of his life in a wheelchair. And that's only because he hit the struts on the way down. Nothing broke Avery's fall but the ground."

I shivered in a moment of déjà vu. The little girl who died in my mom's lawsuit—how far had she fallen from that amusement park ride?

"She said something else," Hester whispered. "If Matt gets out of the ICU, they're going to Baker Act him. So he isn't going far."

I gaped at her, bewildered, but the others seemed to know what she meant.

"That's awful," Mia said. "I knew a girl in middle school who got Baker Acted after she pulled a knife on her mom. They put her in the mental ward, doped her up, and made her stay three days. I think she was worse after she got out."

Hester noticed the confused look on my face. "The Baker Act," she said, tapping my arm, "says they can put you in the hospital if they think you're struggling mentally and might hurt someone— including yourself. Matt tried to kill himself, so . . ." She shrugged.

Just then, Dr. Sweet walked to the center of the stage. "Thank you for coming," he said, his gaze roving over the auditorium. "We have come together to commemorate the life of one of our students, Avery Miles. I'm sure her parents would want to thank you personally for coming, but let's respect their privacy today so they can grieve as a family."

He lifted a program, which featured Avery's school picture on the cover, and began to read the obituary: "Avery Diane Miles was born January 3, 2005, at St. Petersburg General Hospital. . . ."

I leaned back and closed my eyes. I had seen way too many funerals for a girl my age.

At lunch on Monday, Logan dropped into the seat next to me. "Hey," he said, popping the ring on a Coke can. "What'd you do after the funeral?"

I shrugged. "Painted poems on the inside walls of the caboose. You?"

"Slept, mostly. I wanted to go see Matt, but only immediate family can visit ICU patients. So I went back to bed."

I nodded. "I slept a lot after my dad died. Just seemed easier than dealing with stuff."

"What happened to your dad, anyway?"

Score one for Hester—she hadn't blabbed my story. But I didn't care if my friends knew.

"He shot himself," I said. "The day after Christmas."

"Whoa. Bet that was rough."

"The hardest part was that I found him. He'd put a note on the door telling me not to come in but to call 911. How illogical is that?"

Logan snorted. "That's like saying, 'I need help, but not from you.'"

"Exactly."

"And that's why you came to Florida?"

"You nailed it. My mom's working on a huge case and didn't think she'd be able to get anything done if we were both emotional wrecks. We may be messed up, but at least we're messed up in separate spaces."

I smiled when the corner of Logan's mouth quirked. Somebody finally appreciated my humor.

"What was your dad like?" Logan mumbled around his sandwich.

"He was great. He was a salesman, but he was always around when I needed something. Until . . . you know."

"And your mom?"

"She's more into her work, and sometimes she's so focused, she forgets about everything else. But she's good at what she does. Unlike me."

"Whaddya mean? You're good at stuff."

"What, hanging around?"

"Hester says you're smart. And Mia says you're a real artist."

"Sketching's not a big deal."

"It is to guys who can't even draw stick people."

I laughed. "Come on. Anyone can draw stick people."

"Not me."

"You have a different talent. I've heard you read, and you're amazing. You could get a job doing audiobooks."

Logan parked his chin in his hand, looking adorable, especially when his blue eyes peered through the curtains of his dark hair. "I have a talent for driving my folks crazy."

I laughed so loudly that kids at the next table turned to look.

"All of us are good at that," I said. "But you're also good at making me laugh. Very few people have that gift."

"Did your dad?"

I stared at my lunch, remembering Dad's corny jokes, his horrible imitations, and the way he'd tease me until I was ready to explode. He used to make me so mad. But I wasn't really angry, I was only frustrated, just like I'd been for the past few weeks. Frustrated because he was gone and I couldn't do anything to bring him back.

I'd have given my last colored pencil to have him tease me just once more.

"Yeah," I finally said, meeting Logan's gaze. "Dad had lots of gifts, but his best was probably his humor. Everybody loved being around him."

"I think you're wrong," Logan said, his mouth quirking in a small smile. "The way I see it, his greatest gift was you."

Chapter Thirty-Six

Susan

I dumped the laundry basket on the bed and folded clothes while watching the afternoon news. I couldn't help wondering how two suicides, so close together, had affected Maddie.

Frank and I weren't spending as much time with her as we'd hoped. She'd pop in occasionally for a snack and then hurry to the caboose to finish her homework. Friday nights meant pizza with her friends, and Saturdays, according to Maddie, were for sleeping.

When she first arrived, we asked if she'd go to church with us. She said she might, but so far, my Sunday morning knocks had been met with "I have a horrible headache" or "I was up all night writing a paper." I always let her stay home, which upset Frank, but forcing a seventeen-year-old to go to church seemed counter-productive. I wanted her to go because she *wanted* to go.

I pulled a sheet from the laundry basket and forced myself to focus on local news instead of my problems. Fortunately, the noon report mostly featured neutral stories about the influx of winter tourists and the resulting increase in traffic. The "hero of the day" was an EMT who'd administered first aid to a dog dying by the side of the road.

I smiled at the enthusiasm of the grateful owner, then put my folded clothes in piles and dropped Maddie's things into a basket. I told Ike I'd be right back, then walked across the driveway, grateful for the breeze moving in the oaks. February and March offered the best weather of the year, which explained the flood of tourists. I loved the winter months, because I could throw the windows open and finish my spring cleaning, which I intended to begin as soon as I delivered Maddie's laundry.

I punched the unlock code into the caboose door, opened it, and stared.

The cheery caboose no longer resembled the cozy, tiny house Frank and I had envisioned. I hit the light switch, but instead of warm white lamps, glowing purple bulbs highlighted neon words on the black walls. The windows had been covered with painted cardboard.

I dropped Maddie's clothes onto the futon—yes, it was still there, barely visible in the darkness—and ventured into the space, reading words that glowed in the dark:

After great pain, a formal feeling comes . . .
I'm nobody, who are you? Are you nobody too?
Mirth is the mail of anguish . . .

The bathroom door bore these lines:

Pain—has an Element of Blank—
It cannot recollect
When it begun—or if there were
A time when it was not.

And in the back room, on the ceiling above the bed:

Because I could not stop for Death—
He kindly stopped for me . . .

I lay on the bed and stared at the poem. Had Maddie done this alone? She'd invited friends to help, but I had expected a sunny yellow, or perhaps a restful light blue. And though these words read like poetry, I didn't recognize them.

Why was Maddie immortalizing pain and death?

Of course, I knew the answer. She'd lost her father and now one of her friends. She had also left the security of her home, and though Frank and I adored her, we weren't her parents. This caboose was a way station, and though we had promised to help her through her grief, apparently we hadn't done nearly enough, if anything at all.

Cold reality swept over me in a terrible wave. I should call Rachel and confess that we weren't helping Maddie. If anything, we had made things worse by having her mix with kids who obsessed over death and made suicide pacts. Maybe we should send her home.

I flinched when I heard the beep of the lock. Maddie halted in midstep when she saw me. "Nana?" A guilty look flickered over her face. "Are you all right?"

I sat up. "Hi, sweetheart. How was your day?"

She dropped her book bag onto the futon. "It was okay."

"I thought you would go to your friend's house after school."

"I have to study for my history test. It's hard to study at Hester's."

Lord, give me wisdom.

I pointed to the ceiling. "I, um, wasn't expecting this."

I could barely see in the purple light, but I think Maddie flushed. "Yeah, it takes some getting used to. If you hate it, I can

paint over it when I leave. We thought it would be fun to experiment, and the black light makes the neon colors pop."

"Who—what are these words?"

"Emily Dickinson." She smiled, apparently confident of my
approval. "We studied her poetry in English, and we all loved her.
Did you know she never published anything while she was alive?
Now her stuff is classic."

And macabre.

"I brought your laundry." I pointed to the futon. "Guess I'd
better go start dinner."

Maddie seemed okay. She'd come home to study, a sensible
thing to do, and she'd said the black paint was an experiment, not
a lifestyle.

Maybe she would be fine.

On my way out, I stopped and caught her hand. "Did I ever
tell you what happened before you were born?"

Her brow furrowed. "I don't think so."

Still holding her hand, I leaned against the wall. "Your mom
and dad wanted a baby so badly, but they didn't find it easy to get
pregnant. They tried for almost two years and went to specialists.
But they prayed all that time, and the day before their appoint-
ment at a fertility clinic, your mom learned she was pregnant with
you. We were so thrilled! Never has a baby been more wanted,
more prayed for, and more eagerly awaited." I squeezed her hand.
"You are a precious gift from God."

Maddie seemed to make an effort to smile, but in her eyes I
saw both curiosity and bewilderment. She probably thought I was
crazy, but at least she should know she was loved.

I made macaroni and cheese and set three plates on the kitchen
bar. Frank came in, dropped a stack of papers on the dining table,
and winked. "Hello, gorgeous."

"Hello, yourself." I grinned. "How was your day?"

He shrugged. "About as thrilling as freshman English can be.

Brought home a bunch of quizzes to grade—basic grammar. You'd be surprised how many kids don't know the first thing about it."

"I wouldn't be at all surprised." I opened the oven door to peek at the mac and cheese. "I've seen some of their Instagram posts."

He gestured to the three plates. "Maddie joining us tonight?"

"Hope so. She said she'd come over, but she seemed tired."

"No wonder. The poor kid's been through a lot."

"We all have."

"But we're not adolescents." He shook his head. "When I came into the classroom this morning, a group of boys were huddled around someone's phone. I asked what was so interesting, and they scattered like flies. The boy with the phone put it away and said they weren't looking at anything important, but I knew better."

"Did you find out what it was?"

He nodded. "When the bell rang, I asked that kid to show me what he'd shown the others. He didn't want to, but when I suggested he let the principal take a look at his texts, he showed me a picture of a girl. They call it sexting."

I nearly dropped the casserole. "In ninth grade?"

"It can happen at any age—as soon as a kid can persuade a girl to send him a revealing photo."

"How'd you know they were looking at a text?"

"Teacher's intuition. Anyway, the picture had been sent around a lot and had a ton of comments, which I didn't bother to read."

I set the casserole on the counter. "I hope Maddie has never been involved in anything like that."

"I doubt she has. Daniel was a good father, so she isn't desperate for male attention."

"What'd you do about the kid you caught?"

"Sent him to the principal's office. I knew Dr. Sweet would want to shut it down."

I was pulling roasted green beans from the oven when Maddie came in. "Hey, Pop." She hopped onto the stool next to him. "How was school?"

"Pretty good, my one and only." He grinned. "But I'm supposed to ask you that question. How was *your* day?"

"Fine." She crossed her arms. "Mia likes Jackson, but I don't think he likes her."

"Is she the little brunette who looks like Audrey Hepburn?"

Maddie made a face. "Been a while since I saw her picture, but I guess."

"Tell Mia to give it time. These things have a way of working themselves out."

I took the chair next to Maddie. After we had served ourselves, we held hands while Frank said a blessing.

I picked up my fork. "You know," I said, attempting to sound casual, "I've been learning a lot from my support group. Turns out that the leader, Bob Halsey, is a licensed professional counselor. On weekdays he sees individual clients. What do you think?"

Crickets.

Chapter Thirty-Seven

Maddie

We were playing volleyball in phys ed that morning when Coach Miller whistled and told us to shut up. The girl who'd been chasing the ball froze as the sad wail of a siren filled the gym. It wasn't the alarm for a shooter or a fire.

Still, one girl whispered, eyes wide, "What do we do if there's a shooter? Hide or run?"

Coach Miller looked as frightened as everyone else. "Into the locker room now," she said, keeping her voice low. "Everybody move!"

A couple of the girls started crying, and I couldn't help thinking about kids who had brought guns to school and shot anyone who moved. At least we hadn't heard gunfire.

Once inside the locker room, Coach Miller said, "Just keep quiet and dress quickly."

I glanced down the row of lockers. Nearly every girl had pulled out her phone, but who were they calling? I didn't want to call Nana and scare her unless I knew we had a shooter. And Pop had to be somewhere in the building.

I opened my locker and kicked off my sneakers while trying to keep an eye on the window of Coach Miller's office. She was on her radio, probably speaking to security. After a moment, she set the radio on her desk. She wasn't panicking.

Coach walked to the center of the locker room. "Girls, let me have your attention," she said. "I want you to know there's no reason to panic. A student has been hurt, so the ambulance came for her." She lifted a brow. "If you've called anyone outside the school, call them back and tell them everything's okay. We don't want a lot of crazy rumors floating around town."

"Who was hurt?" someone called.

Coach shook her head. "I don't know. But Principal Sweet wants to delay class dismissal a few minutes."

We changed into our school clothes, then crowded into the narrow hallway that led to the outdoor sidewalk. We stood there, staring at each other, and waited for the dismissal bell. Most of us were nervous. I could hear anxiety in our jittery voices and see it in the way some of the girls crowded the door. We wanted out.

When the bell rang at the usual time, the girls next to the door bolted, and the rest of us followed. Who could blame us? That hallway was making us claustrophobic.

A minute later, I realized we were probably the only class that hadn't been detained. We walked through deserted hallways, and the silence freaked me out. I wanted to find my friends.

I was almost to the commons when I passed Dr. Sweet. He was standing in a hallway, one hand on his hip, the other holding his radio. He frowned at me as I passed, and I got the impression he was blocking the area behind him.

A minute later, the door to a girls' restroom opened, and two EMTs came out rolling a stretcher. I stopped, shocked, as I recognized the pale face of a girl whose locker wasn't far from mine. A sheet covered her body, but she was talking to one of the EMTs as they wheeled toward an exit.

Dr. Sweet glanced over his shoulder and spoke into his radio. A minute later, the commons filled with students.

Hester appeared at my elbow. "What's up?"

I pointed toward the exit doors, where I could see the ambulance through the narrow windows. Hester gasped when she saw the EMTs loading the stretcher into the vehicle. "What happened?"

I shook my head. "Maybe she got sick?"

"You girls should get to class," Dr. Sweet said, his voice rumbling through the commotion. "Nothing to see here."

A custodian emerged from the restroom carrying a bloody mop and bucket.

Hester leaned closer. "Must have fallen and hit her head."

"I didn't see a bandage."

"Neither did I."

By lunchtime, the story was all over campus—Chrissy Phillips had skipped class and used a nail file to slit her wrists. Why? Apparently, the quiet freshman did it because Tommy Haynes, the boy she liked, asked her to send him a sexy photo. Chrissy sent him a selfie with her sweater slipping off one shoulder, to prove how much she liked him.

But Tommy posted the picture to his Instagram account with the caption, "If you were stuck on a desert island with this girl, would you?" The trolls went wild, criticizing everything from Chrissy's thin body to her lack of makeup.

Hester and I looked up Tommy's Insty account and read all the nasty remarks. "I'd want to kill myself too," Hester said. "But first I'd punch out Tommy."

"For a long time, my dad didn't want me to have an Instagram or Twitter account," I said. "When he finally said I could, he said he was going to follow me so he could keep an eye on things." I swallowed hard. "I haven't been able to post since he died."

"What happened to Chrissy is awful," Hester said, "but no one brought a gun to school and no one died, so that's a good thing. And though I feel sorry for that girl, you have to admit she was crazy for trying to kill herself at school."

I heard other kids express the same thought.

"The idiot didn't even have the guts to do it right," I heard one girl tell her friend. "But since everybody knows what happened, she'll probably do it right next time."

As I walked home that afternoon, I wondered if Chrissy Phillips would try to kill herself again. I couldn't see any hope for her at St. Pete High.

If I ever wanted to kill myself, I would have to make a fool-proof plan. Just like Dad.

Chapter Thirty-Eight

Susan

That afternoon I found Maddie on the floor, rubbing Ike's belly. "Hi, sweetie. Good day at school?"

She took a deep breath. "We had a little excitement. Pop didn't tell you?"

"He's not home yet. What happened?"

Maddie shrugged. "A girl cut her wrists in the restroom, so they called an ambulance. Everyone freaked out when they heard the sirens, thinking maybe we had a shooter."

"Thank the Lord it wasn't that. Is the girl going to be okay?"

"I think so. But if I were her, I wouldn't go back to that school again." She petted Ike, and her smile went flat. "Nana? Have you looked at Ike lately?"

I blinked. "I see him every day. What do you mean?"

"Last night he was panting really fast, and I thought maybe he'd eaten too much. But he's still doing it."

I knelt and placed my hand on his freckled belly. Breathing was always a concern with short-nosed dogs, so I'd grown accustomed to Ike's panting and snorting. But he was breathing more heavily than usual, and his belly seemed tight.

"I think we should take him to the vet," I said. "We can do it first thing in the morning." I said *we*, hoping Maddie would want to join me, but she stood and backed away.

"Let me know what the vet says," she said, reaching for the doorknob. "I hope he's okay."

The next morning, Dr. Barnett listened to Ike's heart and lungs, then took a blood sample. "He doesn't seem quite like himself, does he?"

"No. He's been sleeping with my granddaughter, so I don't see him as often as usual. But even she noticed he was having difficulty breathing."

"And how old is Ike?"

"Ten."

"He should have several years left. I see he's lost two pounds since his last visit. Does he still eat well?"

"We used to call him the human vacuum cleaner, but lately . . . not so much. I thought it was because he's getting older."

"How's his energy?"

I had to chuckle. "His favorite things are eating and sleeping."

"Let me check his blood test."

I waited as Ike walked to the door, sniffed the doctor's footprints, and turned back to me, panting as though he'd just run five miles.

"Poor boy." I picked him up and set him next to me. My thoughts drifted back to the day Ike arrived at our house. He had been an adorable puppy, and that year we took him with us when we visited Daniel's family. Maddie was seven and fell completely in love with Ike. That was the first time she asked if she could sleep with him, an idea Rachel nixed when she learned the puppy wasn't house-trained.

"You wouldn't want him to wee on you, right?" I asked Maddie, trying to ease her disappointment. "So he can't sleep with you, but when you get up tomorrow, he will *definitely* play with you. When he gets tired, he can take a nap in your lap."

When we pulled out of the driveway that year, Frank waved goodbye, then nodded at Maddie. "She's crying. Does she always cry when we leave?"

"She's not crying because she'll miss us," I told him, sighing. "She's crying because she'll miss Ike." I glanced at the back seat, where Ike was riding in a safety harness. "I wish Rachel would let her have a puppy. Maddie would love it to bits."

"Rachel's not an animal lover." Frank put the car in drive. "Daniel said she thinks animals take up too much time and make too many messes."

"You could say the same thing about children."

"Better keep that to yourself or Rachel might drop Maddie at the nearest animal shelter."

Frank and I laughed, but later I wondered if Rachel would be up to the task of parenting. I consoled myself with the knowledge that Maddie would have Daniel, who wanted three or four kids. He would pour his life into her.

And he had.

Dr. Barnett returned, chart in hand. "We need to do an ultrasound. Ike's belly is distended, and a scan should show us what's going on. Would you like to wait in the reception area?"

"If you don't mind, I'd like to see for myself."

"Come this way then."

Carrying Ike, I followed the vet into another room, where an assistant waited beside the exam table. "If he's quiet, we won't have to sedate him," she said, taking Ike from me. He snorted when she stroked his belly, and I knew he was loving the attention.

The doctor turned on a monitor, and Ike settled back to enjoy his massage.

The doctor ran the scope over Ike's belly and studied the screen. I peered at it too, but couldn't identify anything.

"Here." The doctor pointed to a blob. "I think this is a tumor. This large, white area is the spleen, and it's probably three times as big as it should be. Fortunately, a dog can live without a spleen. I recommend you leave Ike with us for surgery."

Surgery? Ike was only a dog, but he was a member of our family. All three of us loved him.

Please, Lord, we've had too much death in our world.

Leaving Ike with the vet, I headed to my car, the heaviness of bad news cramping my shoulders. Frank would know something was wrong the moment I walked through the door, and Maddie would be upset too. Ike had been her part-time dog for years.

The girl had been through so much in the last couple of months.

What was I going to tell them? And how would the news affect Maddie?

Dr. Barnett's nurse called in mid-afternoon.

"The surgery's over," I told Frank and Maddie. "They removed a tumor, and he's sleeping off the anesthesia. We can pick him up tomorrow morning."

Frank crossed his arms. "Was the tumor malignant?"

"The nurse said Dr. Barnett would explain everything tomorrow."

Maddie dimpled. "Can I go with you? I want to be there when he comes prancing out to meet us."

"I don't know if he'll feel like prancing, but of course you can come."

The next morning, Maddie and I were waiting in the exam room when a vet tech set Ike on the table. He wasn't prancing, but his tail wagged at high speed when he saw us.

."Good boy," Maddie said, stroking the spot between his eyes. "I'm sure you'll be glad to get home."

Dr. Barnett greeted us and said, "He looks good. We'll put a cone on him so he won't lick the incision. In ten days, we'll take the stitches out."

"Wonderful," I said. "My husband wanted to know about the tumor. Was it malignant? Did you get it all?"

The doctor folded his arms. "I'm happy to say Ike is feeling better," he said, his jaw edging forward. "But I'm sorry to tell you the tumor was a hemangiosarcoma. It's caused by a cancer of the cells that line the blood vessels, and it's fairly aggressive. The tumors erode the blood vessels, which leak blood into the abdominal cavity. That's why Ike's belly was distended."

I glanced at Maddie, whose smile had dissolved into a bewildered expression. "What's the bottom line?"

Dr. Barnett drew a breath. "Ike can go home today, but his prognosis is not good. We removed one tumor, but malignant cells have already dispersed throughout his body, so his time with you is limited. I'm sorry."

I blinked in astonished silence.

"Someday, probably within a few weeks," Dr. Barnett continued, "the tumors will make it difficult for Ike to breathe. Or his heart may stop beating. If it's not a sudden event, you're likely to realize Ike is suffering, and then it will be time to do the humane thing."

Maddie lifted her head. "What's the humane thing?"

"Euthanasia," the doctor said. "We don't want Ike to suffer."

Ike barked at Maddie, then smiled when she put her hand on his head.

I looked away, fighting back tears. "But it's okay for us to take him home."

"Of course. Be careful of his stitches, but treat him as you ordinarily would. He may still be a little groggy, but we'll send you home with pills for the pain. And when you need us, don't hesitate to call."

I turned. Maddie was staring at the wall, her face blank, as though her thoughts had shifted to another time and place.

"Thank you, Dr. Barnett."

The tech fastened a cone around Ike's neck, then placed him on the floor. Moving slowly, I paid the bill, then took Maddie and Ike home.

Chapter Thirty-Nine

Maddie

When we arrived back at the house, I carried Ike inside and put him in the living room doggie bed. He hopped up and wiggled his behind when Pop came into the room, but he settled down after Pop examined his stitches. "Poor little man," Pop said, rubbing Ike's forehead. "You don't like that cone, do you?"

"It's too bad," I said, "that God didn't arrange it so our life-spans would match—humans and dogs." I stroked Ike's velvety ears. "Your house won't feel the same without him."

"We'll get another dog," Nana said. "It won't replace Ike, but it'll make the house feel less empty."

Should I get a new dad so our house will feel full again? I didn't say that, of course. I wouldn't. But . . .

The house in Atlanta that used to be home was where Dad arrived every day at five thirty, where he decided whether we should order pizza or Chinese, and where he took long Sunday afternoon naps. It was where he hung a shelf to hold my tee-ball trophy so it could crash to the floor the next day. It was where he once pulled up a toilet to unclog a drain and had to call a plumber to put it back.

Home was wherever Dad lived, so maybe I didn't have a home anymore. Maybe that's why I hadn't minded moving to St. Pete. I loved where Nana and Pop and Ike lived because I loved them. But now Ike was going to leave us, and Nana and Pop weren't getting any younger.

Sadness crept into the room like a fog, and I was surprised Nana and Pop couldn't feel it. "I'm going to the caboose," I said, pushing myself up. "I need a nap."

"Are you feeling okay?" Nana's brows wrinkled. "You could be coming down with something."

I turned toward the door. "I'm okay. I just need some sleep."

Chapter Forty

Susan

"Before we begin to share today," Bob said, looking around the circle, "I thought we would review the basic stages of grief: denial, anger, bargaining, depression, and finally acceptance. Not everyone grieves in the same way, and not everyone experiences these stages in the same order. But they are common to those who have suffered loss, and I think it helps to know what we're feeling is normal." A wry smile tugged at his mouth. "Otherwise, most of us would think we were going a little crazy."

The group shared a collective chuckle and settled back to listen.

I certainly remembered the denial stage—*This can't be; it has to be a nightmare*—that I'm sure Frank and Rachel and Maddie shared. And while I hadn't sent a grocery cart into a parked car or scratched out the eyes of drawings of my loved ones, I couldn't deny my anger at Daniel for abandoning us.

"Anger and even rage are normal," Bob said. "The Bible tells us not to sin by letting anger control us. We can't control our feelings, but we *must* control our actions."

I knew better than to bargain with God to get Daniel back, but how many times had I resolved to do better so I could escape the crushing grief?

"Once you realize you can't bargain your way out of grief," Bob said, "you have to face the hard truth: Your loved one is gone. One day you'll be able to accept that, but first you may go through the next phase, depression. Again, this is a normal part of the process. We mourn. We grieve. And only when this stage is finished are we able to accept our loss and move forward."

Of course I was depressed—maybe not clinically, but I hadn't felt joy in a long time.

A woman raised her hand. "How long will it take me to get to acceptance? It's all I can do to get out of bed every morning. Everyone keeps saying things will get better, but I haven't seen any improvement."

Bob gentled his voice. "There is no set timetable, because every situation is different. A man who spent years supporting his wife as she fought cancer may complete his mourning in a few months, because he experienced these stages of grief while she was dying. But a man whose wife is killed in a traffic accident may need more time, because he wasn't prepared for sudden loss."

I caught Bob's eye. "I think—I'm not sure I'm doing it right," I said. "I felt shock when we learned our son had killed himself, and I still cry when I talk about him, but I've been so concerned about our granddaughter that I have no idea what stage I'm in."

"Don't worry about defining your experience," Bob said. "You will feel what you feel when you feel it."

Helen, who was sitting next to Bob, chuckled. "Excuse me," she said when we all looked at her, "but what Bob said reminds me of a line from *Tootsie*, the old Dustin Hoffman movie."

Bob lifted his brows. "You'll have to explain that one."

She blushed. "Well, Terri Garr—I forget her character's

name—is mad at Dustin Hoffman, and she says, 'I just have to feel this way until I don't feel this way anymore.' I've always thought that was brilliant."

Bob nodded. "Take the time you need to sort things out. You can't hurry the process. Give yourself grace, and extend the same to others going through the process with you."

"My granddaughter—" My voice broke, so I took a second to steady my emotions. "I think my granddaughter's moving from anger to depression. It breaks my heart to see her sad. What can I do to help her?"

Bob rested his elbows on his knees. "We're all different, but God made us with the same emotional needs—to be loved and appreciated and safe. If you want to help your granddaughter, let her know you think she's the best thing since ice cream and you'll never leave her. That's what she needs to know."

Others shared their latest stories. Isabell, whose brother had committed suicide, had finally found the strength to clean out his apartment. John, who had written countless poems to his dead wife, had actually asked a female friend out for coffee.

While I was happy to see that others had made progress, I knew Frank and I were a long way from the finish line. Nonetheless, Bob's encouragement to love and assure Maddie struck me as sound advice.

As I was leaving, Bob stopped me by the door. "I understand why you're so concerned about your granddaughter," he said, "but I'm concerned about you, Susan. You're going through stages too, so keep that in mind. Give yourself grace, and know that God thinks *you're* the best thing since ice cream."

I couldn't stop a smile as I walked out the door.

Chapter Forty-One

Maddie

Whenever Mom called and asked if I missed Emily and Tristan, I truthfully told her no. My new friends offered plenty to do and think about, and I don't know what I would have done without them.

Hester and Sofia were a big help when the time came to write my midsemester English paper. Mr. Wright told us to choose a piece of American literature and explain how it related to a contemporary issue. I had no idea what to do until Sofia found the perfect Dickinson poem, and my fingers flew as I typed my essay. The poem was not one of Dickinson's most famous, but I had no trouble getting the gist when Sofia read it:

> *After great pain, a formal feeling comes—*
> *The Nerves sit ceremonious, like Tombs—*
> *The stiff Heart questions 'was it He, that bore,'*
> *And 'Yesterday, or Centuries before?*

The Feet, mechanical, go round—
A Wooden way
Of Ground, or Air, or Ought—
Regardless grown,
A Quartz contentment, like a stone—

This is the Hour of Lead—
Remembered, if outlived,
As Freezing persons, recollect the Snow—
First—Chill—then Stupor—then the letting go—

Those words put me right back at my dad's funeral. Sofia said the "stiff Heart" referred to Jesus, who died centuries before, but his grief was like our grief because death was as powerful then as now.

The part about the mechanical feet reminded me of how I slogged through the cemetery to Dad's gravesite. Dickinson nailed how it felt to walk in front of all those people and stand silently, not feeling, not thinking, as we all stared at Dad's casket.

The Hour of Lead . . . the chill, the numbness, and the letting go, whether you do it in a crying jag or creep into your room and sleep the hours away. I had done both, over Dad and even over Avery.

I titled my paper "Hour of Dread" and used the poem to introduce my topic. "Death is a horrible thing," I wrote, "but no one can stop someone who really wants to die."

Dad loved me and Mom. If his love for us wasn't enough to keep him alive, what was? He loved God, too, but not even his faith stopped him from ending his life.

I included facts and figures about suicide and ended by stating that death was part of life, and suicide was only another way to die. I concluded: "Suicide can be hereditary, as evidenced by the famous Hemingway family. The tendency may not be genetic, but we cannot deny that a suicide creates ripples that influence other family members for years."

I finished my paper and clicked "Send to printer." The printer was in Nana's office, so I'd have to pick it up over there. But I also put a copy on my iPad so I could show it to Sofia and Hester before I handed it in.

That night at the Pizza Palace, I slid into the booth beside Logan and across from Jackson and ordered a soda while they joked about a sci-fi movie they'd streamed on Netflix. When Hester, Sofia, and Mia arrived, I pulled out my iPad so they could read my paper. "Tell me what you think," I said, resting my chin on my hand.

When they finished, Sofia hugged my iPad and sighed. "It's perfect," she said. "Mr. Wright is going to give you an A+."

"You really think so?"

"How could he argue with the voice of experience? Emily Dickinson would be proud of you. And so would Avery."

Soon Jackson and Mia started arguing about an art film he had taken her to the night before. He had liked it, but Mia was bored. "It made no sense. I didn't see the point."

"It wasn't supposed to make sense," he said, flushing. "It was a metaphor for life. Either you get it or you don't."

"Well, I don't," Mia said. "A movie should have some kind of point. The main character is supposed to learn something; he should change. Even kids' movies have decent endings."

"Movies *are* a metaphor for life," I said. "But life should have a point, shouldn't it?"

Logan whistled. "The woman speaks profundities."

Hester smacked his arm. "So, does it, Maddie? Does life have a point?"

Nana and Pop would say the point of life was knowing God. My parents probably felt the same way, but they weren't as vocal about it.

But me? "I don't know. I think it should. But I haven't figured out what it is yet."

"Me either," Logan said. "I'm still waiting for someone to tell me what it is."

I shot him a smile. Maybe we understood each other.

I groaned as I rolled out of bed at six thirty on Saturday morning, the day of my SAT—which, according to Mom, was "the key to a successful college application."

Nana insisted I have breakfast before leaving and scooped a big helping of scrambled eggs onto a plate, along with two pieces of sausage. "Protein is good for the brain. And you're allowed a snack and a drink, so I packed a bag for you. I know you'll do well, honey. Just take your time and do your best."

"I can't take too much time," I said, sliding off my stool. "I have an average of one minute and ten seconds for each question."

I didn't know why the test was so important to Mom, Nana, and Pop. They acted as though the rest of my life depended on it.

I had news for them—this test wouldn't change anything. I'd always made okay grades, so I'd make an okay score and get into an okay college. Why make such a big fuss about it?

Chapter Forty-Two

Susan

After seeing Maddie off, I went to my office and noticed a stack of paper in the printer. Maddie's term paper. The title caught my eye: "Hour of Dread."

Anxiety spurted through me.

I skimmed the paragraphs. "In our country," Maddie had written, "suicide is the second leading cause of death among people ages ten to thirty-four. In 1995, more teens and young adults died from suicide than from cancer, AIDS, heart disease, pneumonia, influenza, birth defects, and stroke combined."

With growing dismay, I read that suicide rates had been increasing not only in the United States but also across the world.

"Why? Many reasons. More people are using recreational drugs, even when pregnant, and those drugs can affect the fetus so the child might later experience mood and behavior patterns associated with suicide. Others blame the rise in suicide on the decreasing average age of puberty, causing kids to experience depression and anxiety at earlier ages. Some doctors believe the successful treatment of mental illness has encouraged patients to marry and have children who may inherit a predisposition to depression and schizophrenia, two disorders often associated with suicide."

Her final paragraph chilled my blood: "Suicide can be hereditary, as evidenced by the famous Hemingway family. The tendency may not be genetic, but we cannot deny that a suicide creates ripples that influence other family members for years."

Could she believe Daniel's suicide might compel her to follow his example?

I pressed my hand over my mouth as a ghost spider scrambled up my spine. *Dear Lord, guard her thoughts. Protect her from the consequences of Daniel's actions.*

I stared at the pages, my mind racing. What should I do? Should I confront Maddie about this, or would she think I'd been snooping? Should I call Rachel? If I did, would she see this as no big deal, another distraction from her court case?

I finally stacked the pages and slid them back into the printer tray. I would let Maddie retrieve her paper. Perhaps the Lord had led me into the office this morning, because now I knew suicide was still on Maddie's mind, and she had begun to consider it hereditary. Which meant—the thought chilled me—she might have considered it herself.

Chapter Forty-Three

Maddie

March meant an end to the cold weather and brought winds that sent dozens of old branches and acorns crashing to the roof of the caboose while Ike and I were trying to sleep. Every morning, we walked around the train car and marveled at all the bird and squirrel nests on the ground.

March also brought little green worms that appeared to hang in midair until I ran into them face-first. Pop said they were oak leaf rollers, dangling on thin strings of silk because the wind had blown them out of the trees.

Otherwise, I actually enjoyed being the first to step outside in the morning. While Ike ran around looking for the perfect place to pee, I listened to the birds. Sometimes the outdoors felt better than being in the caboose, where the black walls and fluorescent words were beginning to close in on me. I was starting to regret my color choice, but if I repainted, my friends would think I'd succumbed to the pressure of the bourgeois.

The week after my SAT test, I found myself thinking a *lot* about Logan. He ate lunch with me several times and often sat next to me at the Pizza Palace. Sometimes, when one of the others told a joke or made a snide comment, he gave me a private look that made my heart pump a little faster. I hadn't dated anyone since Tristan, but something told me Logan wanted to be more than a friend.

So why didn't he ask me out? I kept hoping he would, but apparently he was taking his time. Or maybe he didn't want to get involved because he knew I'd be heading back to Atlanta at the end of the school year.

What if I didn't go back? Maybe Mom would be relieved to let me stay through the summer. I could find a part-time job or get involved in a community program that would look good on a college application. As long as I didn't give Nana and Pop any trouble, maybe I could stay in St. Pete until fall.

Or even later.

On the last Friday night in March, Hester and I met everyone at the usual spot. Jackson brought his cousin Mason. From the way the other girls giggled, I could tell they thought he was hot. He *was* nice-looking, but he lacked the dark, brooding quality that attracted me to Logan.

Later, when Jackson and Mason offered to give Sofia and Mia a ride home, Hester elbowed me and coyly told the foursome to have a good time.

"Hey." Logan tugged on my jacket. "You want a ride?"

It wasn't exactly a date, but it was something.

Hester leaned close and whispered, "Good things come to those who wait, huh?"

Logan opened the door of his Camaro for me, then drove to Mirror Lake Park and parked near the water. "I come here when I want peace and quiet," he said. "Or when I want to think."

I unbuckled my seat belt and turned to face him. "What do you think about?"

He shrugged. "Life. The future. What it all means." He leaned against the door. "What about you?"

I sighed. "I think about my dad. I miss him."

"I thought you did."

"Really? Why?"

"Because sometimes when everyone is talking, you get this look, and I know you're thinking about something else. And when you mention your dad, your voice gets . . . warmer, I guess. I can hear a smile in it, even when you're not smiling. Unless you're talking about when he died. Then I hear tears."

I stared, astounded. Logan never talked like this when we were with the others. These words were like poetry, and they moved me the same way Dickinson's verses did.

"Wow," I said. "You're more profound than I thought."

He barked a laugh. "Right."

"No, really. Are your parents artistic?"

"What gave you that idea?"

I laughed. "I don't know. I can imagine you all sitting around the dinner table talking about Van Gogh, Dickinson, or some other poor-yet-celebrated artist."

"We don't gather around the table. My dad's usually at the hospital, and Mom stays at her practice until late. We eat whatever the housekeeper fixes."

"I forgot your parents were doctors." I shook my head. "My mind is blown."

Hester had mentioned that, but I'd pushed that out of my head because Logan didn't act like the son of wealthy professionals. I'd pictured him as the son of a couple of wannabe hippies who lived in a school bus or something.

Logan snorted. "I'm pretty sure I was left on their doorstep."

Now things made sense—Logan's car, the expensive sneakers,

and more than once I'd seen him throw more than his share on the table when it came time to pay the pizza bill.

"And I thought your family was normal."

"My family's as normal as everyone else's."

"C'mon," I said, laughing. "You have a housekeeper who cooks!"

He wrapped his arms around the steering wheel. "Sometimes . . . I dunno, I can't help but wonder about the purpose of it all."

"The purpose of what? Family?"

"Life. We're born, we live, we die. Only a few people get remembered. The rest of us are like hands in a bucket. And when the people who knew us die, we're gone forever."

I blinked. "Hands in a bucket?"

Logan smiled. "You put your hand in a bucket of water, it displaces some liquid. But take it out and there's no trace it was ever there."

I understood. My dad had been gone less than three months, and what remained? One kid, and I certainly wasn't going to be noticed or remembered. He sold a lot, but so did the other salesmen. He married my mom, but she was young enough to marry again, unless she decided to marry her career. She was practically engaged to it already.

By the time I went back to Atlanta, everything of Dad's would probably be gone to charity or sold off at an estate sale.

I stared out the window into the darkness. "My grandparents would say God has a purpose for everybody. Nana is always saying that if a sparrow can't die without God noticing, he certainly cares about people."

"What good does noticing do? God may have noticed when Avery and Matthew climbed the water tower, but he didn't stop them."

"He stopped Matthew. Matthew didn't die."

"But he'll be in a wheelchair forever. What kind of life is that?"

"It's better than being dead."

Logan's eyes narrowed. "Have you ever thought about it? You know, putting an end to it all?"

"Sure. I mean, who hasn't?"

"I think about it a lot."

I studied him, hoping he would say more, but he was peering out at something I couldn't see.

This was not the conversation I had hoped for. I wanted Logan to put his arms around me, to tell me everything would be okay, that Dad was somewhere watching me, maybe even praying for me. I wanted to hear that life had meaning and someday I would be happy again.

But despite his pretty words and great voice, Logan had no hope to offer. All he had were questions like my own.

Logan finally asked me out. I knew Nana and Pop would probably want him to come to the house, meet them, and promise to have me home on time, but I wasn't planning to elope or anything. We just wanted to hang out.

So I said yes and told Nana I was going out with a friend and would be back before ten, since it was a school night. Logan pulled up right at four, and away we went.

He grinned. "I've got a surprise."

I was happy to go along with whatever he wanted to do. As we drove, I spotted the Crescent Lake water tower and felt my stomach tighten. Whatever he'd planned, I hoped it had nothing to do with that awful place. I couldn't even glance at it without seeing Avery in her casket.

Finally Logan turned into Mirror Lake Park. The place looked a lot like Nana's yard, with lots of oak trees and palmettos. But Mirror Lake also had picnic tables, and after driving about a mile down the winding road, Logan parked next to one. "I reserved this because I thought you'd like the view of the lake through those trees."

"Sweet." He got out of the car and I waited, thinking maybe

he'd come around and open my door, but he opened the trunk instead. So I got out and walked around to see if he needed help.

Logan pulled a small cooler from the trunk and handed it to me. I followed as he carried a basket over to the picnic table. "There's one more bag," he called, walking back to the trunk. "And that's the last of it."

The other bag turned out to be from Walmart, and when I peeked inside, I saw a bottle of mosquito repellant and a plastic tablecloth. Logan spread the checkered cover over the table and started taking items from the wicker basket. "I hope you like fried chicken," he said, pulling out a bucket of KFC. "I got mashed potatoes and gravy, macaroni and cheese, and corn. There's also biscuits and honey."

"Wow." I stared, honestly surprised. "I can't remember the last time I went on a picnic."

"I know, right?" He grinned. "My parents used to take us picnicking when we were little, before they got too busy. I thought it'd be a fun thing to do before we run out of time."

I sat on the bench, pleased that Logan had been thinking about my return to Georgia. "I might ask my mom if I can stay a little longer," I said. "Maybe she'll let me spend the summer here."

Logan handed me the bottle of mosquito spray. "Better put some of this on. The sun'll be going down soon, and that's when the mosquitoes come out. They can be pretty thick near the water."

I did as he suggested, then tossed him the bottle and watched as he sprayed his arms and neck before pulling ice and soft drinks from the cooler. "I brought bottles of water, if you want one."

I nodded. "Thanks."

We sat across from each other and piled our paper plates high. While we ate, we talked about school, our families, and our friends.

Eventually the conversation turned to Avery and Matthew. "At first I couldn't understand why they jumped," Logan said, wiping his fingers with a napkin. "But now I think I get it. They lost hope."

I nodded, though I wasn't sure what he meant. I didn't know what to say, so I pointed to the leather cuff on his wrist. "I like that," I said, studying it. "I've never seen one with silver worked into it."

"You like it?" He held up his arm so I could see it better.

"I do."

"Then you can have it."

I gasped, amazed, as he slipped it off his wrist and handed it to me. "You didn't—I didn't mean for you—"

"It's yours," he said, his gaze drifting toward the lake. "You can think of me every time you wear it."

Overcome by surprise and gratitude, I put it on. "Whaddya think?" I held up my arm. "Does this mean we're a couple?"

The words had no sooner slipped past my lips than I wished I hadn't said them. "Just joking," I added.

"So," he asked after an awkward minute, "how do you think you did on your SAT?"

I shrugged. "Okay, I guess. I've always been bad at math, so I stuck to the questions I knew. I think I did okay."

"I've never been good at math either," Logan said, shrugging. "I'm the only person in my family to flunk geometry."

I laughed. "I made my first D in geometry. Freaked me out, because I'd never made a D before. Geometry and I did *not* get along."

"And chemistry!" Logan laughed. "I liked the idea of doing experiments, but the minute I saw my first formula, I knew I was in trouble."

"I'll bet you did well in English."

"I like reading and writing. My dad thought I was crazy for memorizing some poems from last year's English class, but I can still recite them. There's something about the rhythm of poetry. I find it soothing."

I propped my arms on the table. "I'd love to hear one. I've always liked the way you read."

He hesitated. "You mean it?"

"I've said so before, haven't I? You may not remember this, but you had to read an Emily Dickinson poem on my first day in Mr. Wright's class. I fell in love with your voice the minute you started reading."

Logan lowered his head, and two pink spots appeared on his cheeks. "Okay. We had to memorize the last verse of William Cullen Bryant's "Thanatopsis." It's not very long; I think I still remember it."

"Go for it."

> "So live, that when thy summons comes to join
> The innumerable caravan, which moves
> To that mysterious realm, where each shall take
> His chamber in the silent halls of death,
> Thou go not, like the quarry-slave at night,
> Scourged to his dungeon, but, sustained and soothed
> By an unfaltering trust, approach thy grave,
> Like one who wraps the drapery of his couch
> About him, and lies down to pleasant dreams.

"When it's my time to go," Logan added, "I want to think of dying as going to bed."

"'Soothed by an unfaltering trust,'" I whispered. "I guess Bryant meant trust in God."

"Probably. But who knows?" He lowered his head. "His father was a doctor too. And his college career didn't take off either."

"Wait—what? *Either*?"

He shrugged. "I'm not going to college."

"Why not?"

"My ACT scores weren't good enough. I got a 22."

"How bad is that?"

"A perfect score would be a 36. You can't get into Johns Hopkins without at least a 33. The lowest Cornell will accept is 32."

"But you're smart! Maybe you suffer from exam anxiety."

"Trust me, I don't. I did great on the English and reading sections, but lousy on the math and science."

"You could find another college. You don't have to go to Cornell or—"

"You don't know my parents. Only the best will do. My sister graduated from Cornell. My parents met at Johns Hopkins."

"Surely they'll consider something else."

He waved my comment away. "What about you? You picked out a school yet?"

"You know," I continued, "we didn't have a science section. Maybe you should take the SAT instead."

"My dad made me take the ACT *because* of the science section."

I blew out a breath. "Have you told them about your scores?"

He looked away. "They don't know. I told them the results haven't been posted yet." He looked away. "They're going to flip out."

I reached for his hand and squeezed it. "I'm sorry."

He shrugged but intertwined his fingers with mine. "I've always been the family oddball." He released my hand and stood. "You want to walk down to the lake?"

We left the picnic table, and Logan grabbed a blanket from the back of his car. He was right—as the sun lowered, a cloud of mosquitoes hovered around us as if tantalized by our scent.

"That bug repellent works," Logan said, spreading the blanket on a patch of grass near the shore. "Now we'll be able to watch the sunset in peace."

I sat and stretched out my legs. Logan sat next to me, his shoulder against mine.

I studied the vibrant shades of purple and orange that shimmered in the water. "Now I see why they call this Mirror—"

Logan leaned toward me. He cupped my face in his hands and kissed me—not roughly, like some guys, but not timidly, either. He kissed me like the poet he was and stirred something in my heart.

His eyes, only inches away, seemed to brim with secrets and deep thoughts. "I could love you, Maddie Lawton," he whispered, "because so much about you is lovely."

I nearly melted. I wanted to say something as profoundly beautiful, but since I would never find the right words, I put my arms around his neck and kissed him back.

A week passed. Logan and I saw each other at lunch and in the hallway, but I looked forward to Friday night when we might have some time alone after the Pizza Palace. I found myself trying to come up with ways Logan could convince his parents to let him apply to a college where he could pursue a degree in literature or dramatic arts. I was certain they'd agree—after all, they were intelligent people—so all I had to do was persuade Logan to try.

One morning as we waited for school to open, Hester noticed I was wearing Logan's leather cuff. "He gave you his bracelet?" she asked.

I nodded.

"So you two are an item now?"

"I don't know." I shrugged. "I kind of made a joke about going steady, but he didn't respond." I lowered my voice. "But he *did* kiss me."

"I knew it!" She grinned. "Congratulations!"

"Shh." I glanced around to see if anyone had heard her. "I don't want to assume anything."

"Don't worry." She smiled, looking like a cat who'd just swallowed a bird. "Your little secret is safe with me."

Friday morning, I met the girls outside the school. Hester was wearing new shoes, so Mia, Sofia, and I admired them. "Avery would have adored those," Sofia said.

Jackson walked up. "Hey, girls."

Hester arched a brow. "Where's your sidekick? Logan oversleep again?"

Jackson shrugged. "He didn't pick me up, so my dad dropped me off."

I hoped my disappointment didn't show. "Hope he's not sick."

"He's probably snoring," Sofia said. "He'll turn up around third period."

"It's April 1," Mia added. "Maybe he was pranking you, Jackson."

"He better not have," Jackson said. "Made my dad late for work."

I looked for Logan all morning. Maybe he *was* sick. Still, it seemed odd that he hadn't told Jackson he wouldn't pick him up.

Hester and I were on our way to lunch when we saw a police car pull up to the curb. "Uh-oh," Hester said. "Somebody's in trouble."

After we left the cafeteria, we saw a cop come out of the office, followed a minute later by Sofia. She staggered out, her face blotchy. Hester called to her, and she burst into tears when she saw us. Hester and I gave each other a quick glance, then hurried toward her.

"What's wrong?" Hester asked.

Sofia drew a ragged breath. "It's Logan. He hanged himself this morning."

The floor seemed to give way and I fell, feeling the cold tile under my hands and hearing Hester say something. I could barely make out the words above the mad buzzing in my ears. My vision blurred until all I could see was Logan behind his steering wheel, his gaze fastened on something in the darkness, where he was thinking about something. Had he been planning to kill himself when I was with him?

Hester managed to pull me up and guide me to a bench, where I collapsed. She patted my back and turned to Sofia. "How do you know this?"

Sofia nodded, her chin quivering. "I was getting some forms for Mr. Wright when the cop came in to see Dr. Sweet. The secretary came out of his office crying and told one of the other ladies. I overheard all of it."

Hester managed a tremulous smile. "That's insane. Logan wouldn't do that." She turned to me. "Would he?"

I blinked, too stunned to do anything else. Had Logan dropped any hints? He was upset about his ACT scores. He said something about Avery and Matt losing hope. He said a picnic would be a fun thing to do before we ran out of time.

What if he *wasn't* talking about my return to Georgia? What if I had misunderstood everything?

"Did he say anything to you?" Hester's sharp eyes drilled into my brain. "Maddie? Don't have a panic attack, but we need you to think. Did Logan say anything about killing himself?"

"I'm . . . I'm not sure." I closed my eyes. "The other night he asked if I'd ever thought about it. But I never dreamed *he* was seriously considering it."

"Maybe he wasn't that night. But if this is true, something must have happened."

He lost hope.

I sagged forward, barely resisting the urge to drop and curl up on the floor. Remaining erect would require energy I no longer had.

"Maybe it's an April Fool's joke," Hester said, her voice rising to an unnatural pitch. "Maybe he's hiding somewhere, laughing at all of us."

Maybe it was a joke, not on us, but on his parents. The oddball of the family demonstrating that he would never fit in their mold.

"The cop wouldn't have come here unless it was true," Sophia said, her voice hollow. "They must have found him somewhere."

"If this is true," Hester said, lowering her voice, "it's going to freak out everybody. Everybody's going to think suicide is contagious."

"Isn't it?" I whispered, remembering the Hemingway family.

Hester pressed her lips together and didn't answer.

Chapter Forty-Four

Maddie

The next morning, I woke up and couldn't move. My arms, legs, and chest felt numb, and I struggled to breathe. I lay in the darkness cast by those black walls as Logan's voice mingled with Emily Dickinson's and William Cullen Bryant's:

> *After great pain, a formal feeling comes . . .*
> *To that mysterious realm, where each shall take*
> *His chamber in the silent halls of death . . .*
> *I could love you, Maddie Lawton . . .*

He could, but he wouldn't. Because he had made other plans.

I had made plans too. I would take my time getting up. Later, when I could move again, I'd text Nana and tell her I didn't feel like coming over. She'd understand. Everyone would.

I reached for a tissue, wiped the tears from my eyes, and blew my nose. That's all I'd been doing for the last couple of hours—emptying tissue boxes.

I needed to stop. I needed to rest.

I closed my eyes and drifted back into a dreamless sleep.

We met at the Pizza Palace that night because we needed to be together. I couldn't explain the urge to be with my friends, but when Nana suggested I stay home to rest, I looked at her as if she'd lost her mind.

As Hester and I slid into the booth where Sofia, Mia, and Jackson waited, I wondered if Logan thought about me when he slipped his head through the noose. He told me he *could* love me, but he must not have. Did he realize that within a few hours we'd be staring at the empty spot in our booth and blaming ourselves for not paying attention?

I stared at the bracelet, *his* bracelet, on my wrist. Had he given it to me because I meant something to him or because he had no more use for it? If he was planning on dying in a few days, he probably would have given me his car if I'd asked for it.

Dad had done the same thing, but I'd been too blind to see. He'd given Mom an anniversary ring five months early, and he'd made me promise to put the star on top of the Christmas tree.

Because he knew he wouldn't be around anymore.

Hester saw me staring and leaned over to give me a quick hug. "I'm so sorry," she said, tears filling her eyes. "I know you two were special to each other."

"Special?" I whispered. "I don't know if I am, but he sure was."

On the TV news, we'd learned more details about Logan's death. According to police reports, Logan got up early, drove to Mirror Lake, and hanged himself from a tree limb. The police said the noose had been perfectly tied, which led the experts to believe he'd been planning his death for some time. "The average high school kid doesn't know how to tie a perfect noose," the police chief said. "This kid took the time to learn."

Julie the waitress said, "I was sorry to hear about your friend. If you guys don't want to eat, you can just sit and talk."

But we ordered food. And when it came to drinks, I ordered water. "That's what Logan always drank."

Hester shook her head. "He was a bit of a health nut, wasn't he?"

Tears slipped down Sofia's face, and I sat in a stupor. What happened to Logan? What brought him to the point where he'd rather end his life than make the best of the one he had?

Finally, Hester said, "I can't figure out why he did it. What do you think, Maddie? You two were pretty chummy."

I shivered. "I know he didn't do well on his ACT. He was worried about disappointing his parents."

Hester turned to Jackson. "You rode to school with him every morning. Did he mention the ACT to you?"

Jackson shook his head. "Not a word. But I know he did better than me."

"Okay." Hester looked around the table. "If anybody else is planning to leave us, tell me now."

"Hester!" Sofia's eyes welled. "That's a terrible thing to say."

"What's terrible is killing yourself without considering your friends!" A tear rolled over Hester's cheek.

Around us, people laughed, silverware rattled, and a child fussed. A jukebox played in the corner, and outside an ambulance shrieked as it flew by. But silence as thick as cotton wrapped around our table.

I rested my forehead in my palm, overcome by a sense of déjà vu.

After great pain, a formal feeling comes . . . This is the Hour of Lead.

I couldn't stay. I slid out of the booth and glanced back at my friends. "I'm not hungry," I said. "Sorry. I'm going to call Pop and ask him to come get me."

The Nerves sit ceremonious, like Tombs—

"Maddie," Hester called, "I didn't mean to upset you."

I waved her away. "It's okay. I'll see you Monday."

The Feet, mechanical, go round—
A Wooden way
Of Ground, or Air, or Ought—

Nana was right. I should have stayed home.

When Pop parked at the house, I got out and told him I wanted to go to bed.

"Are you sure?" he asked. "Nana and I thought we might keep you company tonight."

"Not now," I told him. "I need to get some sleep."

I felt him watching me as I climbed the steps of the caboose. "Maddie? We love you. And we're praying for you."

A sob burned in my chest, but I pressed my lips together. I wanted to call out a cheery "Thanks," but I couldn't.

Inside the caboose, I sat on the edge of the mattress and remembered how I felt when Logan kissed me. That had filled me with hope. Later he kissed me again at the door of the caboose, and I'd felt like singing.

But that turned out to have been a goodbye.

Could this have somehow been my fault? Had he thought, *If that's a date, I might as well kill myself*?

I drew a quavering breath and studied my black walls. *Mirth is the mail of anguish.*

Mail, as in armor.

But there were other tools. . . .

In a basket near the sink, I fumbled through makeup and mascara and pulled out my cuticle scissors. I sat again on the edge of the bed and lifted my skirt to expose my pale inner thigh. No one would see this, especially if I kept the mark well above my knee. I placed the tip of the scissor blade on my pale skin, then pressed and pulled it toward me. The gash stung, but the pain released some of the pressure inside me.

As blood streamed, I pressed a tissue to the cut, then lay back and stared at my dark ceiling.

Cutting wasn't the answer—I knew that. But the pain gave me something else to think about.

On Monday after homeroom, the student body was summoned to a special meeting in the gymnasium. Few of us were surprised. Dr. Sweet had announced Logan's death before the end of school Friday, and while he had said nothing about how Logan died, the local news and the Internet revealed the cause within a few hours.

The news shocked parents throughout the area, and if those parents were anything like Nana and Pop, they gathered their kids around the dinner table and told them suicide was never an answer.

Nana and Pop told me the same thing, but their words didn't exactly overwhelm the evidence. My dad thought suicide was an answer. So did Van Gogh, Ernest Hemingway, and a lot of Hemingway relatives. Apparently a *ton* of people thought the best answer to life was death.

I was still reeling from the fact that Logan chose to die after our one and only date. I had thought we stood on the threshold of a future together, but to him our date was a farewell performance. How could we have been so close and yet so far apart?

Dr. Sweet introduced the school guidance counselor, Dr. Chloe Campbell, a woman in a dark skirt and matching jacket. She told us that Logan had left a note containing personal information for his family, and he would not want us to follow his example.

"If you have ever had thoughts about harming yourself," she went on, her voice low and calm, "reach out to someone. All of us go through difficult times, and it's easy to forget that darkness doesn't last. The sun will rise in the morning, and things *will* get better. Hope reminds us that better times wait around the corner."

As she talked, I thought about what Logan had told me about

his family. They didn't sound close. But his friends would have been there for him, if only he'd let us know he was hurting.

"I've always been the family oddball."

Maybe we should have been better at reading the clues. He had no hope, but I might have been able to offer him some, if only he'd given me more time.

If only Dad had taken time to talk to us . . .

My dad was a wise, mature man. Mom and I loved him and would have stood by him even if he'd done something wrong. Nana and Pop would have forgiven him for anything. He would have agreed with everything Dr. Campbell was saying, but he killed himself anyway. So what made him lose hope?

"Don't give up on yourself," Dr. Campbell said, "because you are part of the human family, and we need you. You bring something to the world no one else can bring.

"Most of you are familiar with Michael Jordan, one of the best basketball players in history, but did you know he didn't make his high school varsity team in his sophomore year? He wasn't good enough. But he found the courage to believe failure could be a path to success.

"He said, and I quote, 'I've missed more than 9,000 shots in my career. I've lost almost 300 games. Twenty-six times, I've been trusted to take the game-winning shot and missed. I've failed over and over and over again in my life. And that is why I succeed.'

"I want to share another true story with you. In 1985, twenty-eight-year-old Ken Baldwin walked out onto the Golden Gate Bridge, suffering from severe depression, and jumped.

"He later told a reporter that when he saw his hands leave the bridge, he knew he had messed up. 'Everything could have been better,' he said. 'I could change things, and I was falling. I couldn't change that.'

"Ken Baldwin hit the water four seconds after jumping, and in that four seconds he saw the faces of the people he loved—his parents, his brothers, his wife, and his three-year-old daughter.

Those were the people he was going to hurt. Profound sadness swept over him even before he hit the water.

"And when he came up, he discovered a fierce will to live. The Coast Guard rescued him, and today Ken Baldwin tells other people that problems are fixable. He quit a job he hated and became a high school teacher. He walked his daughter down the aisle. He held his first grandbaby in his arms.

"Ken Baldwin was fortunate, but others who jumped off the Golden Gate Bridge were not. Don't believe your problems are too big to be fixed. Your *today* is not your *tomorrow*. Your problems are not your future.

"Logan Westfield may be the first person you know who committed suicide. Some of you were close to him, and his death has hit you hard. I've heard enough about him to know he gave up too soon. He hit a roadblock he couldn't see a way around.

"But he could have found a way. His parents loved him, but today their hearts are broken. His friends miss him and did not want him to die. If Logan were with us today, he'd want you to live. He'd tell you to stay strong and carry on. I'm hoping you'll do that. For yourself. And for Logan."

Chapter Forty-Five

Susan

Frank and I weren't surprised Maddie wanted to go to the Westfield boy's funeral. We thought about going ourselves, but we didn't want Maddie to think we were spying on her.

We *had* been watching Maddie closely. I didn't want her to become so depressed she couldn't move forward. I prayed for her all morning, asking God to comfort her and help her understand that suicide was not the answer to life's problems.

Maddie came home around three, her eyes and nose red. I asked about the funeral.

"It was okay," she said, not looking at me. "And I need to get busy on my homework."

A lump rose in my throat. Losing a parent was traumatic. Losing a parent and two friends would be catastrophic.

Wednesday she came home while I was tidying the guest

apartment and asked if I wanted any magazines. "My class is selling subscriptions to raise money for our senior prom."

"But you're juniors."

"Proms are expensive, Nana. We have to start raising money early."

I was surprised she was making an effort on behalf of a class she wouldn't be part of next year. "I barely have time to read the magazines I get," I told her. "But maybe I can take a subscription for my guests."

She shrugged. "Don't feel pressured. I only brought the form home because I promised to help."

I groaned as I unfurled a fitted sheet over the bed.

"Does your arm still hurt?" Maddie asked.

"Sometimes," I told her. "Not the bone, but the muscles."

"I've never broken a bone," she said. "I've always wondered what it would feel like."

"Pain is pain," I told her, my voice flat.

"But the pain eventually went away, right?"

"Sure. But healing takes time."

"Good to know."

Chapter Forty-Six

Maddie

I had to write another essay for English, this one on a book by a contemporary American author. Since I had read *Flowers for Algernon* at my other school, I decided to use *Algernon* for this assignment. I didn't have the emotional energy to read a new book.

I didn't remember seeing my copy in the caboose, so I figured it had to be in one of the boxes Mom had shipped to St. Pete. I went to the garage and found my boxes stashed on shelves. I opened two, both of which were filled with summer clothes. I went through another two boxes—the first held nothing but shoes, and the second was filled with books, but not *Algernon*. I found another box, shook it, and thought it might have books inside, but I found a stack of folders on top. The first contained some of my old English papers, and the next was jammed with blank stationery, envelopes, and stamps. Mom was probably hinting, but who wrote letters anymore? If I wanted to talk to her, I'd call or text.

The last folder was filled with odds and ends—old birthday cards, a certificate from when I made the honor roll, a note from Tristan, a blue ribbon from a middle school art contest, and a printout with Dad's name and birthdate at the top. It was on the stationery of Dr. Michael Turner, a neurologist, and was dated November 30—a little over three weeks before Dad killed himself.

I sat on the floor and skimmed several paragraphs I could barely understand. I knew *hypertension* meant high blood pressure, but I'd never heard of *glioblastoma multiforme*.

Had Dad been sick? I knew hypertension wasn't fatal, but what was that other thing?

I set the paper aside and kept looking for my book. At the bottom of the box, along with a yellowed copy of *The Wizard of Oz*, I found *Flowers for Algernon*.

I grabbed the book and put everything back in the box, then picked up the patient encounter form and tucked it into the pages of *Algernon*. I carried both back to the caboose, planning to write my essay and see if anything serious had been going on with my dad.

According to several Internet sites, glioblastoma multiforme (or GBM) is the deadliest form of brain tumor, killing nearly 95 percent of its victims within five years—more than half of those within fifteen months.

The tumors are extremely difficult to remove because they have finger-like tentacles that invade normal brain tissue. Even if cut out, they almost always grow back with a different molecular profile, so doctors have to design a new treatment each time. "The current five-year survival rate for GBM," one doctor wrote, "is less than 5 percent."

The symptoms of GBM, I read, could include severe headaches, vomiting, seizures, memory loss, dizziness, difficulty reading and writing, and muscle weakness.

Yes, Dad sometimes had headaches, but so did Mom. Dad sometimes vomited, but so did I if I ate something that disagreed with me. Mom and I teased Dad when he walked into the family room and forgot why he'd come, but Nana and Pop did that all the time.

Could Dad have had GBM and hidden his symptoms?

I didn't remember Dad being sick in the last couple of years, except for a week when he stayed in bed with what we thought was Covid.

I trembled as memories played in my head: Dad eating more slowly than the rest of us, saying he wanted to savor his meal. Dad switching from printed to audiobooks because he said he liked to listen in the car. Dad blaming his headaches on clogged sinuses in spring, summer, and fall. Dad calling me to open a pickle jar because he wanted to see if my workouts were having any effect on my biceps.

Maybe these symptoms had prompted him to visit this neurologist. Maybe he had tests or scans, and the doctor told him he had GBM.

I was tempted to call Dr. Turner, but I knew he probably wasn't allowed to tell me anything.

So Dad had gone to the doctor, had some tests, and on November 30—my mouth went dry when I looked at the page again. This patient encounter hadn't taken place *last* November, but two years ago. For over two years, Dad knew he had a fatal brain disease, but he hid his symptoms and carried on, not wanting me to—

Wait. Did Mom know, or did he keep the news from her, too?

I closed my eyes, remembering Mom's face when she came rushing home the day Dad died. I recalled her stricken expression when she told Nana that not knowing why was the hardest aspect of dealing with Dad's death.

Mom hadn't known. Dad hid his illness to spare us.

So how did the printout get into my folder? Dad had to know Mom and I would want to know why. He wouldn't want to leave us without an answer. What better way to make sure we would find out than by slipping this page into a folder I wouldn't throw away?

Dad trusted me to figure things out. He knew I'd tell Mom, but the news would come later, after the initial shock.

I hoped he knew we would never stop missing him.

I dropped onto the bed and stared at the paper, which glowed purple in the ultraviolet light. Ken Baldwin might have had fixable problems, but my dad didn't. By the time Christmas came around, he knew he didn't have many more tomorrows. He pulled that trigger because he saw himself as already dead. His brain must have been riddled with cancer.

I stiffened. The autopsy! I overheard Mom mention the autopsy, so surely she would know the results by now. So why hadn't she told me? I was pretty sure she hadn't told Nana and Pop, either, or they'd have mentioned it.

So . . . should I tell Mom about what I'd found? Should I tell Nana and Pop? Or should I keep the news to myself awhile, allowing the pain of loss to lessen before I told them Dad would have died soon anyway?

I didn't tell any of my friends what I'd learned about Dad. I went through my day quietly, trying to focus on schoolwork. Hester tried to draw me out, but at lunch Sofia and Mia told Hester to give me a break. "She's mourning Logan," Sofia said. "They were sort of together, you know."

Hester didn't bother me for the rest of the day. Instead of going to her place after school, I went home and worked on my English paper. When my stomach began to growl, I walked toward the house, hoping Nana had fixed something good for dinner. My stomach had felt weirdly hollow the entire day, so I hoped a decent meal would give me some energy.

A strange car sat in the driveway, but I figured it belonged to a new set of guests.

I rapped on the front door and opened it, then crossed the foyer. In the living room, I found Nana and Pop on the floor with the vet, who was petting Ike.

Nana looked up, her face blotchy. "Ike isn't doing well. We called Dr. Barnett to come."

"You're putting him to *sleep?*"

Pop gave me a sad smile. "It's time, Maddie. We don't want him to suffer any more."

The vet kept murmuring to Ike—or maybe to Nana and Pop—and after a few minutes the sound of Ike's panting slowed and finally stopped.

I turned toward them again and saw that Ike's chest had stilled. The vet pressed a stethoscope to his rib cage, then pressed it to another spot and listened again.

"He's gone," he said, straightening. "I'm sorry for your loss, but you made the right decision."

The silence made me realize what a noisy little thing Ike had been. We could always hear his breathing, his nails tapping the tile, or his snoring. Now even the house seemed to listen for little dog sounds.

"Thank you," Nana said, wiping tears from her cheeks. "I didn't want him to pass in your office."

The vet nodded as he packed up his equipment. "I'll take him to the crematorium unless—"

"I'll bury him," Pop said, his voice husky. "Leave him with us."

After the vet left, Nana got up and walked down the hallway. She returned a moment later with a worn blanket, which she spread on the floor. Pop set Ike on the blanket, and together they wrapped him like a baby.

I sat in the shocking stillness, wondering whether Ike was okay with having been put to sleep.

Dad certainly would have been.

While Pop was in the backyard, I went to get the printout from the caboose. Nana was making iced tea when I came back, and after a few minutes Pop came in, his shirt damp and his hands dirty.

I figured there was no time like the present. "I found this in one of my file folders in the garage," I told them, setting it on the counter. "It's about Dad."

Pop and Nana bent to read the paper together.

"Look at the date," I said. "More than two years before . . ."

Pop sat and shook his head. "Well, I'll be," he said. "I've heard of that. It's a death sentence."

Nana looked ashen and shaky.

"I think he put that in my folder knowing I'd find it someday. He knew we would want to know."

"It's a relief to know," Nana said, "but it doesn't make it easier. Do you think your mother knew? She would have told us, wouldn't she?"

"I don't think she knew until the autopsy," I said. "But she had to know then."

"I can't believe he didn't want to try some kind of treatment," Nana said, staring at the paper. "I'm sure he could have tried chemo or radiation."

"He wanted to spare us." Pop drew a deep breath. "He didn't want to spend his last years being sick from surgery or chemotherapy, and he didn't want Rachel to stay home and take care of him. He wanted to live his life and go out on his own terms."

Nana burst into tears, covering her face with her hands. "But why couldn't he have let us help him?" she said, her words muffled by her fingers. "I understand what you're saying, but that wasn't his call to make. He should have let us help. We could have supported him. He didn't have to face such a horrible disease alone."

"I don't get it," I interrupted, my voice quavering despite my resolve to stay calm. "You guys put Ike to sleep when he was suffering with a terminal disease. What's the difference?"

Nana and Pop looked at me as if I had just declared myself dictator of the world, and I was sure they were going to tell me all the reasons I was wrong.

But Nana only said, "You need to tell your mom that you know."

Chapter Forty-Seven

Susan

I had awakened that morning with a sinking feeling—the night before, I had noticed Ike moving slowly, and Frank had to carry him to the caboose to sleep with Maddie. After she went to school, I found Ike on the floor, his legs twitching as he whined in his sleep.

Now I had to do what every dog owner dreads.

I picked Ike up, waking him. As he covered my neck and chin with kisses, I brought him into the house and set him in front of his food. But he wouldn't eat or drink. He staggered to his bed, lay down, and closed his eyes.

Dr. Barnett agreed to come as soon as he could.

I spent most of the morning by Ike's bed, stroking him, singing to him, trying my best to thank him for ten years of unconditional love. I thanked him for loving Maddie, for being kind to our guests, and for warming my feet on chilly nights. I thanked him

241

for singing along when I played the piano and for making me laugh with his antics. "Stealing a bag of potato chips?" I said, scratching the spot between his eyes. "You got us in trouble, you dangerous dog."

Then I thanked God for sending him to us.

Dr. Barnett didn't arrive until late afternoon, right after Frank came home.

And Maddie came in.

I wasn't expecting her. I thought she would go home with Hester, but there she was, averting her eyes as the doctor administered the injections.

I found myself grieving for her, too, after far too many encounters with death in the past few weeks. What was this doing to her heart? How was she handling her losses?

Then Maddie showed me that paper—that explained everything . . . and nothing.

Yes, I could see Daniel had a fatal disease. I understood disease. I understood why he wouldn't want to suffer or make his family endure his suffering.

What I could *not* understand is why he thought it necessary or appropriate to exclude us from the greatest trial of his life.

Later I told Frank, "Daniel didn't give us a chance. We could have helped, could have comforted all of them, could have prayed. Who knows? God might have worked a miracle."

Frank wiped wetness from his cheek. "It's easy to blame Danny, but we don't know what he was thinking. Maybe he knew God wasn't going to heal him."

"But there's power in united prayer, and he didn't give us a chance! We could have called on the church. We could have sent emails to everyone we know—"

"Susie." Frank caught my hand. "We can't drive ourselves crazy with what-ifs. You can't worry over the past. Daniel did what he did for his own reasons."

"But he was wrong!"

Frank shook his head. "We have to let it go. We have to be strong for Maddie and help her understand that euthanizing a pet is nothing like what Daniel did."

I gaped at him, struggling to restrain my anger, frustration, and disappointment. When I could speak, my voice emerged as a rusty croak. "And how do we do that?"

Chapter Forty-Eight

Maddie

When I was young and couldn't sleep, I'd pretend I'd been in a car accident and thrown onto the side of the road. I'd lie perfectly still, imagining myself critically injured, and wait for rescue. Then I'd fall asleep and wake the next morning.

When I grew older, my imaginary scene changed. I envisioned myself in a hospital bed with wires attached to my chest, needles taped to my arms, and a machine monitoring my heartbeat. I would again lie perfectly still, listening to the rhythm of my heart, until I drifted away and woke the next morning.

I couldn't sleep the night Ike died, so I lay staring at the words painted on the ceiling:

Because I could not stop for Death—He kindly stopped for me . . .

And it hit me: I didn't want to wake the next morning.

What did I have to live for? Within a few weeks I was supposed to go back to Atlanta, where I'd be living in a mostly empty house.

If Mom had won her case, she would be dealing with even more work, and if she'd lost, she'd be in a deep depression that would last until she got busy with another client.

My Atlanta friends had almost certainly forgotten me. Tris started ignoring me the moment we broke up, and Emily hadn't texted in weeks. Dad, my most dependable parent, had already checked out, so what was I supposed to do in Atlanta?

Though Atlanta held nothing for me, neither did St. Pete. I still had a few friends, but Hester, Jackson, Mia, and Sofia had already proved that they would carry on no matter what. Within hours of Logan's death, we'd been back at the Pizza Palace, eating and talking as usual.

What had Logan said? Only a few people get to be remembered. The rest of us are like hands in a bucket. And when the people who knew us die, we're gone forever.

I was never going to be remembered by anyone but Mom, Nana, and Pop, and they were already more than halfway to the grave. So why did I have to keep going?

Nana and Pop would be upset if they knew what I was thinking, but they were happy with the life they'd made.

But I wasn't happy and hadn't made much of a life. Dad always said he'd get me a job in his company or help me get into a good art school, but why sell pharmaceuticals if they couldn't heal people with GBM? And why paint pictures if nobody would remember the artist?

Avery, Matthew, and Logan had decided to stop living. Suicide was about exiting the pointless, painful thing called *life*.

I understood. And I wanted to exit too.

Who would cry for me? Mom, Nana, and Pop. But how could I hurt people who were already shattered?

Nana and Pop had been watching me like a hawk ever since Logan's great adventure, but I would follow Dad's example. I could put on a happy face and be upbeat. If I acted melancholy, Nana would call a counselor, and that would complicate my plan.

I'd give the world a week to change my mind. Otherwise, on Friday Nana and Pop would assume I was going to the Pizza Palace, and my friends would figure I'd decided to stay home. But I'd be on a rendezvous with death, and I would make him stop for me.

But how? I didn't have a gun and was too young to buy one. Pills could land me in the hospital with a tube down my throat. Plus, the wrong drug might make me retch all over the place, a horrible way to go.

I could cut my wrists and bleed out, but I'd hate for Nana to have to clean up the mess. I couldn't hang myself, because Pop would have a heart attack if he found me hanging from one of the trees.

I had two options: I could take a cab to the beach and swim toward the setting sun, but my body might never be found, and that'd drive my mom crazy. Or I could climb the water tower and jump. Simple. And since the grass around the tower was soft, I didn't think there'd be too much gore. Avery had looked good in her casket.

I wouldn't make the same mistake as Matthew. I'd make sure to jump away from the structural supports.

I rolled onto my side and drew a deep, shuddering breath. Done. I'd made my decision. I might write a couple of notes to wrap things up, but I'd make sure those wouldn't be found until I was finished. Literally.

I believed in God, so it would be nice to wake up in heaven and see Dad again. But if suicides went to hell, as I'd often heard, I preferred oblivion.

Chapter Forty-Nine

Susan

I walked up and down the driveway, swatting mosquitos as I prayed for Maddie. Frank was right: My chief concern should no longer be Daniel, who was with the Lord, but Maddie, who had to be overwhelmed with all that had happened.

The purple glow vanished from the caboose windows at half past ten, early for her.

I found Frank in our bedroom, where, despite the hour, we called Rachel and told her what we'd learned from Maddie about Daniel. "I assume you knew," I added, "since it had to have shown up in the autopsy."

Rachel sighed. "Yes."

"I know you had to have had a reason for not telling us," I said.

She hesitated a long time. "Frankly, Susan, I didn't trust myself not to say what I'm about to say, now that you know. My first thought was that Daniel was an idiot to think I couldn't handle a brain tumor. For heaven's sake, we vowed to support each other in sickness and in health, and I would have done that. I couldn't believe he didn't trust me—didn't know me well enough to realize I'd stand by him no matter what."

"Thanks for being honest," Frank said quietly. "I only wish you'd shared those autopsy results."

"I wanted to," Rachel said, "because I knew how hard it was *not* to know why. But then I thought about it and didn't want you to feel the sting of what I felt—that Daniel didn't believe in us. Didn't think we could handle it."

"He had brain cancer," Frank said, "so the illness may have affected his thinking. Maybe the disease was like a monster he didn't want to unleash on you."

"I think," I said, carefully choosing my words, "he wanted to spare you—all of us—from the torture of his treatment."

"But he didn't get treatment!" Rachel cried. "And why didn't he?"

"I don't know, hon. I've been asking myself the same thing. Did you ever notice any symptoms?"

"Sometimes he'd wake with a headache, but he always blamed it on his pillow. I bought him several different kinds, but none of them seemed to help." Her voice broke. "You and Frank must think I was an awful wife. How could I not notice that my husband had a fatal disease?"

"We don't think that, Rachel. Bottom line: Daniel didn't want you to know about his illness. He didn't want you to suffer with him."

"But that's what marriage is supposed to be," she said. "If we weren't meant to suffer together, I wouldn't have wanted him in the delivery room when Maddie was born."

Frank and I glanced at each other, then burst into laughter. "I'm sorry," I said, still chuckling, "but that was funny."

She sniffed. "Really?"

"Yes." I softened my voice. "If there's a silver lining in all this, it's that Daniel put that medical printout where Maddie would find it. Frank and I wondered how he could hurt us the way he did, but he actually did everything he could to shelter us."

"Well, I didn't want to be sheltered," Rachel said, her voice trembling. "He was my husband, and I would have done anything for him."

"I know, honey," I said, wishing I could reach across the miles to hug her. "Like too many people, he underestimated the depth of genuine love."

For the next several days, Frank and I walked on eggshells, keeping an eye on Maddie as we prayed for her and Rachel. I found myself wishing that Rachel *and* Maddie had come to Florida, so we could care for both of them. We loved them, but it wasn't easy to comfort Rachel when we had no idea what she was thinking and feeling.

So we did what we could. We called her, though we usually ended up leaving messages on her home phone because she didn't like to receive personal calls at work. Once, when I actually got through, I invited her to come stay in our guest apartment, but she reminded me that her trial would begin soon and she couldn't walk away. "Once we get started, the trial should take about three weeks," she told me. "After that, maybe."

I kept trying to find a time to sit and talk with Maddie, but she seemed to have rebounded from her depression of the last several days. She bounced in for breakfast and bounced out again. After school, she went home with Hester and returned to the caboose after dark. She kept her promise about checking in with us, but during those check-ins she always said she had homework to finish, so I never managed to corral her long enough for a conversation.

But we definitely needed to talk, especially after she had compared Ike's euthanasia to Daniel's suicide.

Finally, on Thursday night, she came home in time for dinner, probably because she knew I had made a huge pan of paella. As we filled our plates and set to work on the mountain of rice and seafood, I cautiously broached the subject.

"I miss Ike," I said, looking at Frank. "Maybe we should look into getting another dog."

"Not sure I want a puppy." Frank shook his head. "I think my house-training days are done. Besides, older dogs need homes too. And old dogs won't eat your shoes."

Maddie crinkled her nose. "But puppies are so cute!"

"The young families can take the puppies," I said. "We might look for a dog in his twilight years. Like us."

Maddie looked down, obviously disappointed. This conversation was not going the way I'd hoped. "You know, sweetheart," I said, "euthanizing a pet is *nothing* like helping a person die. Helping your pet is the act of a kind caretaker. Helping a person die is murder."

Maddie frowned. "Not in some states. My history teacher said—"

"I'm not referring to manmade laws," I said, "but God's. God created Adam and Eve to be stewards over his creation. They and their descendants were to take care of the planet, including the animals, and to be benevolent caretakers. When an animal suffers from a terminal disease, we ease its suffering. When we need food, we slaughter animals humanely. But humans are created in the image of God, and killing a human destroys one of God's image bearers. Your teacher might say people are animals, but God says we are his representatives on earth."

"Life," Frank added, "is a gift from God, and we are to honor it."

"But people kill each other all the time," Maddie said.

"The world is filled with people who commit evil," I answered. "That's why God—and governments—have laws against murder. We're not to kill others, and we're not to kill ourselves."

"What if a person's life has no purpose? Like a baby born without arms or legs. Or a woman in a coma?"

Frank tented his hands. "We are not to judge the quality of anyone's life," he said. "Maybe that woman's coma will teach her husband how to care for the weak. And maybe that baby will grow up and discover a cure for cancer. You never know."

"People can surprise you," I said. "Never underestimate the value of life."

"When a person is dying," Frank added, "it's important that we take care of them, ease their pain, and help them retain their dignity. By doing those things, we acknowledge that they are made in God's image. Our goal is always to care, never to kill. Not even when *we* are the person who's dying."

"If killing yourself is wrong, why didn't God stop Dad?"

"Because," Frank said, "God has given us free will. We are free to obey God, and we are free to disobey. People make their own choices."

"So . . . even though Dad was trying to spare us, you still think it was wrong for him to kill himself."

I gasped. "Surely you don't think it was *right?*"

Frank offered a more measured response. "Yes, Maddie, Daniel's choice was wrong, but God forgave him. We were deeply hurt by what Daniel did, but we've forgiven him too." He lifted a brow. "Have you?"

Maddie lowered her head. "I don't know."

"Forgiveness isn't easy," Frank said. "And it's not free. If you break Nana's plate and she forgives you, it costs her the plate. Forgiving your dad will cost you something. Once you realize the cost, you'll be ready to forgive."

A frown flickered over Maddie's face. "I don't understand."

I shared her bewilderment. What did Frank mean?

"I think, honey," Frank said, his voice gentle, "you'll understand when you're ready to forgive."

Maddie left the house without finishing her dinner. Suffocating from a surge of guilt for pushing her too hard, too fast, I stood by the window and watched her go.

Life was filled with teachable moments, but apparently this hadn't been one of them.

I turned to Frank. "I'm sorry. I thought I could try to help her see . . ."

"The girl's not ready," he said sadly. "You can't expect her to accept godly principles when she barely believes in God."

"But Daniel and Rachel raised her in church. She should already understand some of these things."

"Susie." Frank gripped my shoulders. "Look at the world around our granddaughter. The school is secular. Television and movies are secular. The music she listens to is secular. The Internet is loaded with all kinds of godless drivel. All those influences have pushed the things she learned in Sunday school to the back of her mind."

"I don't believe those hours in church were wasted."

"They weren't. But logic isn't going to work with Maddie. We have to wait for the Spirit to move her heart. Let God do his work."

"I wish he'd work faster."

Later I called Rachel and admitted, "I'm concerned about Maddie. I'm pretty sure she's struggling."

"What's wrong?"

I told her everything—about the suicide pact, about Logan, Ike's passing, Maddie's paint job, and the death-centered poetry on her walls. "I think you need to come down. She needs time with her mom."

"I'd like to, but this trial—"

"Honey, may I be frank? I know your work is important, but we're talking about *Maddie*."

Rachel hesitated. "You know, if this isn't working for you and Frank, you can always send her home. She can finish the year at her old school."

My heart sank. I was sure Maddie already felt Rachel had abandoned her. How would she feel if Frank and I sent her away?

"No, no, we're fine," I said. "Frank and I love having her with us. I was just thinking she'd enjoy some time with you."

"As soon as the trial is over."

Chapter Fifty

Maddie

April 15, I sat up, wide awake, at 5 a.m. I hadn't slept much, but what did it matter?

I threw on a dark T-shirt and black pants and went into the garage. I took Nana's car keys from the hook on the wall and slid Pop's five-foot stepladder and a big red hammer into the back of Nana's SUV.

Heart pounding, I backed out and glanced at the house. Still dark and quiet.

I spotted only two other cars as I drove. I could have run every red light but didn't, in case a bored traffic cop was hiding behind a billboard. Finally, I turned onto the narrow street next to the water tower.

I parked, unloaded the stepladder and hammer, and hid them behind some shrubbery, making as little noise as possible. No one lived on this side of the street, but the police had been patrolling the area ever since Matthew and Avery jumped.

I drove back to the house and put the car away.

Never had I done anything so bold. Hester and the others would be impressed once they realized how many details I'd quietly handled. Too bad I wouldn't be around to tell the story.

The sky had begun to brighten by the time I splashed my face and stared in the mirror. I was brimming with adrenaline, not at the thought of dying, but at the idea of completing my plans. By this time tomorrow, if all went as planned, I wouldn't have to wash my face or comb my hair. I wouldn't have to do anything.

Chapter Fifty-One

Susan

Maddie came into the house with a gleam in her eye. I didn't know whether to be glad or concerned.

"Well, look at you," I said. "You seem full of energy this morning."

"It's Friday. The week is almost over."

"There's another week coming, you know."

Frank came out of the bedroom, straightening his tie. "Maddie already? With time to eat!"

"No thanks. I'm not hungry." She grabbed a Diet Coke from the fridge. "Almost ready, Pop?"

"What's your hurry?" Frank took a seat as if he had all the time in the world.

Maddie shrugged and sat beside him. "Maybe I will have a piece of toast, Nana. With butter."

"Yes, ma'am." I dropped the bread into the toaster and leaned against the counter, watching Frank and Maddie. Frank leisurely sipped his coffee, but Maddie seemed antsy. Maybe even anxious.

"You have a test today?" I asked.

"Nope."

"I do," Frank said. "I'm subbing for an algebra class, and I'm giving a quiz. This will be an easy day."

Maddie grinned. "That's because you're not the one being quizzed."

What was up with that girl? She was usually sullen in the morning, but today we were chatting with Little Miss Sunshine.

Maybe my prayers were working.

I hummed while I cleaned the house, and I decided to reward Maddie's much-improved mood. I'd make a German chocolate cake, her favorite. She'd be at the Pizza Palace for dinner, but she'd come home to my surprise.

I welcomed my weekend guests at three, then started on the cake. When Frank came home, he sniffed and smiled. "You're baking! Do you know how long it's been since I've heard the clatter of cake pans?"

I hadn't baked since Daniel died. It didn't seem right to enjoy myself while my son lay in his grave. But this was for Maddie.

"Her ladyship's favorite," I told him. "And I'm doubling the number of pecans."

"May I lick the spoon?"

I gave him a quick kiss. "I tell you what: Stay out of my way and I'll save a spoonful of frosting for you."

After we ate dinner, I frosted the cake, imagining Maddie's delight later.

About the time I figured Maddie and her friends would be finishing their pizza, I grabbed a note card and wrote, *Made a special surprise for you. Come over as soon as you get home. Love, Nana.*

I punched in the code for the caboose and found the interior dark as a tomb. I turned on the lights and moved toward the computer, where I planned to leave the note card. I didn't expect to find another note taped to the screen:

Nana and Pop—thanks for everything, but I'm sorry, I just don't see the point. I hate that you have to be the ones to tell Mom.

Chapter Fifty-Two

Maddie

I managed to get through the entire day without arousing suspicion. Dropping hints and giving things away made sense only if I wanted to be talked out of it. And I didn't.

I went home with Hester but left before dusk, telling her I probably wouldn't make it to the Pizza Palace because I had a headache. I walked to the water tower, watching for police cars as I got closer to the metal monstrosity. I opened a gap in the fence just wide enough to wriggle through, ignoring all the warnings and No Trespassing signs.

I had no idea how a person was supposed to feel in the last moments of her life. I wasn't scared or excited, just determined. Finally, I was going to do something that I planned, controlled, and carried out. If anything, I was proud of myself.

As for Dad, I understood why he did what he did, but I couldn't forgive him for not letting me in on his secret. He thought he was protecting me, but I was seventeen, not a child. Even if I couldn't have helped him physically, I could have been by his side and loved him till his last breath.

To Mom, I was an obligation, another item on the to-do list. She was probably dreading my return home, wondering how much time I would steal from her schedule.

My old friends were only memories. My new friends would be shocked for a day or two, then go back to their lives, worrying about homework and track meets and college. I was relieved to be done with all that.

I knew Nana and Pop loved me. But I was the last thing they needed right now. They were supposed to relax at this stage of their lives, but I'd barged into their world without an invitation. I was only in the way, and they clearly didn't understand me. How could they, when I didn't understand myself? I'd brought them a ton of pain and worry, not to mention frustration.

They put Ike down when he had no future, so why couldn't I do the same for myself?

Logan managed it after he realized he was only a hand in a bucket. So was I.

I can't say I was giddy about what I was doing, but it felt right. And I saw no other option.

The shadows had deepened on the east side of the tower, so I worked in gathering darkness as I walked to the shrubbery, grabbed the stepladder and hammer, and shoved them through the opening between the gates. Then I squeezed through. Any size six could have managed it.

I opened the stepladder beneath the steel rungs that ran up the side of the tower, then climbed high enough to reach the metal cage around the rungs. A wire ran from top to bottom, probably for attaching a safety harness. I wouldn't need one. I was going to fly.

A couple of solid whacks with Pop's giant red hammer took care of the padlock that secured a metal screen across the cage opening. I dropped the hammer, gripped a rung, and climbed to the top step of the ladder. As I took that first step onto a rung, the ladder teetered and fell.

I looked down. I was only about ten feet off the ground. I could have survived a fall from that height, but I wasn't interested in surviving. I wanted to say goodbye from the top.

I started climbing.

I had never been much of an athlete, but I didn't think the climb would be that tough. About halfway up, my heart was thumping like a speed bag, and my arms felt like rubber bands. My palms grew slick with sweat, making me wish I'd have grabbed a pair of Nana's rubber gloves.

I slipped my arm over the next rung and closed my eyes. "Deep breaths," I whispered. "Take your time."

I dried my palms on my sleeves, then started climbing again. I could rest when I reached the catwalk. No one would see me up there, and at sunset I'd climb over the railing and step off.

After that, I'd never have to plan anything again.

Chapter Fifty-Three

Susan

I flew into the house and thrust Maddie's note before Frank's eyes. He turned white. "How—how do we stop her?"

I snatched a breath. "Where would she go? How would she—?"

"We'll start with the water tower." Frank grabbed his keys. "It's where her first Florida friends did it."

"I can't see her climbing that thing," I said, following him through the door. "God, change her mind!"

"My car," Frank said. "It's already in the driveway."

As Frank drove, I punched the button for Rachel's cell phone. I didn't care if she was in a meeting or sound asleep. This was not the time to place anything above her daughter.

The call went to voicemail after three rings.

"Rachel," I said, knowing how frantic I sounded, "Maddie's in trouble. You need to get down here as soon as possible. Don't call me back. Just come."

I also tried calling Maddie. Nothing. Apparently her phone was turned off.

I clutched the armrest as Frank swerved around a slower vehicle. "Careful," I said, but I didn't ask him to slow down.

"Dear Lord"—I clutched Frank's arm—"be with Maddie now. Don't let her harm herself. Do whatever you have to do, but preserve her life. Show us what you want us to do. Please, Lord. You're our only hope."

If Maddie did what I feared she would, we would lose everything. Maddie was the only part of himself Daniel left behind, and we were responsible for her. If she died, Rachel would no longer speak to us. Worst of all, Maddie would vanish—that beautiful, talented, precious little girl who stole my heart the day I first glimpsed her face on a sonogram.

Frank whipped around a corner, sending my phone crashing to the floor. When I picked it up, I remembered Bob's phone chain and speed-dialed Caroline.

Fortunately, she picked up. "Caroline," I said, bracing as Frank sped through a yellow light. "My granddaughter left us a suicide note. We're headed to Crescent Lake water tower. We think she might plan to jump. Please pray!"

The sun lay on the horizon as Frank wheeled up near the tower. I jumped out before he'd even stopped and ran to the fence. The catwalk was so high, I couldn't see anything up there, and for a moment my heart leapt with relief. Maybe I'd been wrong. Then I saw our stepladder in the grass.

Frank hurried over, and we yanked at the gap in the gate. Neither of us could fit through it.

Frank's lips compressed into a straight line. "I've got tools in the trunk."

Shading my eyes from the sun, I couldn't see Maddie on the ground or on the tower. I prayed she had changed her mind, but if she had reached the catwalk, she might have moved to the other side.

Huffing and red-faced, Frank ran back and slipped a crowbar through the padlock securing the gate. He summoned strength he hadn't shown for years and twisted until the lock finally snapped.

When Frank straightened the stepladder, I realized it was just tall enough for someone to access the rungs. The city had installed a grate over the opening, but it dangled uselessly on its hinge. I looked down and saw Frank's red hammer on the grass. Maddie had planned every detail.

"Do you think she's already . . . ?"

Frank took off running around the base of the tower. He kept glancing upward and yelling Maddie's name, but I didn't think she would hear him over the street noise. And unless she decided to dangle her legs over the edge, I didn't think he would see her.

So I climbed the ladder.

"She hasn't jumped!" Frank called, panting as he came around the other side of the tower. He reached up and grabbed my ankle. "Doggone it, woman, get down! You think I want to lose both of you?"

"I can do it, Frank. I have to try."

"Get down! I'll do it."

"Not with your heart!"

His hand tightened around my ankle. "Susan! I'm not going to argue with you."

"I can't lose you, either!"

"Get down and out of my way. Now."

I climbed down as Frank held the ladder. "Maybe," I whispered, "she changed her mind and went to the pizza place."

"Do you want to take that chance?"

I stepped back. I held the ladder steady as Frank rushed up and reached for the first rung. "Be careful!"

"Nothing's gonna stop me." He wiped his palms on his jeans

and began to climb. I babbled in prayer: "Lord, give him strength. Don't let him fall. Let him reach her in time. Please, Lord, we have never needed you as much as we do now."

I felt utterly helpless, but what could I do? I blinked. Maybe I could try calling Maddie again and tell her Pop was on his way. If she even had her phone . . .

I patted my pockets and groaned. I'd left my phone in the car.

I looked up, not wanting to abandon Frank, but he was making steady progress. I stepped back and yelled my granddaughter's name. "Maddie!" I cupped my hands around my mouth, hoping my voice would carry. "Maddie, it's Nana!"

Then I heard the sound of slamming car doors. I turned, hoping someone had called the police, but instead saw Lucio and Ivano running toward me.

I had never been more thrilled to see other human beings. I ran toward them and caught their hands. "Thank you! I'm pretty sure Maddie's up there, but my voice isn't strong enough to reach her."

"I can shout," Ivano said, jogging toward the front of the tower. Lucio ran after Ivano.

Other cars pulled up. I stared as Bob, Isabell, and Helen hurried over.

"You came?" I asked Bob. "I thought this was supposed to be a prayer chain."

"Prayer is good," Bob said, squeezing my hand. "Support can be better."

The three of them walked toward Lucio and Ivano as additional cars pulled up. I stared, tears blurring my eyes, as Ruby, John, and Caroline came over and added their voices to the others calling Maddie's name.

"Hey! Hey, lady!"

A man across the street waved at me from his front porch. He pointed to the tower. "She's over there!"

"She's that way." I pointed west. "Keep walking!"

We hurried around the tower and finally saw Maddie's head appear beneath the railing.

"Hey, Maddie," Ivano called, his big voice booming. "Stay put, 'cause your grandpa is coming to help you."

"Be careful, Maddie," Bob shouted. "We care about you."

Another man ran over from across the street and handed me a bullhorn. "Just smash that button," he said.

My hand shook as I gripped it. "Maddie, it's Nana! Pop is coming to help you down!"

Maddie stood at the railing.

Don't jump, don't jump, don't jump.

Chapter Fifty-Four

Maddie

I was lying on my stomach, head resting on my arms, when I heard my name. I was certain my brain had conjured the voices of my friends. In a moment I'd hear Mom, then Logan, then maybe Hester.

"Maddie! Maddie, it's Nana!"

I frowned. The voice had veered off script, and I couldn't help feeling irritated. Then I noticed that the railing next to me was shivering in a rhythmic tremor.

I held my breath as other sounds came to me—slamming car doors, people shouting, voices mingling with the whistling of the wind through the struts.

I inched forward and peered over the edge of the catwalk. Near the street, Nana was talking to people I didn't recognize.

Like a frightened turtle, I pulled my head back. Maybe if I stayed still and didn't respond, they'd leave.

Other voices filled the air. They called my name and urged me to come down. How did they know I was up here?

I looked around, afraid I'd see a drone, but the sky remained clear. When I lowered my gaze, though, on the other side of the street I saw people staring up from their lawns and porches. They had a clear view of the tower. One man held binoculars, which meant he had a good view of me.

Uh-oh.

Suddenly the group on the ground shifted, moving away from the access ladder and coming toward me. Their voices became clearer, and they were shouting my name.

"Hey, Maddie," one loud man called. "Your grandpa is coming up to help you."

No way. I'd had to stop halfway up to rest, so how was he supposed to manage it?

I couldn't let Pop climb all the way to the catwalk. Nana would never forgive me if anything happened to him.

Then came her voice through a bullhorn: "Pop is coming to help you down!"

Choking on a sob, I kept one hand on the railing and walked slowly to the ladder I had never intended to use again.

I held the railing and slowly moved to the top rung. Pop was carefully laboring up, pulling himself along like the seventy-two-year-old man he was.

I wasn't worth this. I couldn't let him do it.

"Pop!" I yelled, my voice breaking. "Go back and I'll come down!" Our eyes met. "Stop," I said again, so he'd be sure to understand. "I'm coming down."

Keenly aware that we were both risking our lives, I sat on the edge of the platform and waited until he was nearly down.

My foolproof plan had failed. Not only did I not succeed at dying, but I also endangered someone I loved.

Going down was easier, of course, but every bit as treacherous because of my sweaty palms and the slippery rungs. I worried most about Pop making it down safely, and I felt like such a fool as people cheered me all the way. I was anything but a hero.

The sun had set by the time I landed on solid ground. I turned and was relieved to see Nana beside the stepladder. "Oh, Maddie," she said. As the other people smiled and high-fived each other, she wrapped her arms around me.

"How's Pop? And who are all these people?" I asked.

"They're friends," she said, "and Pop is over there."

I saw him lying on the grass. A couple of the women were with him—one was taking his pulse, while another wiped perspiration from his face.

Guilt hit me like a blow to the stomach.

I hurried over and knelt beside him. "Pop, are you okay?"

He grinned up at me. "Never better, now that I see you." His smile gleamed in the gathering darkness. "I just need a minute to catch my breath."

Nana grabbed his shirt, which was drenched with sweat, and struggled to undo the buttons.

"Susan," one of the women said, her voice firm, "I'm calling 911. Don't move him, and don't let him sit up."

"Is Pop okay?"

The woman didn't answer but stepped away, her phone to her ear. I heard her say, "Crescent Lake water tower" and "possible heart attack."

Fear chilled my blood. Nana cradled Pop's head in her lap.

Pop looked up and caught my gaze. "Don't you ever try that again," he said, giving me a stern smile. "I don't think I have another climb in me."

I took Pop's hand. I wanted to say everything was okay, but I couldn't speak. I just couldn't let Pop die because of me.

"Let's go home," Pop said, trying to push himself up. "We have to thank all these people—"

Nana held him down. "Lie still."

Her eyes widened when Pop's face contorted and he put his hand over his heart. "I adore you, Susie," he said, so faintly I could barely hear him. Then he turned to me. "I would climb the Empire State Building for you, my one and only Maddie."

He closed his eyes, and Nana began to sob.

An ambulance took Pop to the hospital. Nana rode with him, and I followed in Pop's car. I found her phone and saw a bunch of missed calls from Mom. *Oh, no.* I tried to call, but she didn't answer.

I hoped she wasn't on a plane. I was causing nothing but trouble.

The entire time I sat with Nana, I kept thinking she would hate me for making her a widow. I didn't see how Pop could survive that climb with a heart condition, and I was pretty sure Nana wouldn't be able to forgive me.

Forgiveness will cost you something, Pop once said. Forgiving me would cost Nana the man she had loved for nearly fifty years, and that was too high a price.

So I sat with her, shifting in an uncomfortable vinyl chair, while cold hands twisted my heart. Life as I had always known it would soon be over. Ironic that I had managed to destroy my life without actually dying.

I would still rather die myself than hurt him.

Chapter Fifty-Five

Susan

I was glad when Maddie fell asleep in the waiting area. The child had to be exhausted. A good rest would help her think more clearly.

As for me, I wouldn't be able to sleep until after I had spoken to Frank's doctor. Either this would be the event that took Frank from me, or they would find a way to give us a few more years together.

When my phone rang, I glanced at the caller ID, then moved into the hallway so I wouldn't wake Maddie. "Rachel?"

"Susan! I'm at your house, but where are you?"

I told her Frank was about to go into surgery.

"My goodness, what happened?"

I drew a deep breath. "It's a long story, but right now you need to come to the hospital as quickly as you can."

When Rachel arrived, I met her at the entrance and put my arm around her shoulder. "Maddie's asleep, and Frank's in surgery,"

I said. "And we need to talk. There's a coffee shop down this hallway."

After getting coffee, I told Rachel everything that had happened.

"Good grief, is Maddie okay?" Rachel rose out of her chair. "Should you have left her alone?"

"She's fine for now," I assured her. "She's going to need help, but she was so upset about Frank, she's not going to hurt herself tonight."

Rachel sat, but reluctantly.

"It's been a rough few weeks," I admitted, "for us, but especially for Maddie. Not only is she still dealing with her grief over Daniel, but she has also attended the funerals of two of her friends."

A melancholy frown flitted across Rachel's features. "She never mentioned any of this when I called."

I shook my head. "I should have seen the signs. I should have paid more attention."

"*You*?" Rachel's voice brimmed with self-incrimination. "I didn't ask any of the right questions when I called. My word, what must have she been feeling?" Rachel stared past me. "May God forgive me for how I've ignored my daughter."

"Maddie doesn't blame you," I said. "But the other night she mentioned something about people whose lives have no purpose. I don't think she's found a reason for living."

Rachel lifted her brows. "What teenager has?"

"When I was her age, I knew Jesus had a purpose for my life. I had no clue what it was, but faith gave me hope for my future."

Rachel took a deep breath. "So how do you give a kid faith if they don't want it?"

"That," I said, pushing away from the table, "is the million-dollar question. Off the top of my head, I'd say you love them, you model faith for them, and you take them to a church that meets their spiritual needs. Ultimately, you ask God to open their hearts to the gospel. I believe he will do that for Maddie, in his time."

"I hope you're right," Rachel said, a look of helplessness in her eyes. "Because I cannot lose my daughter."

Chapter Fifty-Six

Maddie

I awoke shivering in the draft from an overhead vent and walked the hospital hallways, searching for a quiet place to be alone. I took the elevator to the ground floor and finally spotted a door labeled *Interfaith Chapel*.

I sat on one of the small pews and rubbed my arms, breathing in the scents of furniture polish and disinfectant. At the front, an overhead light shone on an empty wooden table, and two pieces of stained glass hung from the ceiling, with differing shapes in shades of blue and a few gold bits for contrast. No real pattern, only pieces of glass randomly placed, but somehow they fit. Chaos under control. Like my life.

This place looked like it had been designed for prayer to any god you pleased, but I only knew the one I'd learned about in Sunday school.

I buried my face in my hands. "Dear God," I whispered, "I

don't know why I'm here. I had everything planned. Did you tell Nana I was at the tower? Did you help Pop climb up there? Why would you do that? I didn't think anybody cared about me, but Pop nearly killed himself because of me. I've never done anything to deserve that. And Nana—why does she put up with me? Why wouldn't you let me do what Dad did? Everyone would be happier if I went away."

I couldn't remember the last time I'd prayed and don't know what I was expecting. It didn't seem as if anyone was listening, let alone God. I stood to leave just as Mom walked in.

"Maddie?" Her eyes lit with surprise. "Thank God you're all right."

I ran to her and cried like a baby in her arms.

Chapter Fifty-Seven

Susan

"Why?" I asked God, staring at the nondescript art on the waiting room wall. "Were we wrong to let Maddie come stay with us? If we hadn't taken her in, Frank wouldn't be on the operating table. The tragedies at the school wouldn't have touched our granddaughter and amplified her feelings of loss. She wouldn't have been suicidal, and she wouldn't have climbed that stupid water tower."

I heard no answer, so I tried another approach. "Lord, Frank and I have always wanted to serve you. Even as a substitute teacher, he tries to love those kids. I do my best to bless the folks who stay in our guest apartment. Are we not doing enough to please you? Have we somehow moved away from your perfect will? Have we harbored some secret sin, and is this your judgment on us?"

Again, no answer.

"Lord," I cried, tears falling on my fingers, "I don't know what to think, but I know this—if you take Frank, you may as well take me, too."

I was grateful Rachel and Maddie were not around to witness my emotional breakdown. I could deal with only one calamity at a time.

I lifted my head as a pair of orderlies wheeled an occupied bed into a nearby room. Two nurses from the central station hurried to care for the patient, and I knew Frank had to be the man on that gurney. He'd spent four hours in surgery.

I moved to the window that looked into the Cardiac Care Unit. The nurses were attaching wires and tubes to the patient while orderlies positioned the bed. I chewed on my thumbnail and hoped the Spirit would pray for me. I had used up all my words.

When a nurse stepped out, I stopped her. "Is that Frank Lawton? He's my husband."

She checked the chart. "Yes."

"Is he going to be okay?"

The nurse's mouth twisted. "The surgery went well."

"Is he going to *live*?"

She walked over to the nurses' station and pulled out a brochure. "Here," she said, giving me a sympathetic smile. "This will help you understand your husband's situation."

I opened the brochure, skimming it as I walked back to the waiting area. The material listed several postsurgical complications, including infection—from visitors, catheters, central lines, ventilators, and multidrug-resistant pathogens. Anxiety spurted through me when I realized that the surgery had been only an initial step. Now Frank would have to avoid or survive myriad healthcare-associated infections, pneumonia, and flesh-eating bacteria.

I sank to the couch as Frank's voice filled my head: "You worry too much, honey."

I had never had more to worry about or less energy to worry with.

Then my phone rang, and I nearly wept with relief when I saw who was calling.

"Bob!"

"Sorry for calling at this hour. How are things going with Maddie and Frank? What can I tell people who've been texting me?"

I brought him up to date, including the news that Rachel had arrived to be with Maddie.

"That's good. She can take some of the burden off you."

"I'm a mess." I burst into tears as all the anxiety, frustration, and fear of the last few hours overwhelmed me.

"Hear this, Susan: 'Fear not, for I have redeemed you; I have called you by name, you are mine. When you pass through the waters, I will be with you; and through the rivers, they shall not overwhelm you; when you walk through fire you shall not be burned, and the flame shall not consume you.

"'For I am the Lord your God, the Holy One of Israel, your Savior.'"

"Thank you," I whispered. "I worry too much. I always want to fix things."

"But remember, Susan—for the believer, hope isn't about solving the problem. Hope is the confident trust that God will carry you through the trial. You can trust him."

"I know." I smiled through my tears. "Now I just need to act like I know."

Chapter Fifty-Eight

Maddie

Mom and I had a long talk in the chapel. She pleaded with me to tell her what had pushed me to want to kill myself. I tried to explain everything, but it didn't make much more sense to me than it did to her. She said she was grieving Dad too, but that he would want us to carry on and be happy.

"I know," I said. "I'll try."

"I would never have forgiven myself for sending you to Nana and Pop's if I thought—"

"No, no, it's not that," I said, not entirely truthfully.

"Tell me the truth, Maddie. Are you still feeling like you want to . . ."

"No," I said. And I meant it. *Not right away, anyway.*

"Because if you do," she said, "we could find you someone to talk to right here—"

"No! I know about the Baker Act, and I don't want to be locked up. I need—I want—to be with my family."

She caught my hand. "I'm going to trust you," she said, her eyes shimmering. "But if you start thinking that way again, you have to promise you'll talk to me. Or Nana, or Pop. *Someone*."

What if I talked to someone and still *wanted to kill myself?*

"Okay," I said. "I promise."

"I mean it, Maddie. You can't go back on your word."

Her phone chimed, so she released my hand to read the message. "Pop is out of surgery, and Nana says we can go to his room. Do you want to do that, or would you like to go home and get some sleep?"

"Let's go see Pop." I stood. "I don't want to leave without knowing he's okay."

The Cardiac Care Unit allowed only two visitors at a time. Nana met us at the door in a sterile gown and gloves and said she'd be in the waiting room. "He's coming around, but he's still groggy. Two arteries were completely blocked. They did an angioplasty and . . ."

She kept talking about the surgery, but all I could think about was what Pop endured because of me. Guilt nearly knocked me over. Pop needed to stay alive for Nana, but he risked his life because he wouldn't let me go. "I would climb the Empire State Building for you, my one and only Maddie."

I lowered my head so Mom and Nana wouldn't see that I was about to lose it. How could I have been so stupid? I was furious with Dad because he didn't think about how he'd hurt me and Mom, but I nearly did the exact same thing.

Mom and I put on protective gear. As we slipped on face masks, the nurse smiled. "I'm glad you've come to see Mr. Lawton. Be sure to speak to him, because he may hear you. And don't be afraid to touch him."

The nurse opened the door, and we stepped into the room.

For a minute I didn't recognize the man in the bed. He was surrounded by machines that beeped, clicked, and whirred, and his arms were covered in tubes and needles. A large bandage lay over the center of his chest, and the surrounding skin was mottled with bruises.

What had I done to him?

A sob crept up my throat, and I wouldn't have been able to speak if I'd wanted to. I reached for his hand and saw that Pop's fingers looked like sausages.

Mom must have seen my expression. "Swelling," she murmured, "from the drugs and such."

I cleared my throat. "He feels cold."

"I think they try to keep the body temperature low. I'm sure there's a good reason."

I leaned toward Pop. "Hey, it's Maddie." My voice cracked. "I'm so sorry, Pop. I never would . . . I never meant for you to come after me."

I didn't expect him to answer, but his fingers closed around my gloved hand.

"He did well in the surgery," Mom said, sitting next to Nana in the waiting area.

Nana sighed. "He's going to spend at least ten days in the hospital; then he'll recuperate at home for six weeks. If he makes it that far, I'm not supposed to let him drive or climb anything higher than a stepstool."

"Isn't he out of danger?"

Nana's brows knitted. "The surgery went well, but so many other things can go wrong. He won't be out of the woods until he leaves the CCU. After that, we can breathe a little easier."

"Okay. But what can we do now?"

Somehow, Nana managed a smile. "The doctor said the best thing we can do is go home and rest. We can always come back tomorrow."

Nana told Mom she could sleep in the guest apartment, but Mom said, "If Maddie doesn't mind, I'd like to stay with her in the caboose."

"Are you sure?" Nana asked. "That's probably a lot smaller bed than you're used to."

"That's okay." Mom slipped her arm around my shoulder. "I'd like to be close to my daughter tonight."

Did she really want that? Or was she afraid I'd try again?

Chapter Fifty-Nine

Susan

When we finally got home at three in the morning, I helped Rachel get situated in the caboose and asked if I could talk with Maddie in the house.

"Now?" Maddie asked.

"Yes, now. Your mother will wait, won't you, Rachel?" I spoke firmly because otherwise I'd dissolve into blubbering gibberish.

"Of course."

Maddie followed me into the house, then stood with the awkwardness of a stranger as I dropped my purse and keys on the foyer table.

"I need to make some calls," I said, thinking aloud, "but first I want to talk to you." I pointed toward the sofa. "Have a seat, kiddo."

She walked over and sat, staring straight ahead. I sat next to her. "Maddie—"

"I know you hate me," she interrupted. "Maybe you didn't before, but you do now, and I don't blame you. I thought my life was worthless, and now you must think the same thing. But I didn't want Pop to climb that tower. I didn't tell him to come after me. In fact, I tried to arrange it so you wouldn't know where I was until it was over."

I drew a shuddering breath and studied my weeping grandchild. How could I make her see how desperately she was loved?

"Maddie," I began, struggling to keep my voice steady, "Pop and I went after you because we love you. Both of us were willing to climb that tower, but Pop insisted. He wouldn't have it any other way."

"Why?" Raw anguish filled her voice.

"Because he loves you."

"My dad loved me too," she said, sobbing. "But he left me. I wouldn't have cared about his cancer. I would have helped him through the treatments. I would have stuck by him no matter what, but he didn't give me a chance."

"Honey, don't you see? We're living through that same situation right now. You're hurting just like your dad, and we want to help. We want you to give us a chance."

I took her hand. "A thousand men couldn't have stopped Pop from climbing that tower. And now that you're safe, we want to help you through whatever problems you're facing. We want you to know you are loved and you are precious. Will you let us do that?"

Maddie blinked away tears. "I guess."

"You *guess*?"

"Okay. I will."

Maddie threw her arms around me. I didn't move, stunned by sheer surprise, then I patted her back. "It's going to be okay," I said, though I wasn't positive it was. "We'll be fine."

And as we passed the kitchen, I pointed to the surprise I'd nearly forgotten. "Take a look at that."

"My favorite! Can I have some now?"

"How about we all have some together tomorrow?"

I locked the door after Maddie left, then cleared the kitchen counter. And as I passed the cake, I realized again how close we had come to losing Maddie. If I hadn't gone over to leave that note . . .

"Thank you, Lord," I whispered, "for always being two steps ahead of us."

Chapter Sixty

Maddie

I couldn't believe Mom let me skip the next week of school, but it was just as well. Hester said my *stunt*, as she called it, was the talk of the place. "Were you really gonna do it?"

"I don't want to talk about it."

"Not even to me? Suit yourself, but I'm taking that as a yes."

We lived in a sort of time warp at the hospital every day. We mostly couldn't be with Pop but stood outside his window and waved. Whenever a nurse or doctor went in or out, I could hear Nana talking to him or reading to him from the Bible.

Once, I saw tears trickling down Mom's face.

"Are you okay?" I asked.

"This is how it should have been for your father," she said, her voice thick. "I should have been by his side. Both of us"—she put her arm around me—"should have made that journey with him."

One day, Nana came out of Pop's room looking worried. "He has a fever," she told us. "They're testing him for an infection and will know how to treat it once they determine what it is. Until then, we'll have to pray." Nana reached for our hands, but I stepped away so I could watch from a distance. I wasn't sure God and I were on speaking terms.

Pop's situation got worse over the next few days. Nurses went in and out of his room more often, their expressions grim. Nana started reading Bible verses about mansions in heaven. Once I was startled to hear her say, "The Lord cares deeply when his loved ones die."

I looked at Mom. "Think that's true?"

Mom blinked. "Of course."

"Then why doesn't he let them live?"

"No one lives forever, Maddie."

I folded my arms. "So . . . if Pop dies—"

"Jesus will welcome him," Mom said. "And his Spirit will comfort you and me and Nana . . . everyone who loved your grandfather." Her eyes grew misty. "I'm sorry your dad chose to die the way he did. Jesus welcomed him, but the rest of us didn't get to say goodbye or thank him for the times he made our lives better. We could have encouraged him in his final days, but he was focused on the suffering. He should have thought about the joy."

I frowned. "There's no joy in dying, Mom."

"There could be," she said, her voice soft. "Because we always find joy when we count our blessings."

Mom was still wearing the diamond circle on her finger—the gift Dad had given her Christmas Day, five months before their anniversary.

Something clicked. The eternity ring was Dad's way of telling Mom he would always love her.

"Have you forgiven him?"

Her brow lifted. "What?"

"Have you forgiven Dad for killing himself?"

She nodded slowly. "Yes. I have."

"Pop says forgiveness always costs something. So what did forgiving Dad cost you?"

Mom sat back. "Forgiving him means . . . I'm not going to be angry with him. I'm not going to trash his reputation. And I'll keep loving him." She lifted a brow. "What about you?"

I shrugged. "I don't know. Pop says that once I realize the cost of forgiveness, I'll be ready to forgive, but I haven't figured that out."

"Maybe," Mom said, her eyes softening, "you'll forgive him when you no longer want to make the choice he did."

Chapter Sixty-One

Susan

One day slid seamlessly into the next, but Frank walked a little too long in the valley of death for my taste. Thankfully, after his infection cleared, he improved a little every day.

Rachel kept in touch with her office and directed an associate through the amusement park trial. To her credit, she spent as much time as possible with Maddie.

The day before Frank was to go home, an orderly got him into a wheelchair so we could take him to the chapel, where Bob Halsey was waiting. Maddie remembered him from the time she went with me to the support group.

I made introductions all around, feeling as though I was leading a support group of my own.

"Bob, I wanted you to meet with us," I began, "because we lost Daniel, and Maddie has lost two of her friends. Then we nearly lost Maddie and Frank. The question we struggle with is *why* God let all this happen. If he's all-powerful and loving, why didn't he prevent all this?"

Bob lowered his head a moment, then looked up with a lop-sided smile. "What I'm about to say may be hard to hear," he said, opening his Bible, "but it comes straight from Deuteronomy 32, and God himself is speaking: 'See now that I, even I, am he, and there is no god beside me; I kill and I make alive; I wound and I heal; and there is none that can deliver out of my hand.'

"We think of God as loving and kind, and he is. He loves and cares for us, he redeems us from sin, and he is always with us, even when we go through the valley of death. But our perspectives are limited, and we forget the big picture: The God who promises to heal also wounds."

He cleared his throat. "A few years ago, I lost my wife after a five-year battle with cancer. During those five years, we prayed for her again and again. Church members came to the house and anointed her with oil, as the Scripture says to do. Yet God chose not to heal her. And when she died, I suffered a severe wound, but I did not lose hope. Because when she took her last breath, her face lit up, and I knew she was completely healed and in the presence of Jesus."

I saw a smile curve Rachel's lips. She had to be thinking about Daniel. As was Frank.

"Jesus promised he would never leave us," Bob added. "And in Isaiah, God said he has called us by name and *we are his*. We belong to God, body and soul. So when a believer kills himself, he has taken what belongs to God—his body—and destroyed it, placing his desire above God's."

"Don't people go to hell for that?" Maddie asked. "That's what I've heard."

Bob shook his head. "Suicide is sin, but Jesus paid the penalty for our sins when he died on the cross. Anyone who believes in him will be forgiven."

"But suicide is the *last* sin a person commits," Maddie said. "So there's no time to ask for forgiveness."

The corners of Bob's eyes crinkled. "Jesus died more than two thousand years ago, right?"

Maddie nodded.

"None of us had been born at that time, so all our sins were in the future. His sacrifice covered the sins we committed yesterday as well as the sins we might commit tomorrow. Those who accept Jesus have *all* their sins forgiven, so a believer who takes his own life *will* go to heaven."

Frank leaned forward. "The Lord knows I've struggled with Daniel's decision—at times I wanted to scream at Daniel, and sometimes I did scream at God. But everybody experiences grief at some point. Why should I get a free pass?"

Bob nodded. "Right. Believers suffer just as Jesus did, but God promises that our pain will one day result in good. Maybe others will learn from your suffering. Your struggle may teach you to adopt a different outlook on life. Trouble may draw you closer to the God who yearns to be close to you."

"That's comforting," Rachel said. "After Daniel died, I tried to concentrate on work so I wouldn't have to deal with my grief. But it helps to know he's waiting in heaven."

"And heaven is not our only hope," Bob said. "Our suffering serves the holy purpose of making us more like Jesus, because he suffered too."

Bob turned. "Maddie," he said, "losing your father and two friends is enough to knock most people off their feet. I've heard your dad's reason, but what about your friends?"

"They were afraid," she said, "of things they didn't want to face."

"And what about you?"

Maddie glanced at her mother and slid lower in her seat. "I didn't think anyone wanted me. Dad didn't care enough to stay, and Mom wanted me gone."

Rachel whimpered and covered her mouth.

"And Logan, who seemed to really like me, didn't think I was worth sticking around for. And while I love Nana and Pop, I felt guilty for making them worry about me."

This time I wanted to whimper. Maddie must have seen me as a worrywart who was constantly checking up on her. I probably made her feel more like a bother than a joy.

"Parents and grandparents are allowed to be concerned about you," Bob said, "because they love you. If the grown-ups in this room didn't love you, we wouldn't be here. Let me assure you of this: When you want hope for your future, you will find it in Jesus. That doesn't mean life will always be easy, but it does mean you'll never be alone."

As Bob gave Maddie the answer to life, I had an epiphany: I *did* worry too much. For years I had clung to fear instead of hope, as if God couldn't or wouldn't take care of my family.

Bob stood and shook Frank's hand. "You have some lovely ladies in your family. I know they're thrilled you're going to stick around awhile."

"I'm thrilled too," Frank said, giving him the broadest smile I'd seen in days. "I was ready to go until I realized I hadn't given Susan all the computer passwords."

I grabbed the handles on his wheelchair. "If that's what kept you here," I said, wheeling him toward the door, "you can keep your passwords forever."

Chapter Sixty-Two

Maddie

I couldn't sleep. I lay awake in the darkness of the caboose and tripped back to the days when every Sunday I went to church with Mom and Dad. I didn't remember much about the preacher's sermons, but I clearly remembered Miss Nancy, who taught the primary Sunday school class.

She had a gift for storytelling. We would sit cross-legged on the carpet in a semicircle, our eyes wide as she told stories about Jonah and the big fish ("How big was that fish? Big enough to swallow a *man*!"); Shadrach, Meshach, and Abednego in the fiery furnace ("The king made that furnace hot—seven times hotter than it oughta be!"); and Noah in the ark ("How many animals? *All* of them, a mama and papa of each!").

She also talked about how Jesus fed five thousand hungry men with only five loaves and two fishes, how he made a blind man see, and how he called his friend out of a grave after he'd been dead *four days*. We'd act out the stories with construction paper loaves and fish or stumble around with our eyes closed, pretending to be blind. But even Miss Nancy never found a good way to bring home the concept of resurrection, because none of us kids had ever experienced the hopelessness and finality of death.

But now I knew what death was. Along with Emily Dickinson, I knew it well.

If Jesus could feed five thousand hungry men with a little boy's sack lunch, if he could bring light to a beggar's darkness, and if he could call his best friend out of the grave, maybe he could do more with my life than I could.

I had nothing to lose by offering it.

Chapter Sixty-Three

Susan

When Rachel suggested that Maddie return to Georgia with her, everything within me resisted. What if Rachel didn't have time for her? What if Maddie fell into depression because she missed her Florida friends? Surely Frank and I had more time to devote to her.

But God loved Maddie even more than I did. My job was to trust him, pray for her, and support Rachel. She assured me she had found a counselor and that both of them would go.

We went outside to wait for the cab. As Frank carefully maneuvered down the stairs, I reached into my pocket and pulled out something I wanted to give Maddie.

"This is for you, Maddie," I said, unfolding a page I had printed from the Internet. "Emily Dickinson *did* write a lot about death, because she lived during the Civil War, and people tended to die young in those days. But she was anything but melancholy. This poem explains what she was really like."

Maddie read it aloud:

I never saw a moor,
I never saw the sea;
Yet know I how the heather looks,
And what a wave must be.

I never spoke with God,
Nor visited in heaven;
Yet certain am I of the spot
As if the chart were given.

Maddie's brows furrowed. "It's pretty. So . . . because of nature, she knew that God and heaven existed, even though she had never seen them."

Maddie put the page in her pocket and lifted her face to the leafy canopy above us. "Speaking of nature, I'm really going to miss this place. Can I visit this summer?"

"You and your mother can both come," Frank said, balancing on his walker. "Just let us know when, and we'll reserve the guest apartment for you."

"We'll do that," Rachel promised. "I love you both."

I frowned when I saw the leather bracelet on Maddie's wrist. "You're still wearing that?" I asked. "I would think it would bring back bad memories."

Maddie shook her head. "I'm not wearing it to remember Logan's suicide. I'm wearing it to remember his *life*."

I pulled her close and kissed her forehead. "Okay."

"Your ride's here," Frank said.

I lifted my head, my heart constricting as a cab turned into our driveway. Time to let Maddie go home. Time to say a temporary goodbye to Daniel's wife and daughter.

We all hugged and kissed and promised to keep in touch. I grinned like a mad clown the entire time, determined not to break down.

But my facade cracked as the cab pulled away. Frank squeezed my shoulder. "They'll be all right, Susie."

"I know," I said, smiling through tears.

Frank and I *had* lived a charmed life, filled with undeserved blessings, until God planted a lesson in the soil of a difficult season and allowed us to water it with our grief. Already I could see the glimmer of new life emerging from the broken soil.

Discussion Questions

1. Susan and Rachel have a chilly relationship as the story opens. How did this change over the course of the story? Why?

2. Grief comes to those who love, because only when we love do we truly fear loss. When have you experienced grief? How did your experience compare to that of Susan, Frank, and Maddie?

3. Many find value in a support group like the one led by Bob Halsey. When you were grieving, would such a group have helped? Why or why not?

4. Effective fiction rings true when it faithfully represents human situations. Did the stories of Maddie and Susan ring true for you? Why or why not?

5. Is it generally easier for a man or a woman to be open about grief? Frank was devastated by a rendition of "Danny Boy." Susan was devastated by photos of her son. What triggers grief within you?

6. Have you ever known anyone who committed suicide? Before you read this book, would you have said Daniel was

justified in taking his own life? Did this story change your opinion?

7. Many have trouble understanding God. To some, he seems angry, judgmental, and unforgiving. To others, he is unending love, light, and sweetness. The Bible tells us he is love, he is truth, he is just, he is holy. He displays wrath against his enemies and grace to his children. Scripture describes God's emotions as eternally constant: He always loves what he loves and hates what he hates. He loves his children; he hates sin. Why do you think God cares so deeply about the death of his people? Why does he collect our tears "in his bottle"?

8. What do you think will happen to Maddie after she returns home? How will her relationship with her mother change? Will her relationship with God grow? Do you think Maddie will attempt suicide again? Why or why not?

9. Think of someone you have forgiven. What did that forgiveness cost you? Did you offer forgiveness easily, or was it difficult? What did it cost Frank and Susan to forgive Daniel for hurting them?

10. "To ease another's heartache is to forget one's own," wrote Abraham Lincoln. How does compassion for others help us through grief? What are some things you could do for others that would help you move forward after a loss?

Author's Note

I'M OFTEN ASKED WHERE I FIND MY IDEAS. Certain elements of this story practically fell into my lap, because I live in an artist's house with a caboose in the front yard and a jungle for a lawn. I'm also a grandmother and a short-term rental host. I have not lost a family member to suicide, but I have experienced grief. In this book, at least, I wrote what I know.

The topic of suicide, however, could have come from any local newspaper, and the numbers are rising not only in the United States, but also around the world. As our society becomes increasingly secular, we have lost hope and a reason for living. Once society eradicates the idea of an eternal God who loves and cares, what's left? Only man, sitting alone at the apex of the animal kingdom, just another mammal whose life matters little except to those in his limited circle of friends and family.

As you read this story, you may have found the idea of "contagious suicides" improbable. But "suicide clusters," as they are commonly known, do occur among adolescents. For example, between August 2017 and March 2018, a period of only eight months, the community of Stark County, Ohio, experienced twelve suicides among middle and high school students. A 1987 study of youth suicide by the CDC found that from 1 to 5 percent of adolescent suicides occur in clusters. Since the death of a friend or peer is traumatic, that death may leave other adolescents feeling suicidal.*

It's crucial that we give children, adolescents, and adults a reason for living.

The most significant thing we can do to guard the lives of our children and grandchildren is to give them hope for the future, and the best way to give them hope is to introduce them to Jesus Christ.

---

*Romeo Vitelli, Ph.D. "When Suicides Come in Clusters," *Psychology Today* blog, August 28, 2012, https://www.psychologytoday.com/us/contributors/romeo-vitelli-phd (accessed October 29, 2021).

Resources

Kay Redfield Jamison, *Night Falls Fast: Understanding Suicide*. New York: Alfred A. Knopf, 1999.

Gary Roe, *Aftermath: Picking Up the Pieces after a Suicide*. Healing Resources Publishing, 2019.

Focus on the Family, *Alive to Thrive: A Biblical Guide to Preventing Teen Suicide*. A free resource for parents, available at https://www.focusonthefamily.com /alive-to-thrive/download/

Michael Jordan quote from Courtney Connley, "Michael Jordan, Serena Williams, and Peyton Manning agree this is the secret to a winning career," CNBC, July 7, 2017, https://www.cnbc.com/2017/07/06/top-athletes -agree-that-this-is-the-secret-to-a-winning-career.html (accessed October 6, 2021).

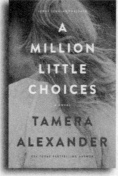